The Listener's
MUSIC BOOK

The Listener's

MUSIC BOOK

OLGA SAMAROFF STOKOWSKI

GREENWOOD PRESS, PUBLISHERS
WESTPORT, CONNECTICUT

The Library of Congress has catalogued this publication as follows:

Library of Congress Cataloging in Publication Data

Samaroff Stokowski, Olga, 1882-1948.
  The listener's music book.

  First ed. has title: The layman's music book.
  Reprint of the 1947 ed. ·
  Includes bibliographies.
  1. Music--Analysis, appreciation. I. Title.
MT6.S25L3 1972   781   72-164473
ISBN 0-8371-6217-3

This book was originally published in 1935
under the title, *"The Layman's Music Book."*

This edition originally published in 1947
by W. W. Norton & Company, Inc., New York

Reprinted with the permission
of W. W. Norton & Company, Inc.

First Greenwood Reprinting 1972

Library of Congress Catalogue Card Number 72-164473

ISBN 0-8371-6217-3

Printed in the United States of America

PREFACE

THE invitation of the publishers to undertake revisions of or additions to *The Layman's Music Book* for a twelfth printing under the new title, *The Listener's Music Book,* has been a matter of considerable concern to the author. The same spirit of humility which caused some fourteen re-writings of the book before its first printing rendered the task of deciding upon the nature and extent of possible revisions and additions exceedingly difficult.

An ever widening and deepening experience of the author in the field of listener education has greatly increased her belief in its importance. The responsibility of those who undertake such a type of education in any form is proportionate. Nevertheless, activities of the Layman's Music Courses, Inc., as well as reports from many sources throughout the United States indicate that *The Layman's Music Book* in the hands of intelligent readers continues to fulfill its original purpose of serving as an initiation into the great world of music which holds such immense possibilities of enjoyment for the human being who takes the time and trouble to become an active and informed listener.

The author has therefore undertaken only such revisions as seem necessary to the practical use of the book. They will be found in the revised appendix.

New York, January 1947   Olga Samaroff Stokowski

CONTENTS

PREFACE   vii

FOREWORD   11

I.   APPROACH TO MUSIC   17

II.   SOUND AND THE FUNCTION OF HEARING   38

III.   WHY SCALES?   50

IV.   WHAT IS POLYPHONY?   66

V.   WHAT IS COUNTERPOINT?   81

VI.   WHAT IS A FUGUE?   98

VII.   OPERA AS A MILESTONE   119

VIII.   FORM AND THE SONATA   136

IX.   INSTRUMENTS AND THE SYMPHONY   160

X.   SHOULD MUSIC HAVE A PROGRAM?   185

XI. OPERA FURNISHES ANOTHER MILESTONE: WAG-
     NER   196

XII. HOW THE LISTENER'S SPHERE OF ACTIVITY
      DEVELOPED   209

XIII. MUSIC WE HEAR IN THE CONCERT HALL   230

XIV. MODERN TENDENCIES   250

      APPENDIX   279

      INDEX   289

FOREWORD

THE WORD "layman" throughout this book is considered
to apply to someone who has not studied music at all.
The book has been planned and written for his benefit.
Its contents and its continuity give in condensed form
an approach to music that has been found helpful to
many laymen in the past seven years.

During that time the author has been attempting,
first privately, then in laboratory classes at the Juilliard
Graduate School of Music, and finally in the public
classes of the Layman's Music Courses, Inc. (founded in
1933),[1] to evolve a simple and effective way of developing active listeners among adult laymen. In the last two
years, over a thousand people of both sexes and of various types and ages have joined classes of the Layman's Music Courses in New York, Philadelphia and
Washington. Many of these laymen could not distinguish one tone from another in listening and some were
monotones in singing. In all this work, there has been
a correlation of lectures with ear-training and theoretical activities that gave the layman a real musical ex-

---

[1] The Layman's Music Courses was incorporated in 1933 as a
non-profit-making organization. It has been conducted (without
subsidy) on a purely co-operative basis. Since 1939 its center of activity in New York has been The Town Hall, 123 West 43rd Street.

perience. Those readers of The Listener's Music Book who wish to develop themselves further as active listeners in such a manner can find the necessary practical guidance in "The Gist of Music," by George A. Wedge, published simultaneously with this volume by G. Schirmer, Inc.

In the Layman's Music Courses, the presentation of information contained in The Listener's Music Book, together with correlated ear-training and theory, has rightly been called the "Initiation Course." It does not claim to be more. But at least eighty per cent of the laymen who have taken the Initiation Course have continued the study of music in some form, either exploring musical literature under the guidance of a qualified teacher, or combining this artistic exploration with the study of an instrument in private lessons. Many have combined it with choral singing.

If the layman who desires to cross the threshold of the world of music would devote the same amount of time and effort to his development as an active listener that most people are willing to give to games, crossword puzzles or picture puzzles, he would soon reap a rich reward in lasting results. To such ambitious readers the author offers the following advice:

Make sure of a thorough grasp of each section of this book before going on to the next.

Remember that results can be greatly increased and strengthened by the correlated reading suggested throughout the book.

Remember, above all, that actual musical experience is absolutely essential. A thorough familiarity with the suggested musical illustrations or similar ones is of the utmost importance.[2]

Most laymen who have studied with the author have enjoyed making the acquaintance of the piano keyboard and finding out all sorts of things for themselves as they did this. Others have obtained a good sense of pitch by familiarizing themselves with the sound of the major diatonic scale on a toy xylophone. But, obviously, the *phonograph* is the indispensable practice instrument of the active listener.

No matter how much a layman may become interested in singing or playing an instrument, the phonograph, intelligently used in connection with musical scores, affords the best opportunity to obtain a broad and comprehensive experience of the great art treasure that lies beyond the possibilities of any individual performer. The layman should learn the difference between what the phonograph can give and what the living performer can give. Neither the phonograph nor the radio can as yet produce music with acoustical perfection. The actual quality of sound suffers from existing limitations of recording and broadcasting. In addition the listener misses the vitalizing magnetic current that emanates from the presence of the living performer. But it is a great mistake to think that *musical* personality does not make itself felt in phonograph records and

[2] For advice to teachers, see Appendix.

broadcasts. Anyone who condemns or belittles the phonograph record and the radio broadcast as "mechanical" must be peculiarly insensitive to the extraordinary power of both agencies faithfully to transmit every musical *impulse* that makes one performance different from another. The phonograph and the radio are doing for the re-creation of our musical masterpieces what the art of printing did for literature. We can study and enjoy the printed dramas of Shakespeare at times when we are not witnessing their performance by living actors. The phonograph enables us to study Beethoven symphonies—not in a bungled attempt on the piano, but very nearly in the way Beethoven intended them to sound, even when the orchestra is not present in the flesh.

If a layman is sufficiently interested to learn musical notation, he will double his possibility of a real activity as a listener because he can then follow records with a score. No matter how imperfectly this is done at first, it is invaluable in building up musical consciousness. The performer learns a piece of music when studying alone. He realizes that the process of practice is one thing and performance for pleasure is another. In like manner, if the layman undertakes to *learn* and *analyze* musical works, whether alone or with a teacher, he should regard it as the *practice* necessary to active listening. He must not imagine, however, that it is necessary for him to dissect and analyze music during a performance he is listening to for enjoyment, any more than a performer mixes up practice with pleasure. All his musical development will function *subconsciously* during a performance listened to for pleasure, and the further he advances, the less he will have to make an effort.

The author wishes to express deep appreciation for valuable assistance to John Erskine, President of the Juilliard Foundation, and to Ernest Hutcheson, Dean of the Juilliard School of Music, for permission to hold laboratory classes through which invaluable experience in teaching music to the layman has been gained; to her young colleagues, former fellowship holders in the Juilliard Graduate School, Gwendolyn Ashbaugh, Ethel Flentye, Caroline Gray, Horace Grenell, Harriett D. Johnson, Huddie Johnson, Paul Nordoff, Judith Sidorsky, Rosalyn Tureck, Yetta Wexler, and Isabelle Yalkovsky, who have faithfully worked with her in developing the Layman's Music Courses; to the laymen who have given time and effort to serve as subjects in the early laboratory classes, notably Mrs. Theodore Steinway, Clark Foreman, Mrs. John Hopkinson Baker, Mrs. Philip Hofer, Miss Margaret Brett and Miss Margaret Sparrow; to Mary Agnes Hamilton for invaluable assistance in proof-reading; to the Junior League of New York which organized the first public classes of the Layman's Music Courses; to the Philadelphia Conservatory of Music, Mrs. Hendrik Ezerman, Director, which organized the first Philadelphia classes of the Layman's Music Courses; to Mrs. William Ayres Borden who organized the first Washington classes of the Layman's Music Courses; to Barnett Byman for his resourceful assistance in evolving charts and equipment for classes; and to Steinway and Sons for supplying the first center of Layman's Music Courses activity in New York.

The finest kind of musical enjoyment occurs when a listener not only surrenders himself freely to the spiritual, sensory, emotional and imaginative experiences great music can give, but is also capable of realizing, through a developed artistic perception, the *complete* significance and beauty of the art work he hears. That is the goal the layman should strive for in developing himself as an active listener.

OLGA SAMAROFF STOKOWSKI

New York, June 1st, 1935

I

APPROACH TO MUSIC

Let him who knows his instrument play it.

SPANISH PROVERB

PRIMITIVE MUSIC throughout the world, so far as we know it, displays certain general characteristics such as the continuous repetition of short tunes, composed of relatively few tones, and the effort to vary this melodic monotony through rhythmic variety. The importance attached to music by primitive man in religious worship, tribal ceremonies and daily life is significant because it proves an instinctive perception of something that civilized man should not lose.

Experts can distinguish between the primitive music of different parts of the globe, and even between distinctive types belonging to different tribes of the same region, but these differences mean little to the uninitiated. The first thing we can learn from a consideration of primitive music is that an expression of emotion in music does not necessarily mean a corresponding response in all listeners. The listener must be attuned to receive the message. Anyone may be highly interested in primitive music but, in order to respond in proportion to the real feeling of the performer, a listener must belong to the same civilization or degree of civilization.

Most primitive peoples have discovered the fundamental possibilities of producing musical tones not only with the human voice but by means of stretched strings, air columns within tubes or pipes, and beating upon elastic surfaces. Their instruments vary in size, shape and decoration, but most of them remain within the limitations that mark the broad general boundary between primitive and civilized life.

In folk music, which forms the great important bridge between primitive music and art music, racial differences become more strongly marked. Mode of life, religion, climate, the invention of typical instruments and the prevailing temperament of peoples create in music recognizable characteristics.

There is no better definition of folk-song than that given by Henry Krehbiel:

"Folk-song is not popular song in the sense in which the word is most frequently used, but the song of the folk; not the song admired of the people, but, in a strict sense, the song created by the people. It is a body of poetry and music which has come into existence without the influence of conscious art, as a spontaneous utterance, filled with the characteristic expression of the feelings of a people."

And he adds:

"Civilization atrophies the faculty which creates this phenomenon as it does the creation of myth and legend."

It would be difficult, even in the most daring generality, to attempt to find an exact boundary between folk music and art music. In a sense they are inseparable since folk music nourishes art music. But for purposes of discussion let us assume that a "musical civilization" becomes established when a selection of musical tones, forming the characteristic material of which music is fashioned, and a specific relation between these selected tones, brought about by what Parry calls a "consensus of instinct" during a folk music development, are *consciously* organized. Such organizations of musical elements form the bases of the distinctive music systems of different races and different ages.

Only mute records of musical life in many ancient civilizations remain, in the shape of instruments shown in sculpture and painting. We have to rely on very imperfect records and literary descriptions in forming any conception of the beginnings of great oriental systems such as those of China and India. We know very little, despite elaborate descriptions of its theoretical basis, of the actual music of ancient Greece. But we can realize, through even a slight acquaintance with music such as that existing today in China and India, how radically it differs from our own.

In examining any musical civilization, we have to

consider the nature of the music, its use in the life of the
race and the type of education practiced within the
system.

The type of musical civilization peculiar to Europe,
North and South America and the European element
of colonized countries, which we shall call occidental
music throughout this volume, is not easy to understand.

Our trained musicians come as near to a clarified
concept of the nature of our music as the degree and
development of their native gifts permit; but it is obvious, in these days of tottering traditions and profound
changes, how far we are from having a complete and
general understanding of the potential *functioning* of
our musical civilization in its relation to the individual
and to the masses. Musical education has suffered from
this lack of understanding.

Occidental Musical Education in the Nineteenth Century

Occidental art music in the latter part of the nineteenth century had reached a high but somewhat dangerous stage of development. Its votaries had settled
down to the peaceful enjoyment of an established order
of things. It was the end of a period so indisputably
great that it is not surprising musicians and music
lovers were completely satisfied and desired no change.
One danger produced by this state of mind was its un-
doubted influence upon the composer who worked in
the shadow of colossal geniuses. Blind adherence to

established methods and the inevitable result of imitation threatened to strangle originality in the composition of music.

Throughout human history most new ideas and new art have at first been deemed "wrong" or "decadent" by all but an adventurous minority. The majority, in most generations, fails to perceive artistic possibilities beyond what has been accepted as right or beautiful; seldom has there been such good reason to cling to an existing order of things as at the end of the nineteenth century. Viewed in the broadest sense, this century was part of a development extending over more than four hundred years, wherein occidental music had become a highly developed and diversified art—an art boasting an amazing number of great creative geniuses. Instruments had developed; abstract instrumental music had come into being; the opera, the oratorio and the orchestra had expanded to magnificent proportions, and the increasing difficulty of music itself had forced performers to acquire a hitherto unequalled technical skill.

In nineteenth-century Europe, the study of art music in some form was acknowledged as a desirable part of general education, and America, still intellectually and artistically nourished by Europe, was awakening to its importance. But in Europe as in America, "music" to the layman of the educated classes meant the performance of a certain well-defined musical literature, especially that of the eighteenth and nineteenth centuries. This music was performed under certain conventional conditions. For the composer, the performer and the listener, in the world of musical art, there was a rounded system, a strong type of musical civilization sufficient unto itself, and apparently immutable. Things were taken for granted; questions were not asked. A knowledge of the long evolution and artistic revolutions leading up to this state of affairs scarcely entered into the scheme of the average musical education. A limited number of musicologists occupied themselves with history, did research work and wrote; but the average professional and amateur musician seldom extended his interest in music far beyond the sphere of his special activity. Within this sphere, he was bound by strong traditions.

To the man in the street, particularly in the United States, so-called "classical" music was a "high-brow" affair, undesirable to some and inaccessible to others. True, there were radicals even in those days. Richard Strauss gave conservatives a series of lively shocks towards the latter part of the century and together with Debussy provided the musical generation in question with the opportunity to sing the age-old refrain of "art is going to the dogs." Since Strauss and Debussy have become classics, we realize that they did not stray so very far afield.

There was some singing in schools, and private lessons on the piano, violin or cello were the lot of the average child who studied music. These lessons, frequently given by individuals whose chief qualification was the necessity to earn money, seldom extended far beyond the physical process of producing sound. Nine out of ten people, if asked what they remember of their instrumental musical education, will speak of how they held their hands, or how their knuckles were rapped by irate teachers. Scales were usually taught as mere technical exercises, and in addition to these and other finger gymnastics, little pieces, often possessing but slight musical value, were learned. As a rule, at the end of eight or even ten years of this procedure, the result seldom exceeded the labored performance of a few easy pieces. Indeed the net result sometimes consisted of a *single selection,* the classic thousand dollar piece that represented an endless waste of time and money. In the overwhelming majority of cases, actual musical experience in the course of such study was so slight, and the technical practice involved was so distasteful, that when coercion was removed the student lost interest or rejected music entirely. A love of music can scarcely be expected to thrive on a diet of ugly sounds produced by a performer possessing neither talent nor skill. There were many exceptions in the shape of talented amateurs who took the trouble to learn to play or sing well enough to give pleasure, but they formed a minority in the general scheme of musical education.

One of the strangest delusions that persisted throughout that romantic nineteenth century was the idea that the *chief* function of musical literature is to serve as a means of *self-expression* for the performer, irrespective of the fact that musical performance is actually the re-creation of a composition in which it is the *composer* who has "expressed" himself. The real and legitimate function of the performer, namely, to interpret through a faithful re-creation in sound the creative message of the composer, was so nearly lost sight of that even the worst performances were encouraged.

Obviously, our type of musical civilization could not be a living art without the re-creation of its literature through performance, and yet nothing in our musical life is more misunderstood.

Let us imagine a state of affairs in which great sculptors had created precious works of art, but fate had decreed that these statues could only assume their rightful shape at times when someone possessing the requisite skill re-created them. Except for this re-creative process, the statues could be nothing but formless blocks of marble. Let us visualize a similar possibility in connection with paintings that could only possess their rightful color under the same condition of re-creation. Then let us form an imaginative picture of millions of sheets of music-paper covered with symbols, mute and futile until brought to life through the most elusive and intangible art medium known to man—sound. To approach this difficult and subtle task with the idea that anything can be gained, for the individual or for art, by a bungling and abortive attempt, seems incomprehensible, and yet it was the accepted idea in the nineteenth century that there was some mysterious virtue in even the worst musical performance, no matter how the composition suffered through mistakes. It was a part of genteel life.

Such an attitude was never taken towards anything else. Let us imagine reading a line of poetry—

"I stood tiptoe upon a little hill."

in the following manner—

"I stood tiptoe upon a little pill."

One wrong note in a single chord can create just as much havoc in music. If any of my readers doubt this statement let them try (or get some musician friend to try for them), playing the first three chords of the *Tannhäuser* Overture with a diminished triad instead of a minor triad as the third chord.

If a single note in a single chord can cause such distortion of a musical composition, the imagination balks at what happened to our musical literature and the sensibilities of all concerned as countless children in the nineteenth century obediently, even if sometimes resentfully, strove to "express themselves" in inadequate musical performances.

In the hands of an inspired artist, performance becomes almost creative. Any *adequate* performance, whether amateur or professional, has real value both to the performer and to those who hear it; but it is a strange misconception to consign musical art works of any significance to the role of vehicles for "self-expression" in *inadequate* performances. Professional musicians are often accused—and sometimes with reason—of evincing a vainglorious desire to display their skill. Perhaps we have never seriously considered how much exhibitionism has entered into the musical education of children and into the psychology of the amateur performer.

Musical education would be much more sound if the true nature of performance—re-creation—were sufficiently stressed. Self-expression in a legitimate degree will always automatically enter into performance. If ten different people set out to re-create a musical composition, with the most faithful and selfless effort to interpret the work in every detail according to its artistic reality, there will be ten different results, according to the qualities and temperaments of the performers. There are so many things in music for which no symbols exist. These things must be found by the intuition of the performer. They must be *felt*. There is little danger of losing individuality in the right kind of re-creation.

The Nature of Our Music

The three things that form the great dividing line between our musical civilization and all others are:

1. Polyphony, or the combining of several simultaneous melodies and the harmonic system that grew out of it.
2. The existence of a great musical literature.
3. Abstract instrumental music.

If other races in other ages had discovered the polyphony that began in Europe towards the end of the ninth century, if they had realized the infinite possibilities of "many-voiced music," they would have produced Bachs and Beethovens and Wagners. The fact that this did not happen renders our musical civilization unique in the known history of the world.

If we comprehend this essential significance of polyphony we can understand why the existence of a great musical literature was so long delayed. Not until polyphony had passed its early stages of experimentation and initial restrictions—not until the latter part of the thirteenth century—do we find the individual composer of music established as an institution.

As composers penetrated further and further into the possibilities of sound as an art form, the difficulties of the *performer* increased and necessitated the development that enables him adequately to re-create musical art works.

Professionalism Becomes the Dominating Factor in the Nineteenth Century

This explains why, when we reached the late nineteenth century, more and more of the music students who achieved any degree of real mastery in the art aspired to become professionals. The effort involved was too great to be undertaken merely for the sake of the much-lauded "self-expression." The social disadvan-

tages once attached to the status of the professional musician had disappeared, the rewards of the successful
virtuoso or singer were great, and so the European cap-
itals in the period under discussion were filled with a
growing army of would-be professional music students.
The American contingent of this army was large. Moderately talented Americans, discovered by kind but
undiscriminating friends, financed by some sympathetic but ignorant relative or patron, and inevitably
doomed to oblivion through sheer inability to hold a
place on the concert or opera stage, became familiar and
tragic figures in the musical life of the day.

As to the audiences of that time, opera houses and
concert halls were only filled, as a rule, when performers of high reputation appeared. Dreary rows of empty
seats, a handful of "dead-heads" and a staggering deficit
greeted the unknown musician. The launching of a
"career" cost a small fortune. Even when concert halls
were filled, the audiences in large cities represented but
a negligible fraction of the population, as indeed they
still do.

The Function of Listening in the Light of Evolution

The truth is that despite the great creative flowering
of music as an art, despite the high standard of performance among professionals, despite the widespread
habit of a certain type of amateur music-study, and a

certain amount of music in the home, there was comparatively little real musical *culture* among laymen.

In all occidental countries, at all times, there have been millions of people who failed to participate in our amazing musical civilization.

One reason for this was that it had not yet occurred to the musical world in general what *active listening to music* such as ours can mean. Listening was considered a passive thing. Emotional response and sensory pleasure were supposed to occur spontaneously; if a human being failed to react emotionally or to derive sensory pleasure from music, he was set down as "having no ear." He either withdrew from any contact with the art of sound or idly visited musical performances for social reasons, but admittedly as a rank outsider. Long years of residence abroad convinced the author that this was true in varying degrees in most European countries.

In the United States, only when the recording and broadcasting of music began to fill the air with sounds divorced from the personality of the performer and the familiar surroundings of opera house and concert hall did the great mass of citizens begin to ask itself what our art music really means. For a time confusion reigned supreme. "Canned music" was often vigorously condemned by professionals, whose material interests were menaced, as well as by more idealistic conservatives who could not see beyond the obvious shortcomings of the new developments. But nothing could stop the flood of music—good, bad, and indifferent--that assailed the ears of humanity from every side.

New Conditions Affect Psychology

Curiosity began to grow among those who had had no previous contact with art music. Increasing indifference on the part of family and friends in the matter of listening to unimportant little pieces performed by unskilled amateurs discouraged the study of music along accustomed lines. The phonograph and radio were preferred with brutal frankness by the family and friends who once formed the audience of the amateur performer.

Parents began to ask themselves whether it was really worth while to give Johnny and Susie music lessons. Often Johnny and Susie were quite sure it was not. It became apparent that something different had to be done in musical education. The first fruit of this realization was called "music appreciation."

In schools and colleges this idea took root and a vast amount of talking and writing began. Lecturers took the field; distinguished writers strove harder than ever to assist concert audiences by means of elaborate program notes to "appreciate" what they heard; children's concerts were instituted to stimulate the enjoyment of coming generations of concert- and opera-goers; music was explained in every conceivable way.

As usual, the pendulum swung too far and many mistakes were made. One of the worst was the constant association of abstract musical compositions with nonmusical ideas—with stories and analogies that really had nothing whatsoever to do with them. The imagination

of the listener, which should be free to function independently unless there is a text or some definite literary
program provided by the composer, was chained to an
arbitrary programmatic conception of the lecturer or
program annotator. This piece was likened to "wind
sighing over the grave"; that symphony to the "victo-
rious march of armies." The listener, thus supplied with
a non-musical crutch to help him through the performance of a work he was incapable of hearing with
complete understanding, gratefully grasped the possibility of some sort of an imaginative experience, responded to the more emotional portions of the music
and, through the power of suggestion, assumed he was
"appreciating" it. One faithful subscriber to Boston
Symphony concerts called Philip Hale's admirable program notes the "how-to-feel book." Religiously, during
the performances of the Boston Symphony Orchestra,
he would read these notes. Once, by mistake, he turned
over two pages instead of one, and according to his own
dismayed account, "was sad . . . at the wrong
time. . . ."

As a concrete example of the absurdities that can
arise through attempts to direct the layman's imagination in music by verbal means, let us examine two totally
different word pictures of the same piece of music.
Henry Drinker, Jr., in a recent book on Brahms' Chamber Music, quotes two musical scholars of repute in the
following descriptions of the final coda of the F minor
piano quintet:

Niemann writes:

The *coda* . . . goes laugh-
ing by till it is finally concentrated still more drastically by
means of syncopations. Yet all
this does not succeed in check-
ing its *joyful* mood; and, in the
concluding lines, it takes its
leave by breaking off abruptly
as though with *bright ringing
laughter*.

Specht writes:

The extensive *coda* where
the themes, dissolved into a
more and more precipitate
triplet motion, chase each other
in the manner of a stretto,
*dashes towards the dark un-
known*. The *composer's heart
must have been desolate indeed when he wrote this study
in black*.

Verbal interpretations of those intangible, emotional and imaginative things in music which *cannot* be
put into words were, and still are, constantly presented
to the layman and nobody seems to give much consideration to the obvious fact that if a piece of music is
really gay or sad, that mood is the one thing that ought
to reach the listener without explanation. When concert
program notes are written with the literary gifts, the
poetic fancy, the wit and real knowledge of a Lawrence
Gilman, they cannot fail to stimulate interest. The
highly-developed musician as well as the layman can
enjoy and profit by them. But nothing can take the place
of an independent grasp of musical fundamentals on
the part of a listener. Lawrence Gilman himself once
wrote:

". . . the sensitive and uninformed layman must
not forget that to be wafted helplessly hither and
thither on a surging, vaguely apprehended sea of
sound, 'an unresisting prey to the composer's every
whim,' is not the same thing as listening to music. It

is only the sensitive and knowing musician, listening with all his special faculties, who ever hears all that there is in a piece of great music."

Even if verbal interpretations of the fourth dimension of music were more effectual than they usually are, the fact remains that the layman continues to need the same procedure for every unfamiliar work he hears. Music must be eternally explained to him. The simple solution of teaching the listener something about those tangible musical fundamentals that *can* be put into words, those things that enable the composer and the performer to function in their art, and are just as indispensable to the listener's understanding and enjoyment of music, is a comparatively recent development.

The concept of music as an art in which a priesthood performs for emotionally responsive (and financially indispensable!) but ignorant listeners is not unlike the mediaeval approach to religion. The concept of music as a mere indoor sport or a vehicle for the self-expression of the amateur accounts largely for the losses of music-teachers, publishers, music-industries, and professional performers in the twentieth century. There are too many other sports, diversions, and means of self-expression in modern life. Music, in competition with these, did not hold its own in times of depression, possibly because recording and broadcasting have caused an inevitable re-evaluation of amateur performance in regard to the relation between effort and result, and because the layman who did not produce or perform music was often unable to find a real place for music in his life or for himself in the general musical scheme of things.

The uninitiated listener who enjoys art music is in reality displaying musical talent just as truly as the possessor of creative talent who improvises, or the possessor of re-creative talent who plays by ear. When we find pronounced creative or re-creative talent in a child, we promptly proceed to develop it by giving the child knowledge and technique as tools to work with. There never has been such a thing as a totally uneducated composer or performer of any signifiance in our musical civilization. But we have very wrongly assumed that the listener needed no education beyond a stimulation of interest.

The possibilities of participating in our musical civilization as listeners and the education necessary to this participation are only beginning to be understood. Only if music becomes an important part of general culture will its rightful place in modern life be assured. Only if the human being, whether child or adult, is made aware of the deep and inspiring experiences that await the human being who possesses a developed musical consciousness, will music become a living part of general culture. Only if music, as a living part of general culture, is placed within reach of all, will our peculiar type of musical civilization with its unique treasure of great art works be justified. We now have, beside the notation that made our literature possible, the means of recording and broadcasting it, so that it is universally accessible. All we need is to understand musical education in the broadest sense.

Aeschylus has given us a powerful picture of man before he received the gift of the divine fire from Prometheus:

> "For, in the outset, eyes they
> had and saw not;
> And ears they had but heard not;
> Age on age,
> Like unsubstantial shapes
> in vision seen
> They groped at random in the
> world of sense."

Have we not left our listeners, bereft of the divine fire of enlightenment, to "grope at random in the world of sense"?

To assume that our great musical masterpieces were created solely for the benefit of those who could perform them would be to limit the value of our musical civilization to a fraction of the occidental world. And by the same token, to reduce the musical experience of the individual to what he can perform himself would be to limit his experience to a fraction of what music can give him.

Remembering the Spanish proverb "let him who knows his instrument play it," we may say to the performer who experiences an urge to make music, Do all you can really do adequately. Let your love of music be so great that it will not tolerate anything inadequate or unworthy. Perform what is within your grasp, even if it is the simplest thing. Enjoy making music, but if you perform the art works of other men, *realize the responsibility of re-creation.*

To the layman who has perhaps been influenced by the theory that listening to music is *passive,* and that the only worth-while thing is to "do it yourself," one might say that in our type of musical civilization

"Someone else can compose music for you.
Someone else can perform music for you.
No one on earth can listen to music for you."

POINTS TO BE REMEMBERED

1. Listening to music is a real musical activity.
2. While others can compose and perform music you hear, no one can listen to it for you.
3. The music a human being can perform is but a fraction of the art treasure we possess. The relation of every musician to all the music outside his specialty is that of the *listener.*
4. Only if active listeners participate in our type of musical civilization can it be justified. If our unique musical literature were regarded as existing only for the benefit of those who can perform it, our musical art life would be limited to a fraction of the occidental races.
5. Just as the greatest creative geniuses and re-creative talents have needed development of their natural faculties in music, so the listener also needs it if he is to function in the highest sense.

SUGGESTIONS FOR CORRELATED READING

Histoire de la Musique, Combarieu, Chapter I
Primitive Music, Walaschek
History of Music, Stanford-Forsyth, Chapter I
The World's Earliest Music Traced to Its Beginning in Ancient Lands, H. Smidt
The Indian Book, Natalie Curtis
Afro-American Folk-Song, Krehbiel, G. Schirmer, New York

MUSICAL ILLUSTRATIONS

Odeon	A 248545	Choir, Yoruba Tribe, Africa
Odeon	A 248549	Awudu Debi, Dodo, etc. Haussa Tribe, Africa
Odeon	A 242091	Swahili Male Song, Africa
Odeon	A 242010	Swahili Female Song, Africa
Odeon	A 248544	Abibu Oluwa Abibus. Yoruba Tribe, Africa
Victor	20043	Chant of the Eagle Dance; Chant of the Snake Dance; Hopi Indian Chanters
Victor	20893	Sunrise Call; Lover's Wooing, Chief Caupolican, Zuni Indian
Columbia	A 3057	Children's Chorus; Funeral Chant, Seneca Indians
Columbia	A 3162	Tribal Prayer; Mohawk's Lullaby

II

SOUND AND THE FUNCTION OF HEARING

"Music stands in a much closer connection with pure sensation than any of the other arts."

HELMHOLTZ

Not until the student who approaches the art of listening to music has grasped the reality of the function of hearing can the nature and scope of his potential activity in music be correctly gauged. The first things to be considered are:

The reality of our sense of hearing.
The essence of musical tone.
The fact that we interpret all sound in the light of experience.

It is possible to have knowledge of certain facts and yet lack complete realization of their significance, as well as the capacity to use—and profit by—such knowledge. Most educated adults have some knowledge of physics but if the layman is to clarify the question of his function as a listener, it is well to review certain fundamental points.

The sound-waves that constitute musical tone are carried to the brain through the functioning of the ear and the auditory nerves, *but not until these sound-waves reach the brain do we actually hear them.*[1]

Not until *after* we have heard—that is, become conscious of sound—can we experience any emotional or imaginative reaction.

We have only to reflect upon these two fundamental facts in order to realize what an important part the *brain* must play in our reception of music. The *way* our consciousness functions will condition all subsequent reactions. It is the door that leads to the world of the imagination. It functions *before* the subconscious and super-conscious experiences music can give. It explains why human beings seldom respond completely to the music of alien civilizations. It explains why conservatives of every generation find difficulty in accepting music that subsequently wins universal recognition.

There is no greater mistake than the supposition that the art of music is *only* sensory and emotional. It has been almost a cult, among musicians and laymen alike, to belittle the function of the brain in connection with music.

"Intellectuality" in music has been a synonym for "coldness" or "dryness" in the vocabulary of the majority. It is well for the layman to clarify this question at once and to realize how illogical it is to attribute "coldness" to mental development. The real cause of "coldness" in music or anything else is a limited capacity for emotion, and, as such, it is found quite as

[1] See Appendix, Function of Hearing.

often in *un*intelligent human beings as in intellectuals.

The function of the brain in music being in reality the final point of the act of hearing, the higher the development of this seat of consciousness, the better can it embrace the manifold contents of a musical art work. Obviously, the same thing is true of other arts. The trained eye will perceive and enjoy things in a painting that are lost to the uninitiated. Emerson was right when he said of nature:

"The difference between landscape and landscape is small, but there is a great difference between beholders."

Without a background of general education the enjoyment of great literary works is apt to be limited, if not actually lacking. We recognize these facts in connection with letters and other arts, but, in concentrating our attention almost exclusively on "emotional response" to sound sensation in music, we have forgotten the fact that *consciousness must precede emotion* in listening to music.

For this reason those who aspire to become active listeners should divest themselves of all fear of so-called technicalities in music. Plain common sense can teach us that it would be just as impossible for a composer of music to convey his essential message to the listener without the specific sounds that he uses and their relation to each other—these things called "technicalities"—as it would be for a writer to convey thought and feeling without the specific words that are intelligible to the reader. The highest value in a musical masterpiece lies beyond mere notes just as the highest value in a piece of literature lies beyond mere words, but we can only get at the highest values in all the arts when we are conscious of the medium employed. Let us therefore boldly approach technicalities and logically begin with the *essence of musical tone.*

In considering sound we can find no better definition than that given by Helmholtz:

"The sensation of a musical tone is due to a rapid periodic motion of the sonorous body; the sensation of a noise to *non*-periodic motions."

He amplifies this by stating:

"Noises and musical tones may certainly intermingle in various degrees, and pass insensibly into one another, but their extremes are widely separated."

Let us here formulate—as an imaginative picture —the actual experience of hearing a symphony by Beethoven. Reducing the component parts of the sound mass sent out by the orchestra to the smallest recognizable unit, we arrive at the single musical tone, only to find that what we consider a single musical tone is in reality a composite sound of the most complex description. Just as a drop of water contains various elements, so the single musical tone contains partial tones, sometimes called overtones, forming what is known in physics as the harmonic series. The pitch of each musical tone, the thing that makes it a recognizable unit in music, depends upon the "frequency" of its periodic vibrations. Measured in time, according to scientific custom, we find that each recognizable musical tone has its unalterable number of vibrations per second, induced in some sound-producing agency such as a stretched string, an air column within a pipe or tube, or the breath within the vocal apparatus of the human being. These sound-producing agencies, however, not only vibrate as a *whole* but in *segments*. The partial tones or harmonic series result from the numerically different vibrations of the various segments of the sound source.

Is it necessary for a layman to dwell upon such things?

Only if he wishes to have some conception of the miracle demanded of his ear by our particular type of music; only if he wishes to understand the reason why an oboe sounds different from a French horn; only if he wishes to follow with real understanding the evolution of music from the succession of single tones that form a primitive melody to the simultaneous sounding of many different tones that he hears in every musical composition performed in our occidental concert halls and opera houses.

Walter Pater says: "Curiosity and the desire of beauty have each their place in art. . . ."

If we seek to satisfy a desire for beauty in listening to art music, we should also have the curiosity to find out and understand the things that can enlarge our perception of it. The following diagrams give examples of the vibrations of different segments of a string corresponding to certain partials of a tone's harmonic series.

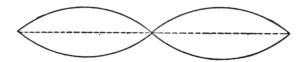

The string vibrating in halves with a point of repose or "node" in the center contributes the second partial of the harmonic series, one octave above the first partial or "generating tone." Each half of the string is vibrating twice as fast as the whole string.

The three thirds of the vibrating string each produce the pitch of the third partial in the same manner.

The five fifths of the vibrating string each produce the pitch of the fifth partial.

There is no known limit to the automatic subdivision of a vibrating string or air column, therefore the series of partial tones also have no known limit but extend far beyond our range of hearing.

The following table gives the first ten partials of the harmonic series of "C":

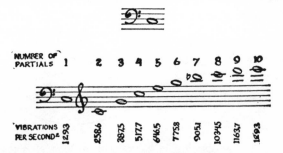

The layman can find these tones on the piano by means of the following keyboard diagram:

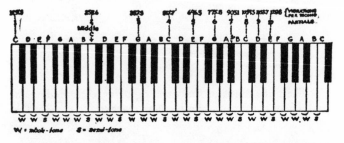

The sounds produced by the keys indicated on this diagram *correspond* with the partial tones of the single tone C in that they have, as separate and individual tones produced by different strings, the same number of vibrations per second as corresponding partial tones produced by the various segments of the string that sounds C at 129.3 vibrations per second. The fact that these tones belong within the harmonic series of the C to

² The numbers of vibrations here given, correct according to the natural law of sound vibration, only approximate those of the given tones on the piano which is tuned according to equal temperament (see Appendix).

the extreme left of the above piano keyboard diagram can be easily proved in the following manner: depress that key gently without making it sound, and hold it down; then quickly strike and immediately release any of the keys indicated as partials of C. The sound of these tones will continue after their key is released because they will have aroused a *sympathetic vibration* of the segment of the low C string which is free to vibrate because the depressed key keeps the hammer off it. If the layman, while still holding down C, strikes and releases any of the black keys, except B-flat, the sound will not continue. They do not belong.

The lowest partial being the strongest is most easily perceived and creates for us the musical identity of the tone. A normal ear can hear sounds ranging from 16 vibrations per second (the lowest tone produced by a large pipe organ) to 16,000 vibrations per second, (a sound produced by jingling keys) but distinguishable musical tones do not exceed 4,138 vibrations per second.

Considered in the light of such numbers of vibrations per second, the function of the ear in receiving a single musical tone would be wonderful enough. It becomes miraculous when we realize that while the partials that form a whole musical tone are unalterable as a series, they do not necessarily all sound, or sound with equal strength. Helmholtz tells us that "the *quality* of a musical tone depends solely on the number and relative strength of the partial simple tones." This of course implies the possibility of weakening or even eliminating certain partials through the conscious control or accidental characteristics of the sound source and the method of producing the sound. For instance, if a string is plucked in the center, the node at that point will not form and the partial created by the vibration of the two halves of the string will be eliminated. The shape and inner bore of wind instruments, the point at which a string is plucked, the build of a human being will determine which segments of the string or air column will contribute to the compound tone, thus creating what might be considered as "a chemical mixture" of partials. Hence the difference between the tone of the French horn and the flute, the clarinet and the trumpet.

The brain, therefore, is capable of determining the pitch (musical identity) of a tone caused by the frequency of vibrations per second received through the ear, and it can also detect the *quality,* caused by the "number and relative strength of the partial simple tones"; otherwise, all the instruments of an orchestra would sound alike.

In addition—to complete the picture of what it means to listen to a Beethoven symphony—the brain must separate the complete sound mass coming from the orchestra, with its myriads of vibrations, into the tonal design and structural form that make one piece of music different from another.

To regard such a process as "passive" seems unthinkable. And if one realizes that it opens the door to a world of the imagination and the emotions conjured up by the enormous suggestive power of great music, it is not difficult to understand that it is within the power of any sensitive listener to become a poet, a dreamer, in truth a *creator* under the spell of such an experience. To be sure, this is an inner experience, not one to be displayed, not one to win applause nor to arouse the admiration easily gained by an exhibition of skill. Listening is the most selfless function in music and yet the one that, next to actual creation, most enriches the inner life of a human being.

If the layman should still entertain any doubt as to the necessity of adequate development for active listening, let him consider one more aspect of the function of hearing—the fact that the brain interprets all sound in the light of past experience. A savage hearing the siren of an ocean liner for the first time, without any knowledge of the ship, would not be able to interpret the sound with any true conception of its significance. He might continue to hear the sound for years without being able to interpret it correctly. A city dweller with no knowledge of the forest would be just as unable to interpret the sounds of its bird and animal life and it is scarcely necessary to point out the loss sustained by a spectator when a drama is performed in an unknown tongue. The phenomenon that most people derive the greatest enjoyment from the music they know is due to the fact that sound can only be interpreted in the light of past experience. Therefore, the greater the experience, the wider will be the field of enjoyment.

The first logical step in the development of the listener is to learn to identify musical sounds, to interpret them correctly and to regard those that form the most fundamental basis of our occidental music system, our scales, as the alphabet of his future musical knowledge.[3]

The author has not attempted to give further information of a scientific nature concerning the element of sound because the correlated reading suggested below affords ample opportunity for extension of knowledge, once the direction is given and the objective established in relation to the entire approach of The Listener's Music Book.

In these days, when every child is becoming scientific-minded, when sound films, phonographs and radio sets bring the general public in direct contact with the mysteries of the sound world, it is very rewarding to learn more about this important part of the vibrational universe in which we live. The student will have occasion more than once to refer back to the harmonic series, as the evolution of the art of music and the construction of the instruments we use demand an understanding of it.

POINTS TO BE REMEMBERED

1. Every musical tone is "due to a rapid periodic motion" of a sonorous body which sets up corresponding vibrations in the air and finally in our ear.

2. Until sound vibrations reach the consciousness (the brain) we do not hear. We must, therefore, think of the art of listening as a function of the brain as well as of the ear through which sound waves reach our consciousness.

3. The musical tone is complex and contains within itself a

[3] For musical experience in building scales, see chapter on scales, "The Gist of Music," by George A. Wedge.

series of partial tones called overtones or the harmonic series.

4. It is necessary for the listener to think of musical tones as entities which he must learn to identify as he would numerals, colors or any other media out of which something can be fashioned.

SUGGESTIONS FOR CORRELATED READING

Sensations of Tone (translated by Alexander A. Ellis), Helmholtz

Broadhouse, *Musical Acoustics*

Music and Musicians, Lavignac, Chapter I

The Science of Musical Sound, Dayton C. Miller

The Physical Basis of Music, A. Wood

Music, A Science and an Art, John Redfield

Grove's Dictionary of Music and Musicians, Article on Acoustics

III

WHY SCALES?

"Music, indeed, like vegetation flourishes differently in different climates; and in proportion to the culture and encouragement it receives; yet to love such music as our ears are accustomed to, is an instinct so generally subsisting in our nature that it appears less wonderful it should have been in the highest estimation at all times and in every place. . . ."

BURNEY

COUNTLESS possessors of ten weary fingers have probably asked themselves this question as they ascended and descended long ladders of notes in striving for the ability to play scales on instruments. And whole-tones, half-tones, this fingering or that, usually occupied the minds of the majority of such students until the playing of scales became a mechanical process and the ambition for speed succeeded the learning of notes.

Only if scales are regarded as the artistic material out of which the music of different civilizations is fashioned can they take their rightful place in our musical consciousness.

Joseph Yasser, eminent musicologist and author of one of the most important books on music published

50

in recent years, "A Theory of Evolving Tonality," has
an amazingly logical theory, embracing the past, present and future of scale-building. He argues most plau-
sibly that the further one goes back in the known history of the world, the fewer the tones that are used in
music. If in primitive music only two or three tones
formed the actual scale-basis of the music, it is logical
to assume that other possible tones existing in the spaces
or intervals between those in constant use, were occasionally sounded—probably without conscious design—and that they gradually came to be accepted and
included in a more highly developed scale.

In order to grasp this idea, let us regard the in-
terval of the octave as *space* between two tones and
realize, for instance, that there are just as many possible tones between C at 129 vibrations per second and

C at 258 vibrations per second as

there are different numbers of vibrations. While this is
strictly true from the point of view of physics, the
reservation must be made that the ear can scarcely
distinguish between a tone having 129 vibrations per
second and one having 130 vibrations per second. For
this reason the space between such selected tones is
apt to be larger in primitive or semi-civilized scales.
The larger spaces between tones render each tone more
recognizable and the larger intervals are easier to sing.
Smaller intervals are more characteristic of highly
developed civilizations. They are more difficult to sing.

The following keyboard diagram from Yasser's

book, "A Theory of Evolving Tonality," gives a clear demonstration of his basic ideas.

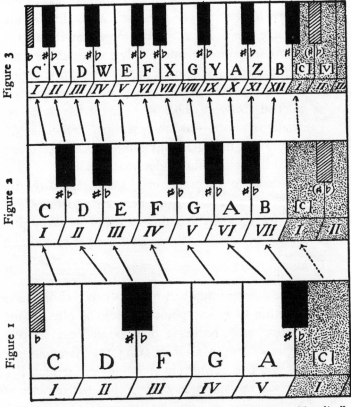

From Joseph Yasser's "A Theory of Evolving Tonality" published by the American Library of Musicology.

The black notes of figure 1 represent musical tones he assumes to have been used by very primitive peoples. Through stumbling upon "passing tones" lying between these tones and using them as auxiliaries for "ornamental" purposes, a five-tone (pentatonic) scale evolved, as shown on the white keys of figure 1. It is undoubtedly true that a five-tone (pentatonic) scale has been found in the music of so many different parts of the world that Yasser is very logical in considering it as a stage of musical development, rather than a racial scale. It is the dominating scale in Chinese music, and yet it also forms the basis of much folk music in Great Britain, Russia, Scandinavia, Northern France (Brittany), Germany, Finland, Rumania, and Bulgaria.

In figure 2, the white and black notes of figure 1 combined, have formed a new scale—what we call our diatonic major scale—composed of whole-tones (larger intervals) and half-tones (smaller intervals).[1] The white keys of figure 2 give this scale. In the space between the tones forming the whole-tones (larger intervals) of this major scale, auxiliary (ornamental) tones, as shown by the black keys, gradually came into general use and eventually combined with the seven tones represented by the white keys to form the twelve equal semi-tone divisions of the octave called the *chromatic scale*.

Yasser offers the theory that this development may be repeated and figure 3 shows a possible scale of the future in which our diatonic scale-tones are found in the auxiliary (black) notes of a new scale that divides

[1] For whole-tones and half-tones see piano keyboard diagram, page 44.

the octave space into 19 degrees with intervals smaller than those that can be played on a modern piano with our present system of tuning. Yasser presents abundant musical and historical evidence to support his theory, and whether we accept it or not, there is no denying its interest as a clear, scientific and logical approach to the vast subject of scale-building.[2]

All musical theory is but the crystallization and description of actual musical experience. The creative spirits of countless generations have been the scale-builders of every musical civilization, whether they were anonymous singers of folk-songs in the shadowy ages of the remote past or modern scientists measuring sound vibration with unerring accuracy, as Yasser has done in the mathematical working out of his interesting theory.

The physical laws of sound have been discovered and used in countless different ways. Buried under a mass of legend and symbolism, we find the music system of China based on the discovery (supposedly in the year 2486 B. C.) that bamboo reeds of different lengths would produce certain tones that had an unalterable relation to the length of the reeds. Gradually a system comprising twelve sounds (lüs) evolved, although most Chinese music employs a five-tone (pentatonic) scale.[3]

[2] The Greek and Mediaeval Modes might be considered variants of the seven-tone scale in figure 2, while scales including intervals smaller than the semi-tone, and occurring in certain Enharmonic Greek Modes and oriental systems—notably India—may be considered to have a prophetic kinship with the 19-tone scale.

[3] The Chinese Scale and its Agreement with the Universe, The

Again one finds in the musical theory of the
Chinese eight different sources of sound-production affecting tone *quality:* metal, stone, silk, bamboo, cala-
bash, clay, animals, and wood. This is the Chinese way
of organizing tone quality.

India affords perhaps the most extraordinary example of the significance of scales. The broad musical
civilization of India, despite many differences in various sections, rests on the use of innumerable scales
called Rags and Raginis. Legend teaches that there
were six original Rags (masculine) and that the Ra-

Five Tones of the Ancient Scale, from "The Yellow Bell" by
Chao-Mei-Pa, Lauréat du Conservatoire Royal de Musique de
Bruxelles, Formerly Instructor of Music of the University of
Shanghai, Author of the "Introductory Course in Western Music,"
Professor (on leave) of the National Conservatory of Music, China,
and Member of the China National Music Committee of the
Ministry of Education:

"Music, this language harmonious to the spirit of lofty and wise
sentiments which was to all people a subtle means of communication with the mystical forces, came to have, in a philosophical
country like China, a very close affinity to spiritual contemplation.
Also since the discovery of sounds, the great principles of philosophy
were applied to it. In China, as in all the ancient Oriental civilizations, numbers played a predominating part in metaphysics. As we
shall see, the number twelve formed a group found in different
combinations of nature or life which allows the establishment of
some symbolical agreement between sounds and natural phenomena.

"We encounter, further, in the study of the FIVE TONES, THE
EIGHT SONOROUS BODIES and the numerous combinations which
preside over the generation of sounds, other singular relationships.
The thing which impresses one, however, in this strange aspect is
the purely mathematical and sophistical science. What question
does this result unexpectedly raise in our minds? Can it be true,
as several claim, that thought can exercise power to regulate itself? Had our philosophers, whose minds exercised themselves in
great antiquity, so profound a prescience of the truth which they
discovered by the sole effort of their brain or by an intuition
obscure but fruitful? Or was the universe ordered according to a
perfectly established harmony and rhythm, which our fathers

ginis (feminine) were their descendants. The Sanscrit word Raga from a root ranj, "to be dyed, to glow," really means "color." The Rags and Raginis (called Ragam in South India) are actually scales that at the same time form *melody-types*. That means that specified musical tones must succeed each other in a specified manner. Not only the pitch of these tones but their duration and the accentual stress of certain ones are involved. The Hindu musician, familiar with the Rags, improvises his song within their prescribed scope. He is at once composer and performer. He has a certain latitude in his use of the Rag, especially in the question of ornamentation of the melodic line which gives the possibility of individual expression, but he must adhere to the melody-type closely enough to make it recognizable. Furthermore the Rags and Raginis are associated with the eight watches into which the twenty-

spontaneously accepted, while we cannot learn it but by material experiences, numerous and often deceiving?

"According to this natural doctrine, MAN conforms to the principle of HEAVEN. HEAVEN follows a LAW; this LAW harmonizes with NATURE. Before the beginning is INFINITY; INFINITY produces the GREAT WHOLE; then followed the DUAL LAW. These two models are YANG, Masculine, and YING, Feminine. The SUN is the synthesis of the Masculine, and the MOON that of the Feminine. From the marriage of the sun and the moon our PLANET is born. The EARTH produces SOIL, and the soil combined with the sun produces FIRE, the soil with the moon, WATER. The union of fire and earth produces WOOD (vegetable kindom). Subterranean fire and soil produce GOLD (mineral kingdom). From these the UNIVERSE exists. Five planets are found in the sky; Mercury, Venus, Mars, Jupiter and Saturn. The earth is divided into five continents, Asia, Europe, Africa, America, and Australia. Man possesses five senses; sight, hearing, touch, taste, and smell. Music is also inspired by this principle F I V E which explains the origin of the five tones, KONG, SHANG, CHUËH, CHIH, and YŬ."

four hours are divided, the seasons of the year, various emotions, and other aspects of human life. Fox Strangways, in his "Music of Hindostan" writes:

"The first thing, sometimes the only thing, that an Indian who is not very familiar with the science of music can tell you about a particular Rag which is being performed is that it is a morning or that it is an evening Rag—though this perhaps does not prove more than that the Rags are as a matter of fact confined in their performance to the appropriate time of day."

A traveller returned from India told the author that he had asked a niece of the poet Tagore to sing a certain Rag, but she replied: "I am sorry I cannot do it. That Rag belongs to Spring* and it is Winter." Reliable authorities claim that seventy-two Rags and Raginis are in actual use at the present time.

Just as the Chinese in legendary antiquity were learning sound laws of nature through bamboo pipes of different lengths, Pythagoras (sixth century B. C.) discovered them for the Greeks by means of exhaustive experiments with the stretched string of the monochord. The elaborate musical theory of the Greeks furnishes one more proof of the fact that organization of musical systems centers around scales.

The terms "scale" and "mode" are interchangeable. Various attempts have been made to define a difference between them, but as it seems most desirable to simplify technicalities for the layman, we will leave such discussion to the musicologist, and assume for our purposes that the Greek *modes* are in reality scales. The Greek modes may be said to have a musical-etymological connection with our scales, just as Greek roots play an important part in our language. It would require too much time and effort to attempt to penetrate the intricacies of the Greek musical system in this course of study, but a brief examination of the main Greek modes can teach us one more fact concerning scales.

Just as families, forming a unit in society, include various relationships between their members, such as the relation of husband to wife, parent to child or brother to sister, so the musical tones constituting a scale or mode have different relations to each other. Some are considered as being more closely related than others. There is no scale that has not its principal tone and its tones of secondary or still lesser importance. Therefore the function of the scale in music not only means the use and "belonging together" of a specific collection of tones, but the *way* these tones are used in relation to each other. There seems to be a definite connection between these tonal relationships and the laws of nature, because the first four partials of a musical tone having between them the intervals of an octave (first to second partial) a fifth (second to third partial), and a fourth (third to fourth partial) [4] correspond in pitch with the scale tones that are most im-

[4] See table of partials, page 44.

portant and have the closest relationship in the tonal families of most known scales or modes.

In order to gain a definite impression of the enormously different results that can be obtained by different uses of the relatively limited musical material existing within our range of hearing (16 to 4,138 vibrations per second) and the immense creative activity that has gone into the various music systems of the world, the layman should listen to some of the records listed below. Even a slight acquaintance with the music of other civilizations will enable him to take a greater interest in the fundamentals of our own system and better understand their significance. The Greek record on the list is one of the few fragments that remain of the music of ancient Greece.[5]

[5] Hymn to Apollo (from "Oxford History of Music").

"Few pieces of the old Greek music are in existence now. There are three inscribed on stone, some fragments written on papyrus and three complete pieces in ordinary manuscript. Two others have been printed; but these may not be genuine.

"The excavations at Delphi disclosed a number of inscriptions on the walls of the Treasury of the Athenians; and two of these inscriptions are hymns to Apollo with music. Both hymns have suffered from the collapse of the wall on which they were inscribed. The first hymn has broken into two large bits and a few little bits, and the second is almost all in little bits.

"Both hymns allude to the destruction of the Gauls at Delphi, and therefore were written after 279 B. C., and the second must have been written after 146 B. C. as it invokes a blessing on the Guild of Artists at Athens—which guild is mentioned in the first as well—and presumably these hymns were sung at Delphi by members of the Guild. It was one of those guilds of poets, actors, singers, musicians—not painters or sculptors—which existed in many parts of the Greek world. History says little of these guilds, but they are well known from inscriptions; and there happens to be an inscription at Athens recording a decree of the Amphictyonic

One very curious and interesting fact in connection with scales is that the Greeks attributed to their principal modes a definite moral influence upon man. The ethical effect of music has been stressed in many civilizations. The Chinese sages had much to say on the subject. Confucius wrote: "Show me the music of a country and I will tell you how it is governed." Religious leaders have realized the importance of music in arousing devotion; secular leaders have used it throughout the ages for military purposes as well as for pomp and ceremony. We vaguely associate sadness with the minor mode, but our emotional reactions to occidental music depend much more on *rhythm* than on the actual pitch relation (scale relation) of tones to each other. The stirring rhythm of martial music, the seductive rhythms of dance music, the impressive slow rhythms of religious music play the most vital part in lending *character* to our music. But for the Greeks, it was the actual *mode* (scale) i. e., a specific collection of

Council at Delphi that this guild was to enjoy some specified immunities all over Greece—unless the Romans objected (the date is about 125 B. C.). This inscription was in the theater of Dionysus, and Dionysus was the patron god of all such guilds. In later times, especially in the age of the Antonines, the Roman emperors became joint patrons with the god, and the guilds acquired great power. They were in control of all the music that the public ever heard at great solemnities and festivals, and thus influenced (though indirectly) the music of the Early Christian Church.

"There are three hymns in manuscripts, usually printed together; one to the Muse, one to the Sun, and one to Nemesis. Two lines of the last are quoted by John Lydus (born 491 A. D.) as coming from a hymn to Nemesis, by Mesomedes. This Mesomedes lived in Hadrian's time, and wrote a piece in honor of Antinous. He was in his prime in 144 A. D. and his reputation must have lasted, as Caracalla put up a monument to him about seventy years afterwards."

tones having a certain relation to each other, that was believed to have an ethical influence for good or evil on the human being. "Dorian" music made men brave and steadfast, "Phrygian" music made them "head-strong," "Lydian" music (our major scale), made them "slack and sentimental."

Table of Seven Greek Modes *

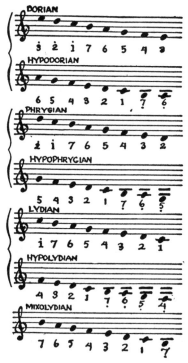

* "The names Dorian, Phrygian, Lydian, etc., belong to certain Greek modes given in the above table in our notation. The layman can find these modes on the white keys of the piano. For his convenience, numerals have been added using middle C throughout

According to Sir Charles Villiers Stanford:

"Greek writers were all agreed that music had a serious *moral value*. They did not say vaguely, as we do, that music was a beautiful thing and had an ennobling effect on the human mind. On the contrary, they said that, according to the way in which it was written, it was actually good or bad; that it had a definitely good or bad influence on the development of personal character; and that therefore the musical means employed was a matter of the most lively concern to educationists and statesmen. This moral character, which they regarded as inherent in the art, was called the *ethos* of music; its value to society in general was known as its *ethical value*. Philosophers differed in explaining why there was an ethos in music; they differed also in discussing its practical application; but none of them ever dreamed of disputing its existence. . . . Their constant subject of discussion was whether this mode or that mode was better suited for inculcating this or that form of moral excellence."

Recently, one of the New York settlement music schools in celebrating the twenty-fifth anniversary of its existence, made the interesting announcement that in this quarter of a century, thirty thousand children had studied music in the school, *and of these not one had ever been brought before a Juvenile Court for delinquency.*

as 1 (one). Numerals of notes lying below middle C have a dot beneath. Those lying in the second octave above middle C have a dot above.

This remarkable record inspired the author to make a private survey of penal institutions in the United States. A form letter was sent out asking the following questions:

1. What is the present population of your institution?
2. How many have had a musical education?
3. How many were trained musicians?
4. Of numbers 2 and 3, what is the nature of their crime and what is their criminal record?

The result of this survey was startling. In eighty per cent of the penitentiaries and prisons in all states of the Union that responded to the inquiry, there were no men or women who had had any form of musical education previous to the time they committed the crimes for which they were imprisoned. In those institutions where musically educated prisoners were found, the percentage was amazingly low. The highest number found anywhere was in Auburn Prison, Auburn, New York, where there were about 50 musically educated prisoners among 1,871 inmates of the penitentiary.[7]

[7] The following letter from the Southern Illinois Penitentiary is especially interesting.

April 5, 1932

Madame Olga Samaroff
New York City, N. Y.
My dear Madam:
   Your communication of March 21 to Warden James A. White was handed to me.

These facts give us food for thought. Perhaps the Greeks understood better than we do, the question, "why scales."

1. Organized musical systems characteristic of different races and different ages have existed throughout the history of the civilized world.
2. The element of musical sound used as the artistic material of these systems can produce results as characteristic as different languages.
3. The grouping of tones having a definite relation to each other is called scale-building, and scales (or modes) are the organized basis of all music systems.

SUGGESTIONS FOR CORRELATED READING

History of Music, Stanford-Forsyth, Chapters I & II
The Art of Music, Volume I
Histoire de la Musique, Combarieu, Volume I, Chapters I & II
Geschichte der Musik Theorie, Riemann
A Theory of Evolving Tonality, Yasser
Evolution of Music, Parry, Chapter II on Scales

During the fourteen years that I have been Bandmaster here there has been but one trained musician convicted and sent here. The charge was child abandonment. There was one here when I came doing life on a murder charge.

There is not one member of our band to-day who ever played a note of music before coming here. Of the many band men who have been paroled, but one has been returned either on a new charge, or for parole violation.

I would not urge musical training as a crime preventative, but the fact remains; trained musicians do not commit crimes, and men who receive musical training in penal institutions, stay out when released.

I find that the foregoing is also true in other prisons.

Yours truly,
(signed) D. E. MUNAL
Bandmaster S. I. P. Band

MUSICAL ILLUSTRATIONS

Chinese Music:
Victor 43756
Victor 43650
Victor 42480
Victor 42815

Japanese Music:
Victor 1232
Victor 4046
Victor 45535

Hindu Music:
His Master's Voice P. 5865

Arabian Music:
Victor 67483
Victor 6–4061
Victor 6–81717
Victor 73429
Victor 67208
Victor 63509
Victor 78609

Ancient Greek Music: Victor 20896-A: *Hymn to Apollo*

IV

WHAT IS POLYPHONY?[1]

"New arts destroy the old."
EMERSON

THIS question is a most significant one for the listener because it is intimately bound up with the necessity for his musical development, with his scope of activity and with the importance of his place in the general scheme of occidental musical civilization.

To listen to a melody, that is, a succession of single tones, presents no particular difficulty. The specific selection of tones in any given melody, their relation to each other, and peculiarities of tone quality due to methods of sound production affecting voices or instruments, may be such that we do not enjoy certain melodic types of music, notably those of alien civilizations, nor respond to them emotionally; but we can *hear* the single line without difficulty. Again, melody that is sung has a text which gives a clue to the meaning of the music. Our consciousness receives not only a simple and easily apprehended sound-impression but associated ideas which direct the imagination and—to a great extent—condition emotional reactions. The

[1] The literal meaning of the word—"many-voiced"—is eloquent. Plural-melody is perhaps the best definition.

66

listener is not called upon for complex or creative functioning.

When two or more melodies are combined a new basis of art begins and with it a new problem for those who listen. Polyphony—"many-voiced music"—brought about changes in musical life no less drastic than those occasioned in the general life of mankind by the discovery of the wheel.

Sweeping generalities are seldom accurate but the eminent German scholar, Riemann, can scarcely be far from the truth, in his summary of musical history:

Music of Antiquity and Primitive Music [2]	Mediaeval Music	Modern Music
Down to 900 A. D.	From 900 to 1600 A. D.	From 1600 A. D. to the present day
Voices & Instruments	Voices	Voices & Instruments
Single line music or melody (occasional "octave" singing or playing).	Polyphony (or the simultaneous sounding of several melodies).	Melody combined with harmony (or polyphonic accompaniment).

Note: Words in brackets are explanatory additions of the author.

[2] It is generally conceded that primitive music is purely melodic even though the melody may be accompanied by several different rhythms on percussion instruments that have no pitch or an indeterminate one, like gongs. The author, however, has heard records of primitive music made in 1930 in Central Africa by Mrs. Laura C. Boulton, in which actual part-singing occurs. While such discoveries would seem to indicate that plural-melody can be found in primitive music, it would be difficult to prove, in the twentieth

Many occidental musicians believe that polyphony must have been known and practiced in other ages and other musical systems, but there is no proof that any type of music other than that of the western world after 900 A. D. was ever based on the conscious combinations of different simultaneous melodies.

Theoretically, most known music systems embody definite (and differing) conceptions of consonance and dissonance. These conceptions fluctuate with the changes occurring in different periods of artistic evolution, but in melodic civilizations they apply solely to the relation of *successive* tones in a single line of melody, not to the *simultaneous sounding of several different tones.*

The Greeks practiced the simultaneous singing of a melody by two voices one octave apart. This practice doubtless originated in the different natural registers of men's voices and those of young boys or women. The practice, extending to choral groups, instruments and combinations of voice and instrument, was called magadizing.[3] Light is thrown upon it in the famous passage in the Aristotelian Problems XIX, 18:

"Why is the consonance of the octave the only one which is sung? For in fact this consonance is magadized but not the others. Is it not because this consonance

century, that the tribes whose singing was recorded by Mrs. Boulton have had absolutely no contact with white man's music. One native making his way to the coast and back could account for the part-singing of twentieth-century primitive tribes.

[3] The name is derived from a harp-like instrument of many strings called the magadis.

alone is antiphonous? For in the antiphones when one of the two notes is sung, the same effect is produced as in the case of the other, so that a single sound of this consonance being sung, the entire consonance is sung; and when the two sounds are sung, or if one is taken by the voice and the other by the flute, the same effect is produced as if one were given alone. This is why this consonance is the only one which is sung, because the antiphones have the sound of a single note."

While this and many other passages in theoretical descriptions of Greek music point to the fact that the duplication of the same melody at the distance of the octave was the nearest approach to polyphony in the musical system of ancient Greece, there is another reason for accepting Riemann's assumption that consciously organized polyphonic music did not exist until after 900 A. D., namely, the absence of musical notation of the kind necessitated by polyphony. It is entirely possible to hand on purely melodic music from man to man, or from generation to generation without any but the simplest letter or character to serve as a written symbol for each single tone in the melody. Folk music was originally handed on without any notation at all. But as soon as men began to sing or play *different* tones at the same time, it was not only difficult for them to memorize their parts, but a practical notation in the shape of symbols that can be conveniently disposed, one above the other, became absolutely necessary. It is not too much to say that the absence of such a notation is the best proof of the absence of polyphony in a musical civilization.

The significance of the discovery of polyphony is admirably and imaginatively described in the Stanford-Forsyth "History of Music":

"From the time of the caveman to about King Alfred's day, music was always 'one-line melody.' Then came a great discovery—the discovery of part-singing. It is no exaggeration to call this the most important invention of the last 2,000 years; for it betokens the existence of a new and hitherto unsuspected human faculty. Naturally in all ages the *accidental* coincidence of voices singing or shouting must have been common. But there was nothing *a priori* to show that these haphazard intersections of speech could be made the basis of a new and complex art-form. To a Roman of the fourth century A. D. such an idea would have appeared to be a fantastic dream. What should *we* say if we were told that in 2900 A. D. there would be a great art, based, let us suppose, on the combinations of perfumes?"

The layman who acquires a clear understanding of the fundamentals discussed in this particular approach to music can logically experience a development along the lines of the evolution of music itself as he becomes acquainted with it.

No picture can be complete without a background, so it behoves us to examine the state of the world, musically speaking, at the time mention of the revolutionary discovery of polyphony first appears in the meager records upon which we must rely for information. The dark ages lying between the beginning of the Christian era and the dawn of polyphony are illumined by a single musical torch—that of the Catholic Church. A great outburst of religious song, gaining momentum throughout the first five centuries after Christ, and probably containing music of Rome, Greece and the Hebrew temples as well as the existing music of many other parts of Christendom, was pressed into the service of the growing ritual of the Church, adapted for liturgical purposes, and preserved. It is the great bridge between our music and that of antiquity.

Four main collections of liturgical music are listed in the treasure house of the Church; the Roman or Gregorian Chant, the Milanese or Ambrosian Chant, the Mozarabic Chant of Spain and the Gallican Chant.[4] Our knowledge of them is unequal because until the ninth century there was no reliable or universal method of recording music in writing. The words were written out; the music was handed on orally. Sometimes a letter notation was used but only the music that survived long enough to be recorded in the musical notation of a later period is unquestionably authentic and much of the Mozarabic Chant and Gallican Chant was lost. The Ambrosian Chant has survived and is still used to a certain extent in the Church. Its founder, St. Ambrose,

---

[4] The generic term plain-song is often applied to all music of this description.

Bishop of Milan in the fourth century, not only compiled an Antiphonary,[5] but also composed simple hymns of real beauty.

By far the most important of the four liturgical collections is the one attributed to St. Gregory the Great (Pope Gregory I, 540–604 A. D.). If we consult various authorities on the subject of this Gregorian music which plays such an important part in the gradually unfolding drama of musical evolution, we find differences of opinion concerning its origin. Waldo Selden Pratt points out:

". . . many able scholars believe the practical completion of the system was not earlier than the 8th century, perhaps under Gregory II (died 731 A. D.) or Gregory III (died 741 A. D.) and that the name Gregorian came from them or was due to the mistaken zeal of those who sought to glorify the earlier Gregory."

This might well spring from the fact that the first mention of a collection of chants occurred about the year 760 A. D. According to "The Art of Music," John the Deacon (about 882 A. D.) was the first to ascribe the existing collections of chants to St. Gregory.

Justine Ward, in the preface of her Gregorian Chant textbook gives the following purely Catholic and fanciful version of its origin:

[5] A collection of antiphons, that is, devotional verse or prose responsively sung as a part of the liturgy.

"This music used by the early Christians was derived in part from that which had been used by the Jews from time immemorial, and partly from the musical system of the Greeks and Romans, but as the Christian liturgy grew richer and more elaborate, new melodies of surpassing beauty grew up out of those early traditional phrases, and were sung by the Christians of those days.

"Pope St. Gregory was a great lover of music. He had been a monk of St. Benedict before he became Pope and had learned to practice the liturgical chant of the Church. Every day, seven times a day, with the other monks, he sang the divine office, praising God in song, and praying for those people who had to live and work outside the monastery.

"One night Pope St. Gregory fell asleep and dreamed that he saw the Church under the form of a muse, clothed in exquisite vesture. She was occupied in writing out chants, and as she wrote, she drew to her all her children from every country of the world and gathered them under the folds of her mantle. And, behold, on the mantle was written plainly all the principles of the art of music,—the notes, the neumes, the modes, and also a great variety of melodies. When St. Gregory awoke he interpreted this vision as a sign from Heaven and undertook to collect together all the beautiful melodies that had been used in the Church since the days of the Apostles, arranging them in order and writing new ones where these were required. These melodies which have come down to us under the name of Gregorian Chant are one of the most precious heritages in the treasure house of the Church, and all her children, young and old, should love to sing them under the folds of her mantle."

If St. Gregory had been able to record his great collection in any form of notation by which the definite pitch of notes was fixed, the study of musical history from the sixth to the tenth century would have been considerably easier than it is. Unfortunately, this is not the case.

Grove describes the "great collection of Gregorian music" as falling into "two principal divisions"—the music of the Mass, with which is grouped that of Baptism and other occasional services, and the music of the Daily Hours of Divine Service. The collection for the Mass comprises over 600 compositions set entirely to scriptural words. A second collection includes the music of the Hours of Divine Service and numbers roughly two thousand antiphons and some eight hundred Greater Responds as well as smaller items.

With regard to the actual music contained in this collection it is certain that when a need for musical development occurs and any sort of musical experience has preceded this need, we are apt to find that the race or generation in question *takes existing musical material* [6] lying at hand, so to speak, and *uses it in a new*

---

[6] "Musical material" is a technical designation for the elements which make up a piece of music, such as scales or modes, melodic design, specific rhythmic values and—in modern music—harmonic or polyphonic structures.

and characteristic way, eventually creating a specific type. We can take Martin Luther as an example illustrating this fact. He possessed real musical talent; he was quite aware of the importance of music in religion; but he also desired to get away from musical traditions connected with Catholicism. Above all he wished to stress the congregational singing which was in line with Reformation ideals and for this he needed tunes that would be easy to sing and even popular in the sense of appealing alike to the initiated and the uninitiated. So he wrote hymns himself, and in addition, he not only re-fashioned Latin hymns, psalms, and liturgical chants for Protestant purposes, but he inaugurated the use of popular secular melodies in religious song. For instance, as Schweitzer writes in his "Life of Bach":

"Luther formed his Christmas Hymn 'Vom Himmel hoch, da komm ich her' out of the melody of the riddle-song 'Ich komm aus fremden Landen her' in which the singer propounds a riddle and takes her garland from the maiden who cannot solve it."

This song which "haunted every tavern and dancing place" was only one of many popular secular tunes adapted for use in the church. The procedure is aptly illustrated:—

". . . by the title of a collection that appeared at Frankfort in 1571; (translated) 'Street songs, cavalier songs, mountain songs, transformed into Christian and moral songs, for the abolishing in course of time of the bad and vexatious practice of singing idle and shameful songs in the streets, in fields, and at home, by substituting for them, good, sacred, honest words.' " [7]

Another example still nearer to us is the use made by the American Negro of musical material which he found in his new environment previous to the abolition of slavery in the United States. Negro spirituals and negro dance tunes are certainly characteristic of the race. The dance tunes form the basis of the whole later Jazz development. If we analyze this music, however, we find in the spirituals melodies and harmonies which in themselves are unmistakably derived from the occidental hymn tunes the negroes must have heard on southern plantations as well as in towns and cities. The negro unconsciously *used* these tunes in a way which made them as characteristic as his use of the English language. In the dance music, he added a distinctive racial contribution, namely, the wide scope of *rhythmic variety* common to primitive peoples. Characteristic and varied rhythm is the racial heritage which the negro brought to the type of dance music that evolved in North America, while the melodies and harmonies he used in connection with it were prevailingly borrowed from European music. The net result, however, is so characteristic that if heard in the remotest corners of the globe by one familiar with life in the United States, its origin would be recognized.

[7] Schweitzer's "Life of Bach."

As a concrete example of what is meant by the "use of existing musical material," the following case actually occurred at a plantation in Louisiana. A daughter of the owner [8] who was an ardent musician, taught the children of the house slaves to sing. During a Christmas celebration they sang the French Christmas Hymn "Minuit Chrétien." The following spring, this same tune, *rhythmically altered to fit other words* was heard in the sugar-cane fields where the slaves were *using it as a work-song.* They had caught the tune and adapted it to their own purposes. This method of procedure plays an important part in all folk music developments while the earliest origins lose themselves in the unrecorded dawn of racial life. Such examples, remote as they are from the Gregorian era, enable us to understand the probable origin of its music.

The "single-line" liturgical melodies of the Church penetrated to the furthest corners of Christendom and Vincent d'Indy is correct when he writes that "for a thousand years they were the sum total of all music." There must have been folk music during this time. We can assume that men have always sung and danced, but we have no way of knowing *what* they sang, outside of the Church, in the first thousand years of the Christian era.

There is something mysterious and dramatic in the way polyphony, destined to create such vast, undreamed-of possibilities in music, crept into the history of the art. Vague and ambiguous references to a "si-

[8] Lucie Palmer, maternal grandmother of the author.

multaneous singing of concords" occur in Latin treatises of the ninth century. The discoverers of polyphony are forgotten men. We can safely assume they were monks but we can only imagine what they would feel if they could come to life and learn what they have bestowed upon the world!

Not until the end of the tenth century do we find the new departure frankly accepted and clearly described. In the famous treatise, *Musica Enchiriadis,* formerly ascribed to Hucbald of St. Amand, but now supposed by leading authorities to have been written by Otger or Odo, Abbot of St. Pons de Tomières in Provence, we find actual musical examples that prove the existence of a regulated procedure in joining two or more melodies. The earliest examples reveal the simultaneous singing of a melody by two voices a *fifth* or a *fourth* apart. This process, called organum, can be visualized as follows:

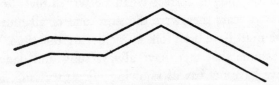

It can readily be seen that the musical effect of this procedure is quite different from the magadizing of the Greeks. When two voices sing the *same* melody an octave apart the listener has the sensation of a single melody because the same notes are merely duplicated in a different register, but when two voices sing a fifth or fourth apart, there is a distinct sensation of *two* tunes sung at the same time. It is like the difference between two shades of the same color and a combination of two totally different colors.

In his "New Resources in Music" Henry Cowell reminds us that the introduction of organum caused a lengthy discussion by ecclesiastical authorities as to whether this departure from tradition was not the work of the devil, designed to sow discontent. Whether his Satanic majesty was the forgotten originator of organum or not, the seeds of divine discontent with the limitations of single-line music were certainly planted. From that time to this, creative spirits have never ceased to evolve new ways of combining different sounds.

Let us see how a well-known tune of our own time would sound with a second voice singing a fifth or fourth below.

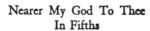

Nearer My God To Thee
In Fifths

In Fourths

Organum, the modern music of the tenth century, is the cornerstone of the great edifice of occidental musical art, a towering art unlike any the world had ever known.

POINTS TO BE REMEMBERED

1. Polyphony means the simultaneous sounding of two or more melodies.
2. The first attempts at polyphony—called Organum, are known to have been in use in 900 A. D. In the earliest strict organum, each note of a melody was combined with a note a fourth or a fifth below sung by a second voice.
3. The discovery of polyphony marks the division between occidental musical civilization since 900 A. D. and all others throughout the ages.

SUGGESTIONS FOR CORRELATED READING

Grove's Dictionary of Music, Article on Gregorian Music
Oxford History of Music, Introductory Volume 1929 edition
    Article on Plain-Song
Oxford History of Music, Volume I, Article on Organum
History of Music, Waldo Selden Pratt, Chapters IV & V
History of Music, Stanford-Forsyth, Chapter VI

MUSICAL ILLUSTRATIONS

Victor 20897-B   Example of Organum

Victor 7180 & 7181   Gregorian Chant
                              Pius X School of Liturgical Music

Delectus Missarum e Graduali Romano [1]
    (published by J. Fischer & Brother, New York)

[1] Gregorian Melodies for Dictation (these melodies are written out in modern notation). Taking musical dictation is an excellent way of developing tonal consciousness.

V

WHAT IS COUNTERPOINT?

*"I taught to them withal that art of
arts
The lore of number, and the written
word
That giveth sense to sound, the tool
wherewith
The gift of memory was wrought in
all,
And so came art and song."*

PROMETHEUS BOUND
AESCHYLUS

A QUAINT definition of counterpoint is contained in the
following description dated 1513:

"A song in our times hath not one voyce alone but
five, six, eight, and sometimes more. For it is evident
that Johannes O Keken did compose a motet for 36
voyces. Now that part of Musick which effecteth this
is called of the Musitians the Counterpoint."

In modern terms, the art of adding different melodies to a main tune is called *counterpoint* while the
generic name *polyphony* is applied to all music composed on the basis of plural-melody. The adjectives
polyphonic and contrapuntal (employing counterpoint) should be added to our terminology at this

point. The literal meaning of counterpoint—"point against point" or "note against note"—well expresses the essential significance of the art by which several melodies are made to fit together.

As our line of study approaches an increasing complexity in music, it is necessary for the layman to have a clear idea of the following fact. The specialized and thorough study of theory, harmony and counterpoint in our occidental musical system requires three or more years. The author does not offer any "get-rich-quick" musical schemes in this course.

The only legitimate possibility within a layman's cultural approach to music is to give a general idea of the most important fundamentals that underlie the great structure of our musical system. If a layman grasps the significance of these realities and they awaken his interest and curiosity, he can later proceed to the specialized study of musical theory, just as connoisseurs of other arts have built their extended knowledge around an initial interest in any particular field.

Counterpoint is usually taught *after* harmony, but the process is here reversed, because, from the point of view of musical evolution, counterpoint actually preceded harmony, and as the layman is not studying for the purpose of using counterpoint in musical composition, but to understand its fundamental significance, it is better for him to build up his musical experience on the basis of the evolution of music itself.

In the last chapter, the simplest form of strict

organum was discussed as the very first attempt at *organized* polyphony. Organum soon followed the course common to new ideas of inherent vitality; it expanded. Enlightening musical examples in the *Musica Enchiriadis* illustrate this rapid expansion that soon followed the initial discovery of polyphony as a musical possibility. The terms "vox principalis" (principal voice) and "vox organalis" (organal voice) were used to designate the main melody and its accompanying melodic line respectively. By doubling both lines, the vox principalis at the octave *below* and the vox organalis at the octave *above,* a composite type of organum using four voices was created around the intervals of the fifth and the fourth.

Example from the *Musica Enchiriadis*

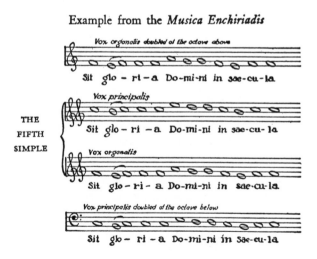

THE
FIFTH
SIMPLE

Example from the *Musica Enchiriadis*

THE
FOURTH
SIMPLE

The development of most music systems involves not only expansion, but—as it crystallizes and rules and formulas come into being—also the element of prohibition. An early instance of the latter, possibly the first one actually recorded in our system of music, occurred during the development of organum. According to some authorities it was based on the inability of the organ of those days to play below [notation]. Whether or not this instrumental limitation was the actual reason, the fact remains that it was forbidden for the organal voice to go below this note. Sometimes the pitch and melodic course of the vox principalis required of the vox organalis a note below this C in order to preserve the traditional distance of a fourth or a fifth between the voices. The fact that the vox organalis *had* to stand still at [notation] while the vox principalis continued to move, may have brought about the realization that two melodic lines were not compelled to adhere to strict parallel motion. We find already in the *Musica Enchiriadis* the following example in which the voices no longer move in parallel fourths or fifths:

Free Organum: *The Fourth Simple*

Composite forms of this irregular or "free" organum, the ultra-modern music of the tenth century, soon arose. This example and one given below from the *Scholia Enchiriadis* [1] in which all four voices end upon the same note (a procedure called "occursus," or running together) both show a free movement of the voices and display a tendency to counterbalance the irregularities incidental to the new-found freedom with the landing on a "home-base," so to speak, giving the listener a sense of *finality* and *solidity*.

---

[1] Another theoretical treatise of the period forming a commentary on the *Musica Enchiriadis*.

The Fourth Composite

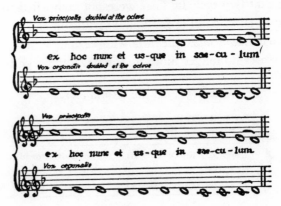

Visually the essence of strict organum and the development of free organum could be illustrated as follows:

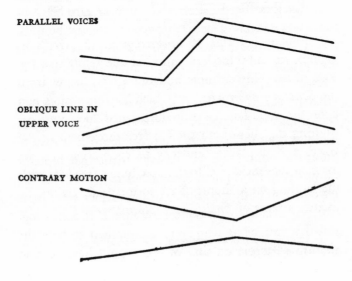

The student should now observe that in all the examples of organum here given, whether simple or composite, in parallel fourths and fifths or in the freer oblique and contrary movements of voices, the *time* value of all the notes was identical in the different parts. No matter how free the speech-rhythms may have been, the voices moved rhythmically note for note *together* because the text furnished the rhythm and affected all lines in the same way. But the creative and inventive spirits of the time had tasted blood and music continued to progress towards its great destiny of an independent art form, just as a growing child develops, logically and organically. By the middle of the twelfth century a new invention of great importance had provided another milestone in the evolution of music—the introduction of the time element or *"measure."* The fact that the duration and rhythmic grouping of tones was entirely dependent on text can best be illustrated by playing a record of Gregorian music (such as Victor Nos. 7180 or 7181) and trying to beat time to it. The layman will find that he can beat neither duple (march) nor triple (waltz) time to it. If we realize that each musical tone must have two elements which distinguish it from others—pitch and duration, it is easy to grasp the significance of the movement that brought music beyond this point. Some scholars believe that the introduction of different texts in the various voice parts was responsible for music measurement. It seems logical that musicians who were accustomed to base the rhythm of music on that of text would have to find some means of keeping the various voices together if different texts were used.

The first known ground-rhythm to be adopted in the establishment of music measurement was triple time. The procedure is supposed to have reference to the Holy Trinity, an assumption that may well be correct in view of the ecclesiastical domination of music. For about a hundred and fifty years there was no music but triple-time music. The possibilities of this triple time crystallized into six rhythmic modes. When we realize that plain-song usually had prose text and that the only metrical singing previous to the time under discussion had been because of employing metrical verse text in hymns or songs, it is not surprising that the musical rhythmic modes took the form of an adaptation of the feet of classical verse.

The following table and examples of the Rhythmic Modes taken from "Oxford History of Music" are enlightening:

Equivalent in Modern Notation

First (Trochee)		
Second (Iambus)		
Third (Dactyl)		
Fourth (Anapest)		
Fifth (Molossus)		
Sixth (Tribrach)		

One of the most interesting documents in musical history is the papal bull issued by Pope John XXII in 1322. Protesting against the measurement of music and the creation of "original melodies," the Pope evidently foresaw that the new developments would lead in the direction of the secularization of music. Part of this historic document reads as follows:

"Certain disciples of a new school, concentrating on time measurement, are applying themselves by means of new notes in creating original melodies at the expense of the ancient chants which they replace by music composed of whole notes and half notes. They cut their music into lengths, weaken it by discant, fill it with vulgar motets and triple figures, and even go so far as to discard the fundamental principles of the Antiphonary and Graduel, thus ignoring the foundation on which they must build, failing to discriminate in choice of tones and often confusing them.

"The great number of notes they use, obscures the modest and temperate methods by which tones are distinguished one from another in plain-song.

"They rush ahead destroying repose, they intoxicate the ear and fail to cure the soul; and thus the devotion sought in music is forgotten while the sensuality which should be avoided is brought to light."

Just as organum expanded to free movement of melodic lines, so the strict triple-time measurement of music could not withstand the pressure of eager creative spirits seeking ever wider possibilities. The description of the introduction of duple time as given in the Stanford-Forsyth "History of Music" is amusing as well as enlightening:

"Towards the end of the thirteenth century, Church musicians seem suddenly to have realized that the world would go mad if it had any more 3-2 rhythm. There was a violent wrench and snap; followed by a period of expansion and confusion which—as far as the Church was concerned—was ended by a decree of the Pope in 1322. From that year we date the introduction of *faburden*. These three sentences give us the main outlines of musical history from about 1280-1400.

"No technical reasons have ever been suggested for the sudden introduction of duple time. However, we shall probably be not far wrong if we regard its appearance as a natural but long-delayed protest against the restriction of human rights.

"But here let the reader pause to consider what a frightfully disturbing element this new rhythm was. No uninvited guest at a feast ever caused such trouble. Imagine the feelings of an elderly musician in 1280, who after being suckled, baptized, and nursed to 3-2 music and after spending his whole life on the supposition,—not that music *could be* written in 3-2 but that music *was* 3-2,—suddenly found from his juniors that it *might be* in duple time. The ground was wiped from under his feet. Our modern innovators who insist that the triad of C-major should include a D-flat and an

F-sharp would be almost harmless beside these mediaeval revolutionaries."

As the development of music became more and
more complex it is evident that dependence on the
memory of musicians in an oral handing on of melodies was not enough. Simple organum might still be
managed on this basis, but when the melody lines began to diverge in the manner we have just discussed
both in pitch and rhythm, some sort of symbol to represent both the pitch and the duration of the musical
tone became an absolute necessity.

The first attempts consisted in memory-aids called
neumes. When these vague signs of pitch really began
is uncertain, but by the eighth century they were definitely serving to remind the singer whether the melody
went up or down.[2] An interesting table in Grove's
"Dictionary of Music and Musicians" gives the development of separate neumes, from the earliest that can be
considered authentic to the symbols used in Gregorian
music at the Benedictine Monastery of Solesmes to-day.
Our notation grew out of this development and, inadequate as musicians still find it, it represents a miracle
of ingenuity. Cecil Forsyth writes that during the process of evolution "the invention of musical notation became a sort of fashionable amusement in monkish
circles; and a frightful confusion reigned in the minds
of musicians." We can imagine one learned scholar
shut up in a monastery working out one system, while

[2] See Appendix.

another invented something entirely different somewhere else and a third musician coming across the fruits of their labors could make nothing of either system.

It was not until an unknown genius of the tenth century hit upon the fundamental necessity of a *horizontal straight line which established the pitch of a single tone* that real progress was possible. This line, called the "F" line, was drawn in red above the text. It gave musicians something to hang on to and other tones were sung in relation to the fixed pitch of the note on the line.

Guido d'Arezzo (990–1050) who contributed more than any other known individual to the final development of our musical notation, added three other lines, one yellow and two black. He also conceived the brilliant idea of placing notes not only *on* lines but in the spaces between them.

Guido did not confine himself to the development of musical notation but also introduced the hexachord, or a scale-group of six tones, as the foundation of the mediaeval modes [3] instead of the old Greek tetrachord idea. To these six sounds he applied, as names, syllables which according to popular tradition he derived from a hymn by Paulus Diaconus in 770 for the Festival of St. John the Baptist. This idea of using syllables to designate musical sounds is called solmization. The *principle* of solmization was known to the Greeks but Guido's method is still in use to-day.

[3] See Appendix.

Hymn to St. John the Baptist

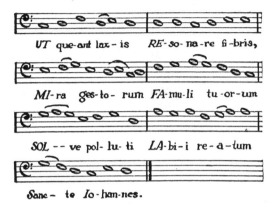

UT que-ant lax - is   RE'-so-na-re fi-bris,

MI-ra ges-to- rum FA-mu-li tu -or-um

SOL - - ve pol- lu- ti LA-bi-i re - a -tum

Sanc - te Io - han-nes.

Numerous inventions gradually came into being as the complexity of music grew. Different clefs which symbolized different pitches for the notes placed on lines or in spaces; sharps and flats to raise or lower a note a semi-tone; double sharps and double flats to raise notes or lower notes a whole tone; ways of writing notes that establish their exact duration as well as their pitch; rests that indicate a pause of definite length; bar lines that exactly define the grouping of notes into a particular rhythmic pattern; and leger-lines, short lines placed above or below the staff [4] which extend its scope in both directions. If the student has a glimpse of this long and complicated development, in which

[4] The musical staff is the collection of lines and spaces upon which musical symbols are placed. Some scholars give as the origin of the modern double staff of five lines each, an old eleven line or "great staff" from which the middle line has been eliminated.

such an immense effort was involved and in which so much ingenuity was required, he will perhaps be encouraged to take advantage of the clear and simplified modern notation now at his disposal and learn to read and write music.[5] The person who cannot read music is in the position of someone who has to be eternally read to. The capacity to read music not only facilitates performance, but a listener can best explore musical literature by studying records with the score. In the development of the listener, this kind of study is just as important as practice is to the performer. Without it the listener can never become independent as well as active.

Anyone who has climbed mountains with a guide will remember how he will invariably stop from time to time to show to his charges special views that can be seen from certain places during the ascent. In a book like this, the author must select from a great mass of possible information those "views" that will mean most to the explorer of music. Regarding the consideration of counterpoint as a "special place" in our ascent, the layman can look out over a wide expanse of musical landscape—one that contains many a high peak of artistic achievement.

From the thirteenth to the seventeenth centuries, musicians were chiefly occupied in cultivating this art of joining melodic lines. At times, ingenuity for its

[5] For a simple and effective way of accomplishing this see "The Gist of Music" by George A. Wedge.

own sake threatened the inspirational quality of music; but enough great geniuses appeared in the course of these centuries to save the art from losing beauty and freedom. In Italy, in the Netherlands and in England great contrapuntal schools arose. The correlated reading recommended below will give the layman an insight into these developments and give him some acquaintance with the names and activities of composers.

Most important is the study of the listed records with a conscious effort to follow the weaving of the various melodic lines. The masses, madrigals,[6] and motets [7] of the contrapuntal era are the forerunners of chamber music and orchestral music. Counterpoint did

[6] A vocal polyphonic type of composition (without instrumental accompaniment), which originated in the Low Countries towards the middle of the fifteenth century. Spreading to other European countries it reached its greatest perfection in Italy and in England where a flourishing Madrigal Society still exists, although the cultivation of the form by composers only extended into the early eighteenth century. Secular in character, the madrigal sets to music a short lyrical poem, pastoral, amorous or descriptive. The name was originally derived from this kind of poem. The madrigal can be written for any number of voices but usually employs from three to eight. It has rightly been called the *chamber music* of its epoch.

[7] The Motet is a vocal polyphonic composition of sacred character, often employing a biblical text. Beginning as far back as the thirteenth century, it had no instrumental accompaniment in its earliest form. Later, the accompanied motet became very popular. The long history of the form contains many curious features, such as different texts for the various voices. This accounts for one definition of it as the "embroidering of a given theme of words-and-music by two or three other sets of words-and-music" ("Grove's Dictionary of Music and Musicians").

Bach and even more recent composers have written motets, which, however, are very different from those of the fourteenth, fifteenth and sixteenth centuries.

not cease in the seventeenth century. It forms an important part of music to-day. While certain types or forms of music may dominate certain periods, it is interesting to realize that in the evolution of music, as in nature, nothing vital is lost. Restrictions may be discarded, the changing of taste may occasion the temporary eclipse of great music, but the major elements and discoveries in music remain and continue—as evolution progresses—to be used in countless different ways by the creative spirits of succeeding generations. So far, the evolution of western art music means the *addition* and *expansion* of possibilities.

POINTS TO BE REMEMBERED

1. The expansion of organum into free movement of different voices.
2. The introduction of the measurement of music.
3. The conception of counterpoint as a note-against-note organization of different melodies or the embellishment of a principal melody by ornamental musical lines in other voice parts.
4. The evolution of symbols to record music in writing or musical notation.

SUGGESTIONS FOR CORRELATED READING

The Oxford History of Music, Volume II, Woolbridge
The Evolution of Music, Parry, Chapters IV & V
History of Music, Stanford-Forsyth, Chapters VI & VII
The Mediaeval Modes, A. Madeley Richardson
Contrapuntal Technique in the Sixteenth Century, R. O. Morris
Music Through the Ages, Marion Bauer and Ethel Peyser

MUSICAL ILLUSTRATIONS

Victor 20897-B: *Hymn to St. John the Baptist*

Roycroft Records by the English Singers:

151—*Sing We and Chant It*
152—*In Going to my Naked Bed*
153—*The Silver Swan*
    The Three Fairies
154—*Now is the Month of Maying*
156—*Hard By a Crystal Fountain*
159—*Sumer Is Icumen In* [a]
160—*Though Amaryllis Dance*
161—*In Dulci Jubilo*
    O Christ Who Art the Light

[a] Famous English Round said to have been composed by John of Fornsete about 1250 and the first important secular composition on record. It is considered a milestone in musical history.

VI

WHAT IS A FUGUE?

"A great master like Bach is instinctively aware that appeals to sensation must be accompanied by proportionate appeals to the higher faculties."

SCHWEITZER

To ATTEMPT to take the terror out of technicalities for the layman is no easy task. The ancient and honorable joke about fugues—that they are compositions in which the voices run away from each other, and the hearer from them all—is no idle pleasantry. Many a listener *has* run away when he saw a fugue coming. And yet there is no type of composition from which the layman can gain more in learning to listen for musical *structure*. The significant designation for architecture, "frozen music," might well be matched by "fluid architecture" as a definition for the big many-voiced musical forms in occidental music.

The fugue is logically the next subject after counterpoint to be chosen for consideration in this book because it grew out of the elements discussed in "What is Counterpoint," and in a measure it may be called the crowning achievement of "the art of joining melodies." In the earliest developments of counterpoint, composers learned that one very effective way of bringing unity into a musical composition was to have one voice imitate a phrase that had been sung by another. This device of composition, as it became a recognized feature of musical building, was given the name "canon," the word being used in the sense of its Latin meaning—law. The rounds such as *Sumer Is Icumen In* formed complete canons inasmuch as each voice imitated in its entirety the song that was begun by the first voice. Few laymen have failed to gain experience in singing rounds in childhood, if only the classic example, *Three Blind Mice.* There is something comforting in being able to link up the formidable fugue form with such a familiar and homely piece of music as *Three Blind Mice,* and yet they have a common ancestry, for the first fugues were called "fuga per canonem," literally a "flight (fuga) of voices according to law (canon)." Nobody could deny that the "flight of voices" in *Three Blind Mice* is absolutely according to law and the author is convinced that any self-respecting fugue would recognize the relationship.

The layman will notice throughout the evolution of music that when a new idea or form comes into the picture, it is first "strict" and then "free." This phenomenon is natural and inevitable. When a good idea is born, creative spirits seize upon and use it. But genius is a veritable Houdini in wriggling out of strait-jackets, and no matter how much theorists may proclaim rules and dictate formulas, genius always insists upon a free and unhampered use of basic ideas and accepted forms. In discussing various forms in this course, the author will describe them as types, seizing the moment when they have become recognizable and "strict." The layman can then have the interest of discovering innumerable exceptions to rules as he explores musical literature.

The fugue in its infancy was merely a strict canon. As it achieved greater scope, it began "canonically" and then proceeded to a free play of the different voices. The earliest fugues were written for voices, but it is one of the first great forms to be transferred to instruments, and in the instrumental fugue the layman will find one of the loftiest types of abstract "architectural" music.

The author now invites the layman to join in the experience of constructing the general plan of an instrumental fugue. The architect who sets out to build a cathedral may have a very emotional nature and the loftiest kind of dreams about religion, but if he is to build a cathedral, no matter how much he is inspired by his emotions and dreams, he will not get very far unless he also occupies himself with style, dimensions, materials and all the other things necessary to the actual creation of the building. Let us assume the first decision of the architect would be style. If he decides upon a Gothic cathedral, the Gothic arch will become the main theme of his building.

The fugue-writer must also find a main theme for his composition. He does not, however, have existing types of theme to call on. He must create an original one. It must be neither too long nor too short, but above all, it must have a "shape" and a character that will make it just as recognizable throughout the fugue as the Gothic arch is recognizable throughout the design of the cathedral.

After the fugue-composer has found his main theme, what next? In that question lies the key to an understanding of all musical forms. There is no such thing as a musical composition of large scope that springs complete from a single inspirational impulse of the composer. If the work is great, the themes—technically speaking the *thematic material*—must be born of inspiration. Creative processes defy analysis. We only know their results. But the composer must know what to do with his inspirational musical material, just as a writer must know what to do with his ideas or an architect with his building materials.

The forms within which artistic material can be used are seldom invented by an individual. They evolve. Countless experiments, born of the necessity for form and developed through the cumulative experience of some great, and a host of lesser, creative spirits, gradually produce an art-type of value, one that has plan, strength, logic and proportion. The Greek Temple, the Gothic Church, the Renaissance Palace, the Tragedy, the Comedy, the Farce, the Novel, the Essay, the Landscape, the Portrait, the Still-life, the Fugue, the Sonata, the Symphony, all these possible forms gradually evolve, and into them, as their value becomes evident, the creative artist pours his inspiration, relying on their inherent qualities to save him from incoherence and communicative impotence. The great genius never allows accepted ideas of form to dominate him. He uses fundamental principles in a thousand different ways, benefiting by their intrinsic value but preserving his creative freedom. The creation—and the perception—of art works demands *all* our powers, super-conscious and conscious, intuitive and rational.

Supposing, then, that our theme for the fugue has come to us by an inspirational process we shall not attempt to define, we again ask the question, "What next?"

Obviously, we can only answer this question if we have a clear understanding of fugue form. We must know that the fugue usually contains a single dominating theme—technically called *subject*—just as an essay has one dominating idea, and a portrait one dominating figure. We must know that, in common with its ancestor the canon, its chief mode of procedure is built on the idea of having different voices take up a theme already given out by one of them. Can this be done in "any old way?" No more than arches can be placed in a haphazard manner in a church.

We must first decide how many voices we want in our fugue. We can have as few as two or as many as we want; but the two-voice fugue will be limited in interest, whereas too many voices will make our musical structure unwieldy. Three-voice fugues can be very effective but four or five voices give us richer opportunities. The layman will notice that the author keeps on talking about "voices." Even if the fugue is instrumental the word "voice" is used to designate each of the separate melodic lines that combine to form the interwoven structure of the work.

Let us decide upon four voices (melodic lines) for our fugue. Any one of these can make the first statement of our subject (main theme) but it is very effective to have the lowest voice begin, because then, as each entrance of the subject will be in a higher register, the sensation of building up, the cumulative feeling so valuable in polyphonic writing, will be given to the listener. We must decide on a key for our fugue, and the nature of our theme will determine whether the composition will be in the major or the minor mode. Assuming that we have settled upon the key of C major, our lowest voice will state our subject. The next voice to take it up will be the tenor. Can that voice begin the second statement of the theme—technically called the *answer*—anywhere? Not at all, if we are writing a strict fugue. Experience has taught fugue-writers that the successive entries of subjects sound best when spaced according to plan, just as the distance between arches in a church must be carefully adjusted and in proportion. It is also experience, consciously or unconsciously based on the laws of nature, there being close connection between the intervals of the octave, fifth and fourth (the intervals between the four lowest partials of the single tone), that determined what the traditional voice-entries in a strict fugue should be. Conventionally the plans for voice entry in ascending or descending order, assuming we start on the tonic of C, would be: [1]

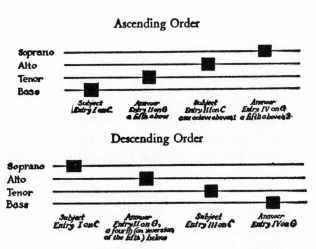

Ascending Order

Soprano
Alto
Tenor
Bass

Subject
Entry I on C.

Answer
Entry II on G
a fifth above

Subject
Entry III on C
one octave above

Answer
Entry IV on G
a fifth above it

Descending Order

Soprano
Alto
Tenor
Bass

Subject
Entry I on C

Answer
Entry II on G,
a fourth (an inversion
of the fifth) below

Subject
Entry III on C

Answer
Entry IV on G

This particular spacing gives the feeling of tonic and dominant, the strongest tones of the scale. The voice entries can also proceed in a mixed order so far as ascent and descent are concerned, but the space between the subject and answer must be retained if we are to remain within the law.

If we decide to have the proper voice-entries in ascending order, the question arises: what is the bass voice to do after it has stated the subject, while the tenor enters with the answer? Obviously, every one of the four voices must continue throughout the fugue. There

[1] The horizontal lines in this diagram represent the melodic lines of the four voices in the fugue, not the lines of the musical staff.

may be occasional short pauses, just as windows may be placed in a wall, but if each voice does not keep up its end, our tonal structure will collapse.

When the second voice-entry occurs, the first voice can go on with any independent melody that sounds well, as counterpoint, with the second entry of the theme (answer); but if we hit upon something that sounds so particularly well with the answer that we would like to use it throughout the fugue in conjunction with the main subject—as one might use a certain motif of carving on the Gothic arches of a cathedral— we elevate it to the position of an important element of the work and—because it is convenient for recognizable things to have a name—we call it a *counter-subject*.

In textbooks we read that a fugue should have three sections. The first—logically called *exposition*— contains the entry of the main subject in all the voices. If we want to extend this section we can repeat all these entries, calling the repetition *counter-exposition,* but in order to avoid monotony, we change the order of the entries and instead of having the order consist of subject (in C), answer (in G), subject (in C) and an- swer (in G), we begin with the answer (in G) and follow with the subject (in C), etc. We must clearly realize that the difference between subject and answer is merely one of *key* inasmuch as the theme remains the same whether called subject or answer. The second sec- tion of a fugue is one in which the composer is free to be as interesting as he can be, playing around with the main theme (and counter-subject if there is one) in all sorts of different ways and different keys. Any voice not occupied with the essential thematic material continues making agreeable counterpoint which might be likened to the background of a tapestry.

The third section of a fugue is not always easy to find. Indeed it seems as though some composers thumbed their noses at the formulator of rules by deliberately concealing the point at which a third section should normally begin. But other fugue-writers with a stronger dramatic sense manage to introduce the main subject at the psychological moment in the original key in such a way that the listener is aware of something significant and the final section of the fugue gains the aspect of a climax.

The question now is, how can we avoid monotony in a composition where a dominating theme is constantly cropping up? Johann Sebastian Bach left one great comprehensive answer to this question. At the time of his death he was working on *The Art of Fugue,* an amazing demonstration of the possibilities of fugue-writing.[2] The greatest of all fugue-writers bequeathed

---

[2] The full title which appeared in the first printed edition read (translated from the German) as follows:

THE ART OF FUGUE

by
Mr. Johann Sebastian Bach

Former Conductor and Musical Director in Leipzig
On the inner side of the page was printed the following notice:

NOTICE

The late composer of this work was prevented through his loss of sight and subsequent death from finishing the last fugue; one has, therefore, tried to lessen the consequent loss to the friends to posterity from his treasure-store of experience manifold possibilities that enable a composer to use a single theme in so many ways that the danger of monotony is eliminated. Bach shows that we can turn a theme upside down (*invert* it) without loss of identity; we can *augment* it by giving each note *twice* the duration it had in the original form of the theme; we can diminish it by giving each note *half* the duration it originally had; we can use fragments of the theme, so characteristic that they make its presence felt; we can use the theme in different keys that seem to alter its color. Again, in the exposition of a fugue, each voice waits until the preceding one has finished stating the entire theme, before making the next entry. A favorite device in the later use of the theme is to crowd the voice entries, i. e., begin each entry *before* the preceding voice has finished stating the theme. This can produce an exciting effect—technically called *stretto,* not unlike the set-backs of a modern skyscraper. This favorite device, often used in the final section of a fugue, although it can be used at any point after the exposition, demands the greatest ingenuity on the part of a composer, because not only must he accomplish a feat of tonal

of his muse by adding the four voice Chorale which Bach during his blindness dictated to one of his friends.

This *"Art of Fugue"* was therefore Bach's last great work. It contains thirteen fugues (each called a "Contrapunctus"), all for four voices except VIII and XIII which are for three; four two-voice canons; two fugues for two claviers, which are Bach's own four-voice version of No. XIII (three-voice) and the final unfinished fugue, probably mistakenly entitled "on three subjects," as the whole lay-out fits with the original main theme and works out (as proved by Nottebohm, Riemann, Tovey et al) as a four-voice fugue.

building, but it must *sound well*. The following example occurs in the Bach B flat minor fugue from the first book of the *Well-tempered Clavichord*.[3]

Stretto from the B flat minor Fugue

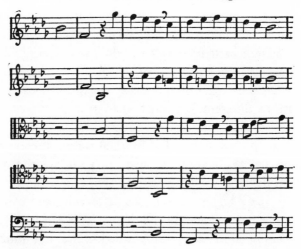

This stretto occurs in the last nine bars of the fugue. The theme extends as far as the comma in each voice part.

[3] The author has found that the curiosity of laymen is aroused by the title of the great collection of Bach Preludes and Fugues, the *"Well-tempered Clavichord."* It is obvious that on instruments such as the violin family, where the pitch of tones is created at the moment of performance by the player, a great number of intervals is possible. The player can at will produce tones differing from each other by only a few vibrations per second. But on a keyboard instrument where the depression of each key must produce a tone of fixed pitch from the string (or organ pipe) it operates, the number of playable tones must be limited enough for the instrument to be practical in respect to size and performance. The earliest examples of keyboard instruments were tuned in the *natural* scale. (See Appendix.)

As the old modal system weakened and the new Ionian and Aeolian modes—our major and minor scales—became dominant

A glance at the examples of augmentation and diminution and inversion from Bach's *Art of Fugue* on
pages 110, 111 and 112 clearly reveals the possibilities
alluded to above, and through the records listed below [4]
we can hear the examples as well as see them.

All these things create a distinctive musical *texture*.
Vaughan Williams aptly points out that one might
speak of a composition being written "in fugue" just
as one speaks of a poem being written "in hexameter."
The musical texture of a fugal weaving of voices with
the effect of canon in successive voice-entries is often

factors in a development that included a rapidly expanding harmonic sense, it became clearly apparent to musicians how desirable
it would be to tune keyboard instruments so as to divide the octave
space into *twelve equal semi-tones*. By doing this they could build
a major or minor scale on each of the semi-tones without encounter-
ing any of the slight differences in pitch which result from building
these scales according to pure acoustical law. Zarlino, a sixteenth-
century Venetian organist, started the ball rolling by investigating the
possibilities of the new scales, and the system of equal temperament
was approved and developed later by Neidhardt, Werckmeister and
Johann Sebastian Bach, who crowned its general adoption by writing the collection of forty-eight Preludes and Fugues called the
Well-tempered Clavichord. The collection is divided into two
Books, each of which contains one major and one minor Prelude
and Fugue to every one of the twelve tones in the division of the
octave known as the *chromatic* or semi-tone scale. For further explanation of *equal temperament* see Appendix.

[4]   BACH—250th Anniversary Album

ART OF THE FUGUE

(transcribed by Roy Harris and M. D. Herter Norton)
Played by the Roth String Quartet

Columbia Recording   Set #206

Record illustrating Augmentation and Diminution:

Part 8, (Contrapunctus VII)

Record illustrating Mirror Fugue:

Part 16, (Contrapunctus XIII)

Using the above measures taken from Bach's *Art of Fugue* as an example of the rhythmical device of augmentation and diminution, it is easy for the layman who can read musical notation to observe that each note in the second and third bars of the soprano voice is exactly twice as long as the notes of the same theme (inverted) in the first bar of the tenor voice.

(Mirror Fugue) Inversion

III

In this famous example of inversion from Bach's *Art of Fugue*, observe that the intervals between the successive tones

112

used by composers in certain portions of miscellaneous works such as symphonies, sonatas or even operas. *Fugato* is the name given to those transient passages that do not develop into a regular fugue, but lend a passing interest and distinctive character. Without attempting a further exploration of fugal possibilities at this time, let us examine one more salient type, the fugue that has independent counter-subjects appearing not in the exposition in conjunction with the main subject, but in the middle section of the fugue, and continuing through the final section. A famous example is the five-voice fugue in C sharp minor from the first book of the *Well-tempered Clavichord* of Bach. By following the chart on page 114, while listening to the record (His Master's Voice Record, DB 2081 #5, Edwin Fischer, pianist), the student can gain a very real conception of what a fugue can be:

Subjects of the C sharp minor Fugue of Bach from the first book of the *Well-tempered Clavichord.*

Note the different character of the themes. The main theme is composed of a few sustained tones. The

of the two voices are identical except that they proceed in opposite directions, one going up and the other going down.

Chart of the C sharp Minor Fugue of Bach from the first book of the Well-tempered Clavichord

From *Fugue* by J. Higgs

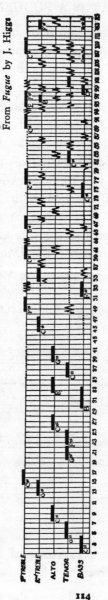

The principal subject is indicated throughout by —
The first counter-subject is indicated by ......
The second counter-subject is indicated by ⌇⌇

114

first counter-subject, with many more tones, constitutes a flowing melodic line, while the second counter-subject has a much stronger rhythmic character than the others and a sharply defined, almost jagged outline. Obviously the different character of these themes makes them stand out even when Bach uses them simultaneously.

If the layman discovers the fascination of exploring these intricate tonal edifices which one student of the Layman's Music Courses declared to "beat cross-word or picture puzzles all hollow," one more question will probably be asked: Can a fugue appeal to the emotions?

It is quite understandable that a layman, becoming really aware for the first time of the processes of musical composition, should get an impression that all these complexities might destroy spontaneity and the expression of emotion. The answer is that the skill and ingenuity, the knowledge and mastery necessary to the actual process of musical composition avail but little if the mysterious thing called inspiration is lacking. Used by an inspired composer, these technicalities become his tools, and very necessary ones; for the type of art music that has evolved in the occidental world cannot be improvised, any more than cathedrals or great dramas or great literature can be improvised. The composer must have the *means* to create an enduring art work. The *way* he uses these means gives a certain kind of pleasure to those who can perceive it. This particular kind of pleasure has its own emotion; not joy nor sorrow, love nor hate, but *realization of purely musical beauty.*

Many fugues in addition to beauty of sound and form also have a pronounced mood, sometimes of gaiety, often of grandeur, as in the great organ fugues of Bach. Evolving at a time, however, when art itself was rated higher than using music to express something else, the fugue is not a form most composers would choose for the direct expression of human emotion. The layman should seek something else in becoming familiar with this particular form of music; nothing is more valuable in accelerating his development as an active listener. If a listener can actually *hear* a fugue with consciousness, he can hear anything.[5]

In connection with this first discussion of a specific form in music, let it be well understood that no listener should attempt to analyze music at a concert. Just as the orchestra rehearses and the performer practices, so the listener should analyze and learn music during hours he devotes to his own development. Just as the performer must study from the printed page, so the layman should have his scores at hand and let his eye help his ear in penetrating to the realities of musical art works.

A musical composition is painted on the canvas of *time*. It moves by us, and we must seize its beauties as they pass. Preparation is as necessary as intuition if we are to perceive these beauties before they vanish. Listening is an art.

[5] It is recommended to precede the study of the fugue with an examination of Bach's first two-part invention, noting the richly varied use of a single motif.

POINTS TO BE REMEMBERED

1. The concept of fugue form as one in which two or more voices moving in horizontal lines combine to form a tonal structure usually built around one main subject, but sometimes including one or more counter-subjects.
2. In fugue form we find purely polyphonic music most perfectly transferred from voices to instruments.
3. The strict fugue has three main divisions—an exposition, a development section and a final section.
4. These sections are *not* divided by formal cadences.
5. The form can neither be used in composition nor listened to with complete enjoyment without intellectual insight; but in the hands of creative genius it can be endowed with beauty and mood, just as a cathedral built on the most formal and traditional plan can be emotionally stirring. The fugue more than any other musical form can be considered as *architecture in music.*

SUGGESTIONS FOR CORRELATED READING

Grove's Dictionary of Music and Musicians, Article on Fugue
Fugue, J. Higgs [*]
Fugue, E. Prout
Fugue Writing, A. Madeley Richardson
Contrapuntal Technique in the Sixteenth Century, R. O. Morris
J. S. Bach, Albert Schweitzer
Bach, a Biography, Terry

RECORDS

Bach   250th Anniversary Album—*Art of the Fugue* (transcribed by Roy Harris and M. D. Herter Norton)
Played by the Roth Quartet
Recorded by Columbia

[*] Some layman students have reported this book to be unavailable, but others have been able to procure it in 1935.

Bach [7]   The Bach Society records of the Fugues from *The Well-tempered Clavichord*
Played by Edwin Fischer
Recorded by The Gramophone Co. Ltd. (His Master's Voice) London

[7] Two volumes of the Fugues have been issued. Others to follow later.

VII

OPERA AS A MILESTONE

*"The sensibilities of a given age
are all directed toward the same in-
visible goal; they seize upon the relationships which another age would
not seize upon; they erect systems
which satisfy the obscurest and the
strongest of their desires."*

ELIE FAURE

OPERA affords endless opportunities for discussion. It
has been reviled and reformed, glorified and popular-
ized more than any other art form within the realm of
music.

It has been pronounced dead as often as the German Crown Prince in the World War, and yet it lives
on. Despite the fact that violence and murder, death
and destruction are so prevalent in operatic plots that
it would seem as though most librettists were bent on
creating the gloomiest kind of entertainment, no
musical institution is so perennially gay, social and
festive as the opera house. The magic of music can
apparently dispel any amount of dramatic gloom.

In Continental Europe, if royal or official personages are to be entertained, if a historic event is to be
celebrated, if a gala atmosphere is to be created for the
public by astute government officials, opera is pressed

into service. Washington, so far, is the only western capital that has not recognized its value in this respect. If we study the early history of opera, we find that the festive possibilities of the form were immediately recognized by political and social leaders in Europe. The first opera on record, produced in 1597, was *Dafne,* music by Jacopo Peri, libretto by the poet Rinuccini. We know very little about it. But the same composer and librettist collaborated in an important music drama —*Euridice*—that makes the year 1600 a milestone in musical history, and it is significant that this opera was created for the especial purpose of gracing royal festivities on the occasion of the marriage of Marie de Medici and Henry the IV of France. Thus the form immediately began its brilliant worldly career.

From a purely musical point of view, critics of opera as an art form might well be reminded that without the effect it had on the evolution of occidental art music, we might not have our existing harmonic conception of music that has given us so much of the musical literature we most highly value. Again, who knows if we would have had the symphony orchestra, or that important instrument, the piano, without the particular development inaugurated by opera? Part of a discussion along these lines must take place in the field of conjecture. We can never do more than guess about a different outcome if certain things had not happened. But if we realize that melody alone sufficed for mankind in general for so many *thousands* of years, it seems possible that the joining of different melodies in purely vocal polyphony which dominated occidental music from 900 to 1600 might well have continued for *hundreds* of years more without any radically new departure. In that case we should still be composing and singing and listening to little more than vast choral works filled with endless complexities of a contrapuntal nature.

What caused the change in 1600 from purely polyphonic vocal music to the harmonic conception that brought about such important later developments? First we must understand the nature of "harmony" and realize how it differs from polyphony or counterpoint. From 900 to 1600, while the art of joining melodies was growing and expanding, we find, even in the earliest Latin treatises on music, a constant pre-occupation with the problem of *consonance* and *dissonance*. When musical tones are combined, both the composer and the listener demand that the result of the combination should sound well. But the conception of what sounds well is as far from being universal or unalterable as taste in the matter of feminine beauty. Despite the natural law of sex attraction, the American or European man would not be apt to respond to the "beauty" of the central-African belle with a flat nose adorned by a nose-ring, any more than a Rubens, who loved ample proportions in a woman's figure, would passionately admire a slim flapper with a boyish bob. These things, even though affected by natural laws, change with race, custom and age.

Natural laws of an acoustical nature are always

advanced by musicians who have accepted certain ideas of consonance and dissonance as the reason behind their credo, and there is truth in a fundamental connection between the natural laws of sound vibration and harmony,[1] but a glance at the table on p. 123 shows an evolution that cannot be disregarded if we are to understand music in the deepest sense, and include in that understanding the unmistakable creative tendencies of our own time.

Why did opera help to bring harmony into music? The originators of opera, a band of ardent "modernists" at the close of the sixteenth century, doubtless very much under the influence of the Renaissance, were avowedly seeking a way to a revival of the combination of music and drama used by the Greeks.

The actual music used in Greek drama has not survived. The fact of its being used is mentioned and the text remains but there is no way of knowing what the music actually was or how it was performed. We can, however, with considerable certainty assume that it was *single-line music,* at the most magadized (see Sound and the Function of Hearing), and possibly accompanied by a duplication of the melody played on the aulos, lyre or kithara.

Even if the modernists of the late sixteenth century had been able to find authentic Greek melodies for their operas, they could scarcely have succeeded in

---

[1] The tones constituting the "chord of nature"—the major triad —are to be found in the first five partials of the single tone. "Harmony" exists in nature, even though it took thousands of years for man to find it out.

CHART OF CONSONANCES AND DISSONANCES IN WESTERN EUROPE

10th Century	12th Century	15th & 16th Century	17th Century	18th Century	19th Century	20th Century
Only Octaves, Fourths, and Fifths accepted as consonances	Thirds and Sixths admitted as "imperfect consonances"	Passing notes create habit of other intervals but all "dissonances" are "prepared" "first composer" Dunstable (died 1453)	Monteverdi uses unprepared dominant seventh. —	New instrumental forms demand freer modulation made possible by equal temperament —	Increasing use of chromatic harmonies and complicated discords —	Smaller Intervals ¼– ⅛– 1/16ths of tones experimented with. —
			Gesualdo, Prince of Venosa, uses chromatic progressions Foundations of modern harmony laid —	Rameau publishes famous treatise on harmony 1722 Key relationships play important part in development of larger musical forms. —	Whole tone scale admitted. —	Atonality —
						Polytonality —

123

rendering a single melodic line completely satisfying to ears that had become attuned to the rich tonal mixtures of polyphony. At the same time, they evidently realized how much more eloquent the single-line (melody) could be in the direct expression of human emotion so indispensable to the union of music and drama. After experimenting with shorter vocal forms called canzonetti, and performing them at the palace of Giovanni Bardi, Conte di Vernio in Florence— which served as a center for the new art movement— the Peri operas were finally written and in them the tonal mixtures of polyphony were replaced by tone-groups (chords) that accompanied the prevailing single-line melodies of the operas. These tone-groups were built on the basis of the conceptions of consonance and dissonance that had grown up in polyphony. A harmonic accompaniment (chords) is entirely familiar to us, but it was a most revolutionary novelty in 1600. As we have seen in a former chapter, polyphony incorporates, musically speaking, the idea of several horizontal melodic lines, each pursuing a separate course of its own, but at the same time, joining harmoniously with others. In *harmonic* music, a melody or theme is supported by progressions of chords (tone-groups) considered by musicians in the light of "vertical" entities. The distinction can be visualized by the layman as follows:

Each of these lines represents a separate melody joined with the others to produce polyphonic music.

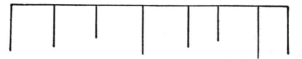

Here the horizontal line represents the melodic (or thematic) part of a composition while the vertical lines represent the chords upon which the melody rests.

Needless to say, the elaborate system of harmony we now have did not spring into being overnight, but the growing and changing conceptions of consonance and dissonance throughout the era of polyphony had brought about a *"harmonic sense"* that is already apparent in the greatest works of many contrapuntal composers preceding the milestone of 1600, notably Palestrina, that extraordinary genius who crowned the "Golden Age" of polyphony in the sixteenth century. These composers, however, were using their harmonic sense unconsciously. They were *thinking horizontal music*.

Opera is the first great form in which harmony took its place as a *major element* of music and, for that reason alone, no one could deny its importance in the evolution of the art. By the time Rameau brought out his famous treatise on harmony (1722) the foundations of a system had been laid in which the relation of tone-groups (chords) to each other had become just as definite as the relation of single tones to each other in melodic systems, or the relation of words to each other in language. Rameau based his theories on natural laws as far as he could work them out with the mono-chord.[2]

Let us now consider opera's other serious claims to consideration.

The fact that music lends added eloquence to words has never been a secret. The savage knew it. That is why, from time immemorial, chanting has formed part of religious ritual; that is why song has always ex-isted and can never die; that is why the Greeks used music in their dramas; why the Chinese still use it, and why we could scarcely escape using it.

Just as many streams contribute to a river, so all kinds of previous developments may be regarded as part of the evolution of opera. The mediaeval miracle and morality plays within and without the Church, various types of secular song such as the troubadour song,[3] popular song, notably the frottole in Italy, the early ballet, and the madrigal (secular part-song) all

---

[2] A single string stretched on some kind of resonating sounding-board. Pythagoras based his tonal theories on experiments with the monochord and it has since played an important part in the study of sound phenomena.

[3] The troubadour movement, beginning in the late eleventh cen-tury and lasting about two hundred years, emanated not from the people, as most song developments do, but from the upper classes. The name is derived from the French *Trover* (old form of the verb *trouver*) or Provençal *trobar*, meaning "to find" or "invent."

The troubadours in Provence (south-eastern France), the trou-vères in northern France and the minnesingers in Germany, while differing somewhat in the style and quality of their poetry and music, were all aristocratic poet-singers, whose artistic impulse to express the sentiment of love, to celebrate the beauty and virtue of woman, to recite deeds of chivalry and declaim epic tales whether of

played a part in the development towards opera. The troubadours and their prototypes in other parts of Europe proved the possibility of setting verse of a secular and cultivated nature to music. This had been

human or mythological character, takes an important place in the secularization of music.

A significant feature of this development is that its music is secondary to text. The verse-making impulse was primarily responsible for the movement, but the desire to render the text more eloquent through the addition of music is another demonstration of the same realization of the expressive power of music as that which caused primitive man to chant. Pratt writes:

"Wherever this minstrelsy penetrated, it fixed a taste for styles quite diverse from that of the Church, one close to the feeling of the common people and apt for their use."

A link between the aristocratic poet-singers and the lower classes was the "jongleur"—the "juggler"—and "minstrel" or "gleeman" who sang, played accompaniments (of an unknown nature) on rather crude portable instruments, notably the early harp, lute and viol, and incidentally used other accomplishments such as dancing and gymnastic and sleight-of-hand tricks to provide amusement in castle halls or market-places. The low social status of these first "professional performers" has influenced the standing of musicians until very recent times. The minstrels or jongleurs were officially frowned on by the Church but, nevertheless, even monasteries gave them a warm welcome in days when diversion was scarce. Gradually the jongleurs began to write music as well as perform it. Often they were retained to write love-songs for which their princely employers took credit. Finally they obtained permanent posts at the courts of princes. In the household accounts of Philip the Bold, Duke of Burgundy in the fourteenth century, for instance, it is recorded that he maintained singers of both sexes (called menestrals de bouche), boys for his chapel at Dijon and players of old instruments such as the harp, the gittern, the psaltery, the rebec, the viol family, the challemelle, cornemuse, and trumpet.

As time went on, towns had their permanent minstrels and peripatetic "schools of minstrelsy" were held during Lent, when weddings and feasts were in abeyance. Gerald Cooper, an English authority on the subject, maintains that "these meetings led eventually to the recognition of music as an honorable profession." Jean

lost sight of during the centuries of ecclesiastical domination of music. It had only been kept alive by the un-
cultivated popular song. The madrigal—which formed
the vocal chamber music of its period—came strongly
into the picture of development towards opera at the
end of the sixteenth century when the tendency of the
times took the form of stringing together a *series of
madrigals* to form the musical setting of a dramatic
plot. Sometimes they were combined with dramatic
action illustrative of the poetic text. The best known
work of this type is *L'Amfiparnasso* (for five voices) of
Orazio Vecchi, performed at Modena in 1594. Because
of old wood-cuts with which the original score is illustrated it has been asserted that Vecchi used certain
voices as later composers would use instruments; when
two characters were on the stage, three were kept out
of sight and sang in the wings; when a single character
occupied the stage, the four other voices sang behind
the scenes, supporting the solo singer. Many authorities
disagree with this idea and insist that a purely musical
performance in the manner of an oratorio was intended.
Vecchi called his work a "Commedia Armonica" and it
is filled with the spirit of the "Commedia del Arte" of
his age. In the quaint prologue to this important work,
Vecchi points out to his audience that even if his
comedy lacks a rich and spacious stage, it contains real

Beck has published an important work—with the generous financial help of Mrs. Edward Bok of Philadelphia—containing an
extraordinary collection of Troubadour melodies and valuable information concerning them.

novelty because it must reach the public through the *ear* and not the *eye*. The last lines of the prologue read:

> "And now be silent—
> Instead of looking—listen."

In Vecchi's *Amfiparnasso,* all the utterances of the individual character are sung by the combined voices in true madrigal style.

Another important development stemming from early opera, the orchestra, owes a great deal to that daring modernist of the early seventeenth century, Claudio Monteverdi, whose love for instruments caused a considerable expansion of the list of instrumental forces in opera. Seven years after the production of Peri's *Euridice,* this extraordinary genius, who was at that time Maestro di Cappella to Vincenzo Gonzaga, Duke of Mantua, took up the new form. Again on the occasion of a princely marriage, he composed the music of two operas, *Dafne* and *Arianna,* using libretti by the prolific Rinuccini. They contain music of real dramatic power.

Monteverdi had already composed madrigals of great originality; he used what his contemporaries considered daring and even reprehensible harmonies (notably the unprepared dominant seventh) and invented the tremolando on strings which has been in use ever since but which was apparently obnoxious to the reactionaries among his contemporaries. In short,

Monteverdi and another amazingly "modern" composer, Gesualdo, Prince of Venosa, were distinctly radicals of their day. Monteverdi's innovations were severely attacked in a book by Artusi of Bologna, entitled: "On the Imperfections of Modern Music."

The form of opera prospered, allied itself with the ballet which Lully, a Florentine who had settled at the court of Louis XIV, was busily developing in France, and entered upon the long and varied career that is still occupying a conspicuous place in western musical life.

There are picturesque details in the history of opera. During the Roman Carnival of 1606, Pietro della Valle—as he himself writes in 1640—conceived the idea of an ambulant theatre, a cart surmounted by a movable stage which was driven from street to street. On it, five masked players enacted a drama with music composed by one Paolo Quagliati. The success was great. From four in the afternoon until midnight, enthusiastic crowds surrounded the players. The first public performances of serious opera outside the palaces of princes and nobles took place in Venice in 1637. From that time on, opera was a public institution, second to none in popularity in Italy.

As the form expanded, many different styles evolved. Opera Seria (serious opera) and Opera Buffa (comic opera) vied with each other in the affections of the public. Spectacular opera reached fantastic proportions. Domenico Freschi wrote an opera called *Berenice,* performed in Padua in 1680, which according to the printed book includes:

Chorus of 100 virgins
       100 soldiers
       100 horsemen in iron armor
        40 cornetists on horseback
         6 mounted trumpeters
         6 drummers
         6 ensigns
         6 sackbuts
         6 flutes
        12 minstrels playing on Turkish and
             other instruments
         6 pages
         3 sergeants
         6 cymbaleers
        12 huntsmen
        12 grooms
        12 charioteers
         2 lions led by two Turks
         2 led elephants
           Berenice's triumphal car drawn by
             four horses
         6 other cars drawn by 12 horses
         6 chariots for the procession
           A forest filled with wild-boar, deer,
             and bears and other scenic splen-
             dors.

This list points to a strange public taste and reminds one of the excesses in spectacular entertainment in ancient Rome of which Horace so bitterly complains.

Alessandro Scarlatti added to the resources of
operatic composers by clarifying the use of three important forms of dramatic vocal expression—the simple
recitative, or as the Italians say, *recitativo secco*—the
accompanied recitative or *recitativo stromentato*, and
the regular aria.[4] The recitativo secco was supported by

[4] The following description of a typical opera of the early eighteenth century is given in the article on opera in "Grove's Dictionary
of Music and Musicians":

"The orthodox number of *personaggi* was six—three women
and three men; or, at most, three women assisted by four men.
The first woman (PRIMA DONNA) was always a high soprano, and
the second or third a contralto. Sometimes a woman was permitted
to sing a man's part, especially if her voice, like those of Mrs. Bar-
bier and Mrs. Anastasia Robinson, happened to be a low one; but,
in any case, it was DE RIGUEUR that the first man (PRIMO UOMO)
should be an artificial soprano (see CASTRATO), even though the
role assigned to him might be that of Theseus or Hercules. The
second man was either a soprano, like the first, or an artificial
contralto; and the third, a tenor. When a fourth male character
(ULTIMA PARTE) was introduced, the part was most frequently
allotted to a bass; but operas were by no means uncommon in
which, as in Handel's Teseo, the entire staff of male singers consisted of artificial sopranos and contraltos, who monopolized all
the principal songs, and upon whose popularity for the time being
the success of the work in no small degree depended.

"The airs entrusted to these several performers were arranged
in five classes, each distinguished by some well-defined peculiarity
of style, though not of general design; the same mechanical form,
consisting of a first and second part, followed by the indispensable
DA CAPO, being common to all alike. These were, with variants,
the ARIA CANTABILE, ARIA DI PORTAMENTO, ARIA DI MEZZO CARATTERE,
ARIA PARLANTE, and ARIA DI BRAVURA, or D'AGILITÀ.

"The sequence and distribution of these varied movements was
regulated by laws no less stringent than those which governed
their division into separate classes. It was necessary that every
scene in every opera should terminate with an air; and every member of the DRAMATIS PERSONAE was expected to sing one, at least, in
each of the three acts into which the piece was almost invariably
divided; but no performer was permitted to sing two airs in succession, nor were two airs of the same class allowed to follow each
other, even though assigned to two different singers. The most

simple chords which were usually played on the harpsi-chord. Accompanied recitative has been handled in many different ways, but has always remained an in-tensely vital form of dramatic musical declamation. Wagner used it constantly in his operas.

A discussion of opera would be incomplete with-out some reference to its twin sister, oratorio. Originally given with scenery and dramatic action and stemming from the same sources as opera, oratorio, employing chorus, orchestra and soloists in the unfolding of a dramatic story, renounced theatrical pomp and confin-ing itself almost exclusively to texts of a sacred char-acter, withdrew to the soberer precincts of the concert hall. Great masterpieces have been written in oratorio form and it has maintained a dignified and—especially in Great Britain—important place in occidental musical life.

It cannot be denied that opera has been dragged to the depths of absurdity by idiotic libretti and by stupid

---

important airs were played at the conclusion of the first and second acts. In the second and third acts, the hero and heroine each claimed a grand scena, consisting of an accompanied recitative followed by an ARIA D'AGILITÁ calculated to display the power of the vocalist to the greatest possible advantage; in addition to which the same two characters united their voices in at least one grand duet. The third act terminated with a chorus of lively character, frequently accompanied by a dance; but no trios, quartets or other concerted movements were permitted in any part of the opera, though three or more characters were sometimes suffered—as in "Rinaldo"—to join in a harmonised exclamation at the close of the recitative. "It seems strange that with so many voices at command, so little advantage should have been taken of the opportunity of combin-ing them; but the law was absolute, and no doubt owed its origin to the desire of popular singers rather to shine alone, at any cost, than to share their triumphs with rival candidates for public favor."

conventions born of vanity and exhibitionism. It has been exploited by greedy impresarios and complacent composers on the basis of "giving the public what it wants." It has been used and abused in every possible way, but so far it has survived all evils and its literature already contains enough great music to warrant its continued existence even if ultra-modern composers were less interested in it than they are. Above all, opera stands, inseparably bound up in its initial stages with the introduction of harmony into music, the development of the orchestra, and the final secularization of occidental art music, as a milestone in musical evolution.

POINTS TO BE REMEMBERED

1. The gradual growth of secular music, notably through the troubadour and madrigal developments.
2. The development of liturgical drama and miracle plays leading towards a combination of drama and music.
3. How opera was preceded by madrigals joined together as in *L'Amfiparnasso* of Vecchi.
4. The birth of opera in 1600 A. D. when Renaissance disciples were striving to revive Greek dramatic musical declamation.
5. The fundamental importance of the single-line music or melody combined with harmony, i. e. tone-groups (chords) having a definite relation to each other.
6. Three or more tones of different pitch sounded at the same time form a chord, considered a "vertical" entity in music.
7. The science of building chords on each degree of the major and minor scales is called harmony.
8. The gradual classification of sound combinations as consonance and dissonance has a definite connection with the harmonic series in nature.

9. The gradual awakening of harmonic consciousness came through vocal polyphonic music.

SUGGESTIONS FOR CORRELATED READING

History of Music, Stanford-Forsyth, Chapter XI
Grove's Dictionary of Music, Article on Opera
Evolution of Music, Parry, Chapter VI
A Short History of Harmony, Charles MacPherson and Combarieu
The Evolution of Music, Alfredo Casella
Grove's Dictionary of Music, Article on Harmony
The Art of the Singer, W. J. Henderson

MUSICAL ILLUSTRATIONS

Victor Record 21752 A & B: Peri's *Euridice* (First Opera 1600)
Victor Record 6219   A: "Mad Scene" from *Lucia di Lammermoor*

For other operatic selections see catalogues of leading phonograph companies.

VIII

FORM AND THE SONATA

"The basis of all artistic genius lies in the power of conceiving humanity in a new and striking way, of putting a happy world of its own creation in place of the meaner world of our common days."

WALTER PATER

THERE must have been a time in the history of man when a certain word in each known language became the recognized designation of the edible cereal mixture generally considered to be the staff of life. We do not know when this happened but we do know *why*. Not until each word by which we identify objects and express thought became a recognizable unit in language, could specific and extended communication between men take place. An analogous process went on in the building up of musical systems. We can study music in no better way than to discover when and why certain uses of certain musical tones and combinations of tones formed a "language," not one that can convey abstract thought, but one that has definite *musical* meaning. This musical language and its meaning is obviously just as indispensable to the listener who would understand musical literature as a grasp of ordinary language is to the comprehension of books or the drama. The selection and grouping of tones into scales, the conceptions of consonance and dissonance in polyphony and harmony, the measurement of music—grouping tones rhythmically by means of ordered duration and accentual stress—all these things went into the creation of musical "language." But even as the primary elements of ordinary language have to be disposed with plan and purpose in order to make sense and convey meaning, so the elements of musical language need the equivalent of sentences and subdivisions of sentences, paragraphs and still larger recognizable divisions of compositions in order to achieve an eloquent and coherent communication of musical meaning.

Colles has well expressed the simplest fundamentals of musical form:

"Every attribute of music, relationships of pitch and rhythm in succession (melody) and concurrently (polyphony and harmony), plays its part in establishing the form of a musical work by creating a series of identities and differences which the ear can recognize. As long as musical sound consists solely of repetition, the monotone, it remains formless. On the other hand, when music goes to the other extreme and refuses to revert to any point, either rhythmic, melodic, or harmonic, which recollection can identify, it is equally formless. Repetition and contrast, therefore, are the two twin principles of musical form."

These principles of repetition and contrast are to be found in the simplest folk-songs. By what Parry happily calls "a consensus of instinct" they took root in the long development which preceded art music. But in order to penetrate to the why and wherefore of musical form in its larger manifestations, we must logically turn to the instrumental types where the problem of conveying purely *musical* meaning, shorn of all association with other things, becomes one of paramount importance.

In many manuscripts of the vocal polyphonic era preceding the seventeenth century we find the significant caption, "apt for voices or viols." [1] The playing of melodies on instruments is as old as music itself. But the viols that took over the function of voices in *part* songs were entering a domain in which it was discovered that the possibilities of instruments far exceeded the human voice, not in the expression of emotion, but in range, flexibility and the variety of tone quality that proved invaluable as musical *building material.*

Musical architecture, once it had come into the picture, exercised increasing fascination upon creative genius. Musical language had to be extended to meet the new possibilities and new methods of procedure had to be evolved.

Early opera composers were among the first to pay attention to purely instrumental forms. They learned that overtures, frequently called "sinfonia" or "toccata," and interludes or dances at various points in an opera,

[1] The family of string instruments that were direct ancestors of the violin family.

added interest and provided variety. Just as the earliest types of song were short and rarely contained more than two contrasting divisions, followed by a repetition of the first—the classic A—B—A [2] of the textbooks— the earliest instrumental pieces were limited in scope and content. After all, man first used caves as a shelter. Then he constructed huts or tents, before he learned to extend and ornament his dwellings and gradually evolve the art and science of architecture. In music, he began with the short, incessantly repeated tunes of primitive music; then came folk-tunes with two or three divisions in which the elements of contrast and repetition sprang from an intuitive artistic impulse like that which caused him to introduce the element of beauty into buildings. The distance travelled by man between the savage's hut and the Cathedral at Cologne is no greater than that between primitive song and the Beethoven symphony. The great art and science of occidental music that developed within the last three hundred years is often called the youngest of the arts because while music always existed and took an important place in human life, abstract, occidental instrumental music is unique in its complete independence as a musical art form. Not until the great forms we are considering had come into being, did we have a type

---

[2] Musical theorists have adopted the convenient method of using letters to designate themes or sections of a musical composition for purposes of analysis. The formula A—B—A would mean: A, first theme or section: B, contrasting theme or section: A, recapitulation of first theme or section.

of music completely sufficient unto itself. Parry gives a wonderful picture of musical evolution when he writes:

"The achievements of art are the unravellings of hidden possibilities of abstract law, through the constant and cumulative extension of instincts. They do not actually exist till man has made them; they are the counterpart of his internal conditions, and change and develop with the changes of his mental powers and sensitive qualities, and apart from him have no validity. There is no such thing as leaping across a chasm on to a new continent, neither is there any gulf fixed anywhere, but continuity and inevitable antecedents to every consequent; the roots of the greatest masterpieces of modern times lie obscurely hidden in the wild dances and barbarous howlings of the remotest ancestors of the race, who began to take pleasure in rhythm and sound, and every step was into the unknown, or it may be better said not only unknown but non-existent till made by mental effort."

The progress, discernible throughout the history of music, from small beginnings to rich expansion is well illustrated by the opera overture. Monteverdi's *Orfeo* (1607) begins with a "Toccata" only nine bars long. Serving as an overture, although little more than an introductory flourish of instruments, this Toccata was supposed to be played through three times. By the end of the seventeenth century, Lully [3] was writing overtures containing two, three and even four different pieces joined together. Lully's type of overture—called the French overture—usually began with a slow movement,[4] followed by one or more quick ones, sometimes including dance forms and sometimes ending with another slow movement. The Italian overture, evolving about the same time, usually consisted of a quick first movement, a slow middle movement and a quick final movement.

Composers had not yet learned to construct extended and continuous compositions that would have both variety and unity; therefore they satisfied their impulse towards expansion by stringing together a number of short pieces. This basic idea, discernible in the French and Italian overtures, was amplified in the instrumental suites. Thomas Morley (1557-1602) in his "Plaine and Easie Introduction" (1597) alludes to the desirability of alternating the Pavan "a kind of staid musick ordained for grave dancing" with the Galliard "a lighter and more stirring kind of dancing."

[3] Jean-Baptiste Lully, born at or near Florence in 1639, became a naturalized Frenchman and was a leading figure at the Court of Louis XIV. As leader of the famous "Petits Violons" and as composer of ballet music for the court, he achieved fame and fortune. He collaborated with Molière and one of his important achievements was the music for the first legitimate French opera (1672) *Les Fêtes de l'Amour et de Bacchus,* text by the poet Quinault.

[4] The word "movement" is used throughout musical literature to designate a single piece within a collection of pieces that bear a collective title and are considered in the light of a whole (composite) work.

This idea of grouping pieces of contrasting character and considering the collection as a harmonious whole grew from the early joining of Pavans and Galliards into the definite and extended plan of the suite. In this form we find another proof of long musical evolution in the fact that it was built mainly on *dance* forms. If we conceive the dance as an outgrowth of primitive tribal life, as a part of the ritual that was combined with chanting, it is interesting to realize that one of the first important instrumental forms grew out of it. The socialized dances, such as the minuet and the gavotte, furnished the rhythm and character of the individual suite movement, but they stemmed from folk-dances in various parts of Europe; therefore the ancestry of the suite is fairly clear. In the height of its development in the eighteenth century, the instrumental suite not only included various dance forms but miscellaneous pieces entitled Prelude, Intermezzo, Rondo, Caprice, Fantasia, etc. Naturally, such a variety of pieces brought in many different styles of composition, but in order to give the layman something definite to serve as a point of departure for the investigation of the genus, the author will describe a typical suite of the period when a well-defined tradition had come into being.

Uniformity of key is a marked characteristic of the typical suite. The single movements, to quote Parry—

"are almost invariably constructed upon the simple principle of balanced halves, each presenting the same material in different phases and each strengthened by repetition. The first half sets out from the tonic key and without any marked pause or division modulates so as to settle into the key of the dominant or relative major and closes in that key. The second half begins afresh from that point and proceeding in most cases by way of the key of the subdominant settles well back again into the original key and concludes.

"The only break therefore is in the middle; and the two halves are made purposely to balance one another as far as may be without definite recapitulation . . . the general principles in the average number of cases are the same, namely, to diffuse the character of the principle figures and features throughout rather than to concentrate the interest of the subject in definite parts of the movement."

The layman, therefore, must not look for entry of different voices at stated points as in the exposition of a fugue, but should examine the motives (tonal patterns) which give the keynote of rhythmic quality and general character to the piece. Modulations and various uses of the thematic material should also be noted, preferably while following records or performances with a score. It should also be noted that most classic suite movements are polyphonic in feeling and "texture," that is, several lines move (horizontally) together. Chordal quality is rare although it occasionally makes itself felt in the sarabandes and gavottes of Bach's suites.

The most typical classic suites, no matter what else they include, are apt to have the following *four* pieces based on dances originating in different countries:

1. The ALLEMAND, originating in Germany. (According to some authorities it is of Suabian origin.) It is written in moderately slow 4/4 time employing a type of theme or motive of a quiet and sober character. The rhythmic flow is smooth and regular, using, as a rule, sixteenth note figuration.

2. The COURANTE. This species subdivides itself into two types, of Italian and French origin respectively. The Italian Corrente is quick and light with regular rhythm in 3/4 time.

The French Courante, nominally in 3/2 time, has as its chief characteristic a curious mixture of 3/2 time and 6/4 time which, although equal in duration values, represents different grouping of notes in the matter of natural accents.

In a 3/2 bar the division of the bar would be six quarter-notes grouped 1–2 ‖ 3–4 ‖ 5–6, the three groups of two each representing the three half-notes, and having only *one* natural accent—on the first beat of the bar. A 6/4 grouping of six quarter-notes would be: 1–2–3 ‖ 4–5–6 with a main natural accent on the first and a secondary accent on the fourth beat of the bar. If these different rhythmic groupings are combined in a single bar, one used in the treble and the other in the bass, the effect can produce a strong contrast to the smooth flow of the Allemand. The crossing of time, however, is in many cases more for the eye than for the ear.

3. The SARABANDE, which is of Spanish origin, with a possible Moorish ancestry, has the characteristic of a distinct accent or rhythmic pause on the *second* beat of the bar in slow 3/4 time. The character is majestic and rather melancholy, even though elaborate ornamentation of the melodic line is frequently used.

It is in the sarabande that chords progress more as entities and serve as accompaniment to a line of melody. They thus display a tendency towards the harmonic conception that developed so tremendously in the last three centuries.

4. The GIGUE, usually based on some rhythmic variety of triple time, i. e., 6/8, 12/8 or 3/8 has a merry character and according to some authorities derives its name from the French word gigue (ham or gammon) used satirically to designate the violin. It is essentially a "fiddler's dance" and was so popular in England—where it was called jig—that some musicians pronounce it to be of English origin. In any case it forms a lively and often brilliant conclusion to a suite.

Between the sarabande and the gigue, composers often inserted light dance pieces such as the minuet, the gavotte, the bourrée, the rigaudon and others. Of these the minuet[5] in moderate 3/4 time was the most im-

[5] The first section of the typical minuet is divided into two parts, each of which is repeated. A contrasting section called Trio—

portant as it was later transferred from the suite to many sonatas and symphonies and finally transformed into the much more rapid scherzo, retaining little more than its structural ground plan.

Of all the additions to the traditional nucleus of the four ubiquitous dances—the allemand, the courante, the sarabande and the gigue, the most important is the Prelude. In this type of piece an expansion of form already shows itself inasmuch as there are often more than two sections. In some examples the treatment is fugal; occasionally a complete fugue is combined with other elements of a more rhapsodical character. Some of the finest examples in Bach's suites show three distinct sections of which the first and last are identical, while the middle section introduces new material as well as development of existing thematic material and interesting modulations. This type of prelude practically follows an extended A—B—A ground plan. The A minor English Suite of Bach contains such a Prelude as well as characteristic examples of the four main dance-forms and a charming bourrée thrown in. This work, excellently recorded by Harold Samuels, will give the student a clear idea of the solo instrumental suite in its finest form.

Suites for orchestra, similarly planned, preceded the symphony just as the suite for solo instruments preceded the sonata.

supposedly because three instruments were employed in early examples—follows. At the conclusion of the trio, custom demands that the two parts of the first section should be played again, but without repeats.

Now let us consider the essential difference between the suite and the sonata. Each piece in a typical classic suite had a certain character indicated by its title which furnished, if not a programmatic suggestion, at least a clue to its significance. But the creative impulse of imaginative musicians was pressing forward towards the infinite possibilities they dimly felt in sound as a still more abstract art-form, one capable of a unique beauty and a potential musical value lying apart from any association with other ideas.

Students should not confuse the issue of "absolute" music and "program" music by applying to it the idea of right or wrong—better or worse.[6] It is much more fruitful to study the essential *difference* between the two. Some of the greatest music we know has been written as a setting to a verbal text, but on the other hand veritable miracles have been wrought in evolving and perfecting those musical forms that make it possible for composers to create works in which all the elements necessary to art—proportion, balance, contrast, repetition, recognizable (musical) ideas and infinite resources in handling the fluid medium of sound—combine to convey emotions, imaginative conceptions and even the suggestion of all sorts of things in nature and in life *without* the aid of words, specific titles or any implied program. Parry says of the sonata:

"The history of the sonata is the history of an at-

[4] Absolute music is abstract instrumental music without any programmatic title or implication. Program music essays to convey non-musical meanings.

tempt to cope with one of the most singular problems ever presented to the mind of man, and its solution is one of the most successful achievements of his artistic instincts. A sonata is, as its name implies, a sound-piece, and a sound-piece alone; in its purest and most perfect examples it is unexplained by title or text, and unassisted by voices; it is nothing but a concatenation of musical notes. Such notes have individually no significance; and even the simplest principles of their relative definition and juxtaposition, such as are necessary to make the most elementary music, had to be drawn from the inner self and the consciousness of things which belong to man's nature only, without the possibility of finding guidance or more than the crudest suggestion from the observation of things external. Yet the structural principles by which such unpromising matterials become intelligible have been so ordered and developed by the unaided musical instinct of many successive generations of composers, as to render possible long works which not only penetrate and stir us in detail, but are in their entire mass direct, consistent and convincing. Such works, in their completest and most severely abstract forms, are sonatas. . . ."

Historically speaking, the name sonata was applied in the seventeenth century and even earlier to miscellaneous compositions having little in common with later developments. The name is used to-day in two different ways.

1. To designate a whole work containing several contrasting movements.

2. To designate, when combined with the word *form,* sonata-form, or sonata-*allegro*-form, a particular *plan* of *composition.* This plan is always found in at least one movement (usually the first) of a collection bearing the name sonata and sometimes in more of the various movements that make up the collective work.

   Sonata-form as a plan of composition is also used in movements of symphonies, concertos, chamber music and overtures.

Sonata-form is intimately bound up with the conceptions of harmony, tonality and modulation that evolved throughout the seventeenth and the first half of the eighteenth centuries. In tracing this development historically we find that Corelli (1653–1713) in Italy produced twenty-four Sonate da Chiesa (Church Sonatas) for strings, lute and organ, twenty-four Sonate da Camera (Chamber Sonatas) for the same instruments and twelve solo sonatas for violin, cello or cembalo alone. These works form a landmark in the history of the sonata but they are seldom performed.

Kuhnau (1660–1722), a German pioneer in the form, left quaint collections of so-called sonatas, one entitled "Fresh Clavier Fruits" and another set of amusingly descriptive "Biblical" sonatas that show an awakening sense of key-relationship, but also betray, through a pronounced programmatic approach to his task, how far this composer still was from the abstract type of sonata achieved by his great successors.

Karl Philipp Emanuel Bach, the gifted son of Johann Sebastian, is sometimes called the inventor of sonata-form. While this is far from correct, it is certain that he is eminent among those who developed the possibilities and clarified the form of the sonata. It remained, however, for Haydn, Mozart, and Beethoven to lift it to the high place it has since occupied.

One reason why sonata-form became so important is because it permits of great expansion without losing coherence. It hangs together. If an orator makes a speech in which all sorts of different ideas are loosely strung together, and he winds up in a manner that leaves his listeners wondering what the end of his speech has to do with the beginning, he is hardly a successful speaker. It is just as impossible to treat musical ideas in a haphazard, incoherent manner.

The layman can obtain a clear idea of sonata-form by studying the following plan of *sonatina* form (the simplest sonata-form of small dimensions):

EXPOSITION	DEVELOPMENT	RECAPITULATION
Part One	*Part Two*	*Part Three*
1. Principal subject or main theme in the tonic key.	a. Free treatment of preceding thematic material.	Recapitulation.
2. Intermediate group or link-episode.	b. New material can be introduced but not in a way to sound like major themes.	Repetition of all groups of Part I.
3. Secondary subject or second theme (sometimes called song group) in a related key.[7]	c. Free modulation can be employed.	*All* groups in this section must be in the principal key and the coda—closing in the tonic key—is usually extended so as to produce a greater sense of finality.
4. Closing group.	d. The development section must never be longer than Part I. Can be very short in early works of the species.	
5. Coda.[8]	e. It must lead to a return of the main theme in the tonic key.	

[7] If the movement is in a major key the second subject will be in the dominant; if the movement is in a minor key, the second subject is in the relative major.

[8] The close of the first section is not in the tonic, but in a different key, thus preparing the way for what is to come. In major movements the first part closes in the dominant; in minor movements in the relative major. The word coda designates any "tail-piece" whether of a whole composition or of the first section of a movement in sonata-form. Its function is to "round off" and establish finality.

A comparison of this ground plan with the fugue chart in Chapter V will at once show the wide difference between the two great forms. The fugue with its several horizontal lines is polyphonic in texture. The sonata-form is harmonic and could never have evolved before the understanding of tonality [9] and the possibility of modulation from one key to another had been firmly established. The use of several themes within the single movement affords rich variety of mood while the division of the piece into three sections, the third being a recapitulation of the first, and the middle section providing contrast, produces the ideal conditions of A—B—A [10] on a grand scale. The fact that each thematic group and each section can be expanded at will explains why this form has been used more than any other in the greatest works of musical literature.

The true significance of sonata-form can only be grasped if studied in conjunction with musical illustrations. Records can be used for this purpose, although the living performer can take a work apart and analyze it with much better results for the listener. The layman should note that the outline given above is *strict* sonata-

---

[9] In a limited sense *tonality*—sometimes called *key*—refers to the harmonies of the scale employed as the tonic of a piece of music. Taking the chord belonging to No. 1 of the scale, as a point of departure, modulations can include all chords built *on* and *with* the remaining scale degrees. In a broader sense a tonality may include other chords so long as they do not destroy the sense of a tonic which serves both as a point of departure and a point of finality.

[10] See page 139.

form. It gives the fundamental principles as used at the time when the form was first recognized and accepted. No musical form is ever rigidly adhered to for any length of time by great composers even though type is preserved. Exceptions and free interpretation of principles soon creep in—luckily for the growth of art. But types remain as long as they fit the life and art of a civilization. A piece or movement in sonata-form is a type of composition which may be regular or irregular, long or short, just so the general plan conforms enough to the principles of the form to make it recognizable and distinct from other forms. The different ways in which composers have used the fundamental principles of this great form furnish a study of inexhaustible interest in a vast musical literature.

The first movement of a typical sonata, employing sonata-form, is followed by two or more movements of contrasting character. A poetic slow movement, a lively final movement and sometimes a shorter movement of light and pleasing character such as a minuet or a scherzo between the last two, usually make up the group. Sonata movements which are not in sonata-form can be written in song-form (A—B—A) or minuet (scherzo) form,[11] variation [12] or rondo form.[13] Sometimes composers introduce the element of program

[11] See page 145.
[12] Variation form, as its name implies, is made up of variations on a single theme.
[13] Rondo form, originating in the *round* and retaining from that early form the repeated use of a single theme, can be con-

music in a single movement, as Chopin and Beethoven have both done in including funeral marches in otherwise abstract sonatas.

Let us now consider the following analogy. If we listen to a drama, we are given some clue to its contents by:—

1. The title of the drama,
2. The names of the characters and their status in life,
3. The time and place of various scenes or acts.

We understand the plot, motives, events, ideas, etc., through the medium of language as well as visual impressions. Our emotions respond to the content of the drama as revealed by the actors.

In listening to a musical instrumental composition in a large form such as a sonata or symphony, *if we are musically educated* we can grasp and enjoy the work through a somewhat similar process.

structed in many different ways. The general idea is that between several repetitions of a principal subject, contrasting subjects are introduced. Using letters as formulas the following examples illustrate types of rondos frequently found in sonatas, symphonies and chamber music:

A—B—A—C—A — Coda
A—B—A—C—A—B—A — Coda

The second example bears a resemblance to sonata-form, except that its middle section presents new thematic material instead of a development built on preceding themes. The textbooks give further variations of the basic idea.

The title of the composition gives us a clue to its type.

The titles of the various movements might be said to correspond with the given information concerning scenes or acts of a drama.

The "personages" of each movement are its themes: the main themes are the most important ones; lesser episodic ideas occurring in the transitions and development section represent the minor characters of the play. Modulations and changes of tonality represent the "action" of the drama. It is not enough to have themes. They must take part in musical "action."

We recognize Lady Macbeth by the way she looks, every time she comes upon the stage after her initial appearance. But we must *remember* the way she looks or we would fail to realize her presence in later scenes. So the listener must be capable of retaining the sound of a theme at least for the duration of the piece. This does not mean that the listener can sing the theme the next day or play it by ear, any more than he would be apt to memorize the appearance of Lady Macbeth in a manner that would enable him to draw her picture. He must simply be able to listen with sufficient consciousness to recognize the main themes when they recur. For this reason the immediate repetition of the first part of a movement in sonata-form is usually indicated by the composer. Nowadays the custom of making this repeat is often abandoned, especially in very well-known or lengthy movements. But there is one excellent way for the layman to acquire the pos-

sibility of recognizing his themes, and that is by studying the works he wishes to enjoy. It is proved beyond
any doubt that the music most enjoyed by audiences is
music with which they are familiar. If the listener will
study musical masterpieces in the light of the knowledge he is here acquiring, he will soon find himself
assisting at musical dramas in which the characters are
old friends. A knowledge of form will enable him to
recognize the significance of the particular theme he is
listening to by the place it occupies in the general plan.
The quality or beauty of the themes and the *way* the
composer handles and develops them, correspond with
the *way* writers express ideas and develop them in
literature.

To continue our analogy with the drama, the
dramatist has much more freedom in building his plot
than the composer of a musical work in one of the
strict forms. The dramatist can have his character enter
upon any scene at will, while the musical composer, in
order to make the type of form he has chosen recognizable, must conform in some degree to a traditional
plan in the disposition of thematic material. He is, in
this respect, somewhat in the position of the architect
who cannot build a cathedral on a bungalow pattern.
But the *listener* at a musical performance is imaginatively and emotionally much more free than the *spectator* at the drama. The attention of the spectator at a
drama is engrossed by definite things. He must follow
them closely and his imagination is not called upon to

function creatively as it must in response to the more elusive, suggestive essence of music. In abstract music, although there is a reality of sound and form which gives *musical* meaning to the work, this meaning stirs both imagination and emotion to a function that is not chained to any definite idea. The human being who listens to such music has the world before him in an imaginative sense, and there is no greater enrichment of the inner life, the life of the spirit, the imagination and the emotions than that which great art music can give.

One of the author's listener-students expressed the possibilities of developed listening as follows: "When one has learned to listen to music it seems as though a world of the imagination that has been dark has had a light thrown on it."

That is what gives the *performer* of music such great joy; digging down to a *real* acquaintance with musical works and then being able to bring to life— through sound—the beauties they contain. *After* the listener-student has learned to know a musical work, he can sit back without any conscious effort and surrender himself to an experience, imaginative and emotional, as well as purely musical, which will be entirely different from that of the untutored layman. A great reward lies in store for the layman who has the vision and imagination to realize that what many shun and belittle as "technicalities" are really the living and exciting manifestations of a creative power that has found the way throughout the ages to produce the enduring art treasures of our occidental music.

POINTS TO BE REMEMBERED

1. The fundamental necessity of contrast and repetition in musical form.

2. The gradual evolution of larger forms, the suite and the sonata.

3. The difference between the *sonata* (a number of different movements combined to form a collective work) and *sonata-form*, musical-architectural *ground-plan* used in single movements of sonatas, symphonies and chamber music.

SUGGESTIONS FOR CORRELATED READING

Grove's Dictionary of Music and Musicians, Article on Form
The Scope of Music, Percy C. Buck, Chapter IX
Musical Form, J. H. Cornell

MUSICAL ILLUSTRATIONS

Victor Record 1193—A: *Harmonious Blacksmith*—Handel
              B: *Turkish March*—Mozart
Victor Record 1199—B: *Le Tambourin*—Rameau; *Le Coucou-Rondo*—Daquin
Victor Record 1424—B: *Gavotte in G minor*—Bach
Victor Record 6635—B: *Adagio* (from *Toccata in G major*)—Bach—Siloti—Casals
Victor Record 6786—B: *I Call Upon Thee, Jesus*—Bach
Columbia Record 2063—M (145543): *Gigue* from *Fifth French Suite*—Bach

Victor Record 6771—A & B ⎱*Pathetique Sonata* (Op. 13) Bee-
          6772—A & B ⎰   thoven
                    Played by Wilhelm Bachaus
His Master's Voice: Records of Beethoven Sonatas played by
    Arthur Schnabel. Issued by The Beethoven Sonata Society.

IX

INSTRUMENTS AND THE SYMPHONY

*"To perfect that wonder of travel
—the locomotive—has perhaps not required the expenditure of more mental
strength and application than to perfect
that wonder of music—the violin."*

GLADSTONE

No GREATER proof can be found of the fact that music is a science as well as an art than a parallel consideration of the evolution of musical instruments and the evolution of musical art. Man could never have soared into the ether without the means provided by science, and the great symphony writers could never have taken their inspirational flights into the stratosphere of abstract music without the instrumental "wings" evolved by countless generations of workers on the scientific side of the sound world. The history of instruments, long and confused as it is, contains many curious facts and developments. Aristotle found instruments "only fit for hirelings" and "unworthy of free men." At that time the musical instrument was the humble handmaiden of the human voice. The human voice at its best is undoubtedly the noblest sound-producing agency for a melodic line. It also possesses the unique power to combine musical tone with words which create the possibility of the direct expression of extra-musical meaning. Men have learned throughout the ages, however, that the human voice at its best is rare. An ugly or feeble human voice cannot compare with a fine string or wind instrument. Even the more percussive piano can "sing" better than the rank and file of undeveloped or inadequate voices. Again, it is much more possible to develop skill on an instrument than it is to change the quality or extend the scope of the human voice. Therefore the importance of instruments grew with the evolution of art music itself, and as the *structural* sense developed in the larger forms, it became increasingly apparent that aggregations of instruments could undertake musical functions for which aggregations of voices were not fitted.

The author has found that the layman sometimes recoils from the idea that music contains so much of science and of mathematics. Elie Faure in the introduction to his "History of Art" admirably expresses the truth that art and science are inseparable when he writes:

"He who believes only in science is like an orchestra musician who imagines that the whole symphony resides in the mechanism of his instrument. He who believes only in intuition is like an orchestra musician who imagines that the whole symphony continues when all the players break their strings and their bows."

And again he comforts the emotional music-lover

who fears a loss of inspiration in the contemplation of more rational things:

"It is in vain that pure science advances; it thrusts back the mystery, it does not destroy it. Once the threshold of mystery is crossed, art regains its whole dominion."

At the border-line between science and art we find a question; did the evolution of art music create a demand that explains the development of instruments, or did new instrumental possibilities inspire composers to write in a new way? History cannot answer that question clearly. It is certain that the early organ builders [1] could not foresee anything like the great

---

[1] ". . . we have to turn to the west for the true development of the organ in the dark ages. In those days a monk or bishop who wished to stand well with society could not take up essay-writing or social-welfare; what he *could* do was to lay hands on all the available timber, metal, and leather, and start organ-building.

"We hear of the results of such organs as those of St. Dunstan at Malmesbury, of St. Alphege at Winchester (tenth century), and later (in the twelfth and thirteenth centuries) at Cologne, Erfurt, and Halberstadt. The accounts almost frighten us.

"In those times, before the invention of the lever and long before the English invention of horizontal reservoirs and feeders, a man was wanted to every bellows or at least to every two bellows. The Winchester organ had four hundred bronze pipes and two manuals of twenty keys. Each of these keys—fit in size for the hand of a giant—was lettered with its note-name and, when struck, gave the wind to ten huge diapasons tuned in octaves or perhaps in octaves and fifths.

"What a picture of dark relentless mediaevalism this mere catalogue summons up for us! Surely the world can never have known such a strange holiday as Winchester knew every time its organ was played one thousand years ago. We can imagine the organists—all men picked for their physique—darting madly to

Bach fugues and yet, by the time Bach wrote the fugues, there was an instrument on which they could be played. The delicate and fragile Cristofori piano in the Metropolitan Museum in New York [2] could not be heard above the Philharmonic Orchestra in one of the concerti that appear on modern programs, and yet it is built on the fundamental scientific principle that eventually produced the powerful concert grand, capable of holding its own in the largest auditorium. Thus we find once more, this time in the history of instru-

and fro at the keyboard, screwed up to the excitement of smiting the right key at the right moment, and attacking it with all the force of their bodies gathered into their thickly gloved hands; the toiling, moiling crowd of blowers behind, treading away for dear life to keep the wind-chest full; the frightful din of the heavy timber mechanism, creaking and groaning like a four-decker in a heavy sea; above all, the diabolical blare as the wind suddenly poured into a huge metal diapason and let loose their appalling series of empty fifths; while in the church the congregation cowered with a terrible astonishment."

Cecil Forsyth in the
Stanford-Forsyth "History of Music."

[2] The keyboard stringed instruments, roughly grouped in the eighteenth century under the collective heading, *Clavier*, were constructed on three different methods of tone production. In one type, stemming from the Psaltery, the string was plucked by a plectra, either of quill, leather, metal or wood. This group included the harpsichord, virginal and spinet. In the piano-forte, stemming from the dulcimer, the string is struck by a hammer. Cristofori (1665–1731) invented the first instruments of this type. An authentic Cristofori piano is in the Crosby Brown instrument collection at the Metropolitan Museum in New York. The third method of tone production in a keyboard stringed instrument was that of "pushing" a small piece of metal called a "tangent" against the string. This was the method employed in the clavichord, which was much more expressive than the harpsichord, but its tone was very limited in volume. All the other clavier instruments eventually gave way to the piano when the demands incidental to public concerts proved it to be the only one that could meet the new conditions.

ments, that same process of evolution and expansion that is apparent in music itself.

Why anybody ever wanted to construct an instrument like the Tromba Marina, a huge wooden pyramid six or seven feet high on which a single playable string was stretched, is difficult to imagine. It is true there were "sympathetic strings" [3] but the bow of the player could only play upon the one string. Why this monstrosity was called "Marine Trumpet" and why it should have become so popular in convents and churches in Germany that it gained the nickname of "Nonnengeige" (nun's fiddle), nobody has satisfactorily explained, so far as the author knows. It stands out in the history of instruments as typical of the innumerable queer efforts made to harness the elusive element of sound, before the science of instrument-building had advanced to the point of understanding cause and effect. The list of such efforts is endless.

Cecil Forsyth, in his authoritative book "Orchestration," lists one hundred and nineteen more or less modern orchestral instruments. Of these, one hundred and seven have definite pitch while twelve (percussion instruments) have indeterminate pitch. Of the total

[3] Sympathetic strings, used in some oriental instruments and on the viola d'amore, are strings that are not touched by the bow, but are so placed that they vibrate in sympathy with the strings that are actually played. If they are tuned up to the pitch of partials belonging to the fundamental playable tones of the main strings, they add a faint and delicate sound like the jingle of tiny chimes to the tones produced by the performer. The Tromba Marina sometimes had as many as fifty sympathetic strings.

list, nineteen are *recently* obsolete, and forty-seven are rarely used in symphony scores or opera although they are occasionally called for in the current repertory. If we realize that every instrument in this list represents an evolution extending throughout centuries, we can feel respect, not only for a Stradivarius or a Cristofori, but for all the nameless workers whose ingenuity and striving gradually brought into being the musical "wings" of Beethoven and Wagner.

The layman can easily graduate from the stage in which he anxiously inquires of his neighbor at a symphony concert, "What is that instrument to the left of the man with the red hair?" All he has to do is to invest in the records and charts recommended at the end of this chapter and study them. But for the benefit of those who are more curious, the following facts about the instruments of the modern orchestra are given.

The grouping of instruments into "families" is obviously occasioned by the desire to extend a valuable tone quality throughout high and low registers. For instance, the piccolo extends flute quality far above the possibilities of the "parent" instrument, and three string instruments of increasing size—viola, cello, and contrabass—extend "violin tone" down to the lowest register of the orchestra. Some of the orchestral "families" have more instruments than others but the tendency to extend the range of any given tone quality is general. The following charts give the principal "families" of the orchestra.

VIOLIN FAMILY

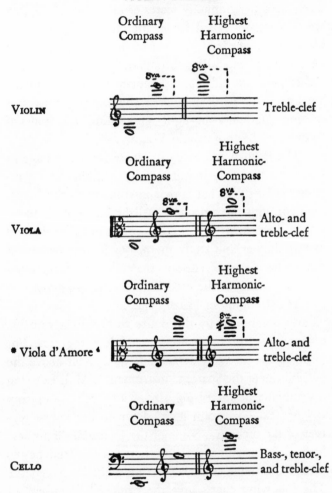

[4] Asterisks indicate that an instrument is obsolete or semi-obsolete.

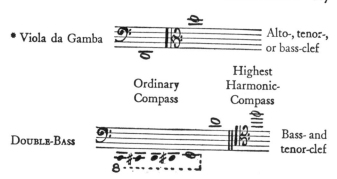

* Viola da Gamba Alto-, tenor-, or bass-clef

Ordinary Compass   Highest Harmonic-Compass

DOUBLE-BASS Bass- and tenor-clef

HARP

HARP Treble- and bass-clef

FLUTE FAMILY

PICCOLO Treble-clef

* Flageolet Treble-clef

FLUTE Treble-clef

Bass-Flute  Treble-clef

OBOE FAMILY

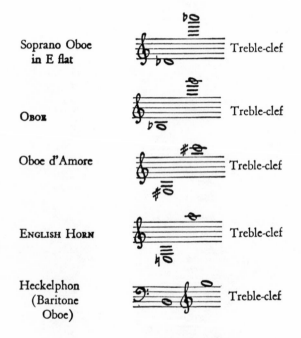

Soprano Oboe
in E flat · Treble-clef

Oboe · Treble-clef

Oboe d'Amore · Treble-clef

English Horn · Treble-clef

Heckelphon
(Baritone
Oboe) · Treble-clef

CLARINET FAMILY

Clarinet
in E flat  Treble-clef

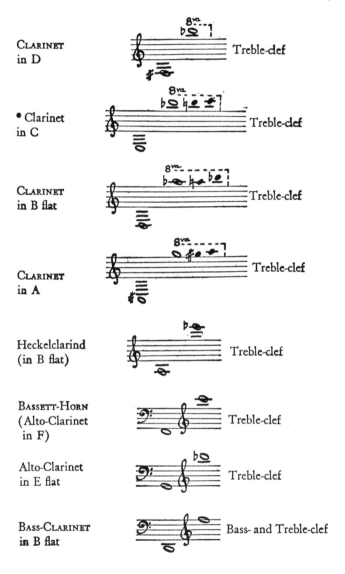

Bass-Clarinet in A  Bass- and Treble-clef

Pedal-Clarinet in B flat 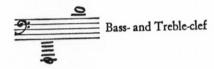 Bass- and Treble-clef

BASSOON FAMILY

  Bass- and Tenor-clef

DOUBLE-BASSOON 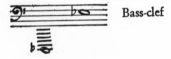 Bass-clef

TRUMPET FAMILY

According to crook used
the possible extremes were

* Natural-Trumpet  Treble-clef

VALVE-TRUMPET in F  Treble-clef

VALVE-TRUMPET in C  Treble-clef

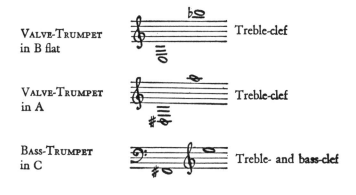

VALVE-TRUMPET in B flat — Treble-clef

VALVE-TRUMPET in A — Treble-clef

BASS-TRUMPET in C — Treble- and bass-clef

HORN FAMILY

According to crook used
the possible extremes were

* Natural-Horn — Treble- and bass-clef

VALVE-HORN IN F — Treble- and bass-clef

TROMBONE FAMILY

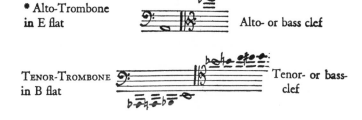

* Alto-Trombone in E flat — Alto- or bass clef

TENOR-TROMBONE in B flat — Tenor- or bass-clef

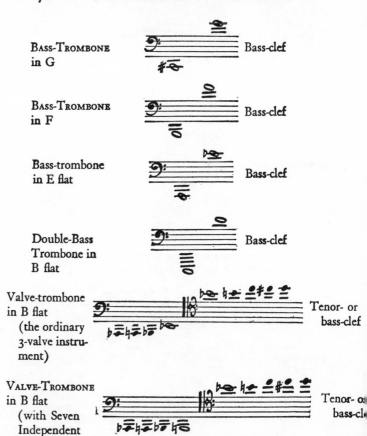

BASS-TROMBONE
in G — Bass-clef

BASS-TROMBONE
in F — Bass-clef

Bass-trombone
in E flat — Bass-clef

Double-Bass
Trombone in
B flat — Bass-clef

Valve-trombone
in B flat
(the ordinary
3-valve instru-
ment) — Tenor- or
bass-clef

VALVE-TROMBONE
in B flat
(with Seven
Independent
Cylinders) — Tenor- or
bass-clef

TUBA FAMILY

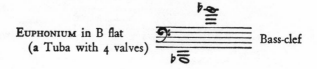

EUPHONIUM in B flat
(a Tuba with 4 valves) — Bass-clef

ORCHESTRAL TUBA in F
(with 4 valves)
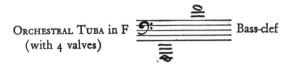 Bass-clef

E flat Military
Brass-Bass
  (a Tuba with 4
  valves)
 Bass-clef

BB flat Military
Brass-Bass
  (a Tuba with 3
  valves)
 Bass-clef

More
correctly
Modified—
Horns

Wagner's
"Tenor-Tuba"
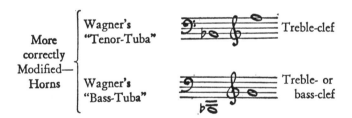 Treble-clef

Wagner's
"Bass-Tuba"
Treble- or
bass-clef

Wagner's "Contrabass-Tuba"
  (a Tuba with 4 valves)
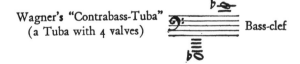 Bass-clef

DRUM FAMILY INCLUDING TYMPANI

SIDE-DRUM	Pitch indeterminate	Conventional treble-clef or a single line
BASS-DRUM	Pitch indeterminate	Conventional bass-clef or a single line

Small Drum

Middle Drum *or*

Large Drum

KETTLE-DRUMS — Bass-clef

PERCUSSION FAMILY—PITCH INDETERMINATE

TAMBOURINE	Pitch indeterminate	Conventional treble-clef or a single line.
TRIANGLE	Pitch indeterminate	Conventional treble-clef or a single line
CYMBALS	Pitch indeterminate	Conventional bass-clef or a single line
GONG	Pitch indeterminate	Conventional bass-clef or a single line
CASTANETS	Pitch indeterminate	Conventional treble-clef or a single line
RATTLE	Pitch indeterminate	Conventional treble-clef or a single line
WIND-MACHINE	Pitch indeterminate, but with some variation possible	Conventional bass-clef or a single line
ANVILS	Pitch generally indeterminate	Treble- or bass-clef or a single line

PERCUSSION FAMILY—WITH PITCH

Bells (ordinary)

Treble- or bass-clef

Bᴇʟʟs (tubular)

Treble-clef

Gʟᴏᴄᴋᴇɴsᴘɪᴇʟ

Treble-clef

* Keyed Harmonica

Treble-clef

Cᴇʟᴇsᴛᴀ

Treble- and bass-clef

Dulcitone
(or Typophone)

Treble- and bass-clef

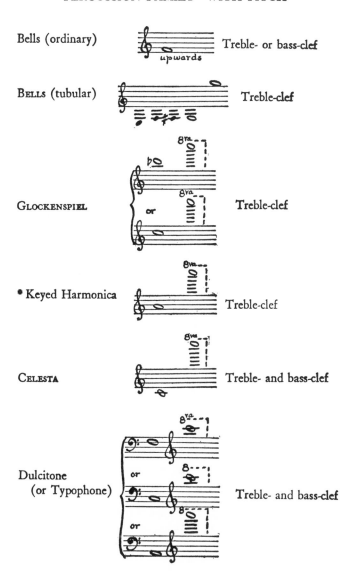

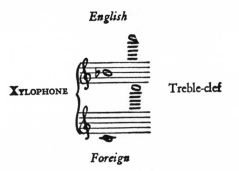

English

XYLOPHONE Treble-clef

Foreign

The above details of instrumental pitch and clefs are given for the benefit of those who wish to learn to read scores.

The essence of polyphony demands that the various horizontal melodic lines should stand out clearly. This probably had a great deal to do with the constantly increasing use of dissonance (in composition) in the evolution of the art. Dissonant tones stand out much more clearly in polyphonic weaving of melodies or in chord progressions than harmonious ones, just as a startling and unexpected bit of color will stand out in a painting. By the time the symphony came into the picture of musical evolution (second half of the eighteenth century), and the orchestra was a recognized factor in musical life, the harmonic basis of music was firmly established, but counterpoint—polyphonic texture—continued to form an important part of composition in general, and it can readily be seen how easily a rich variety of instrumental tone quality could enable the component parts of an orchestral composition to make themselves distinctly discernible within a complex tonal mass. Different tone qualities and a certain amount of dissonance are equally valuable for this purpose, and the art of orchestration,[5] which determines how instruments are used and combined, has become increasingly important.

The art of orchestration, fixing the role of each instrument in the symphony, must not only take into consideration the nature of the instrument's tone, but also the register in which it is most effective, the kind of passage that can best be played on it, and the technical problems of the player. If the layman could once hear a familiar symphony played with an interchange of roles between the instruments, he would realize how subtle and important is this art of orchestration.

Having gained a realization that the *tone* quality of instruments is supremely important in musical structure, the layman's curiosity is usually aroused as to *why* instrumental tone quality differs so greatly. In order to find that out, we have to cross over into the scientific side of music. Paraphrasing Helmholtz's definition of sound quality: "the quality of a musical tone depends solely on the number and relative strength of its partial simple tones," into less scientific language, we might say that the particular *combination of partials*

[5] Years ago the author heard a critical lady say on leaving the Metropolitan Opera House: "I cannot stand so-and-so's (mentioning a leading operatic conductor's name) *orchestration.*" The remark was promptly added to the author's collection of musical jokes, but since then the same idea has cropped up so often in conversations with laymen that a foot-note in The Layman's Music Book may well be devoted to explain that orchestration is not an attribute of conductors. It is the *composer's* art of using and combining instruments in an orchestral score.

that creates the tone quality of a particular instrument could be likened to a mixture of chemical elements that produces a given result. The laws of nature—notably the harmonic series—furnish the reason why the "chemical mixtures" of instrumental tone quality differ so widely. Through understanding them we learn that it is possible to alter the shape of sound-waves through construction of instruments and through the method of producing their possible tones. In the wind instruments, the inner bore (conical or cylindrical), the presence or absence of reeds in the mouthpiece, or the size and shape of a "cup" mouthpiece (on brass instruments) determine tone quality, just as the length of a vibrating air column or string determines its pitch. The material of which the wind instrument is fashioned is relatively unimportant. Flutes can be made of ebony, silver, or gold. Experiments have been made in which our so-called "brass" instruments were constructed of wood and even porcelain. So long as the construction, mouthpiece and method of playing causes the sound-producing air-column inside to vibrate in the way it should, the tone quality is not altered by the material used. The vibrational thing we call musical tone is an elemental force like electricity. Potentially it is all around us, but, like electricity, it must be harnessed to do the bidding of human genius.

Let us now examine examples of the inevitable expansion from small beginnings in the history of the orchestra. The instruments used in the opera *Euridice* by Peri (1600) were:

The Harpsichord
The Chitarrone
The Lira Grande or viola da gamba
The Theorbo
    and
Three flutes used in an interlude

In Monteverdi's *Orfeo,* produced only seven years later, the list of instruments had grown enormously. Here it is:

 2 Gravicembali
 2 Contrabassi de Viola
10 Viole da brazzo
 1 Arpa doppia
 2 Violini piccoli alla Francese

 2 Chitarroni
 2 Organi di legno
 3 Bassi da gamba
 4 Tromboni
 1 Regale
 2 Cornetti
 1 Flautino
 1 Clarino

As the importance of the "Sinfonia avanti l'Opera" —the rapidly developing overture—grew, all kinds of instrumental combinations were tried. Among the innumerable instruments combined in seventeenth- and early eighteenth-century scores, we find the ancestors of our modern types, but none, except perhaps the trombone and the drum, had a mechanism approaching those we know. The viols, the early horns and other wind instruments were crude and awkward. As music advanced and made increasing demands for flexibility and "playability," as music became an independent art and people began to gather for the sole purpose of listening to it, as this inauguration of public concerts in larger auditoriums demanded both a literature and instruments possessing greater volume as well as refinement of tone, the science of constructing perfected instruments gained momentum and gradually furnished the means to the creative geniuses whose works form such an important part of musical life to-day. The large forms discussed in Form and the Sonata were obviously ideal for orchestral purposes.

The history of the sonata and the symphony—developing simultaneously—demonstrates how eagerly the "moderns" of the eighteenth century grasped the new ideas of these larger forms. Karl Philipp Emanuel Bach, while respecting his father's memory, spoke slightingly of his compositions, and of the "old" contrapuntal style of writing. His one idea was to develop the "new" sonata and symphony. In Mannheim, the industrious Bohemian violinist-conductor-composer, Johann Wenzl Anton Stamitz, and his prolific son Carl, produced, between them, over a hundred symphonies before Beethoven reached manhood. Their followers were numerous enough to enable historians

to point to a "Stamitz School"—a well-known landmark in symphonic development. The actual music of
these men who loomed so large in the esteem of their
contemporaries lies mute on the shelves of libraries.
They were builders in the great project of symphonic
music but they only worked at the foundation of what
was to come. When Haydn, composing for the orchestra he directed at the great country estate of Prince
Esterhazy in Hungary, produced symphony after symphony, fresh with the tang of the folk-like themes he
knew so well how to introduce into art music, a development was begun that is unsurpassed in the history
of art. Here is the orchestra Haydn used in his later
symphonies:

> 2 Flutes
> 2 Oboes
> 2 Fagotts
> 2 Horns
> 2 Trumpets
>   Tympani
> First Violin
> Second Violin
> Viola
> Violincello
> Contrabass

In the typical Mozart score we find the same list
but with the addition of two clarinets. This introduction of an existing but hitherto unused instrument into
the symphonic picture is characteristic. It is a bit like

the introduction of a human being at court in a monarchy. Once introduced and sponsored by a genius the instrument was universally accepted and instrument builders promptly began to furbish it up and give it newly perfected features to fit it for its higher estate, much as a beauty would be groomed and outfitted for entrance into court life. Sometimes the introduction of an instrument can only be traced to accidental circumstances, as for instance in the case of the French horn. Long used as an outdoor instrument for military purposes and the chase, it was "brought indoors" to lend an appropriate atmosphere to hunting scenes in French ballets. Arriving in England in this capacity it acquired the title "French" horn, although it was perfectly familiar to the British as a perennially useful descendant of that homely instrument of our semi-civilized ancestors—the animal's tusk.

Sometimes an instrument already admitted to symphonic scores would receive special distinction from some composer, lifting it to a new and more important position. Mozart conferred such a distinction upon the viola, which, until his time, had been little more than a filler-in of harmonies. Beethoven extended the function of the hitherto limited tympanum. Until he occupied himself with its possibilities it had only been expected to produce two tones, tonic and dominant. Beethoven is responsible for the demands which cause the tympani player of modern times to do so much anxious tuning during a concert. Since Beethoven, he has considerably more than two tones to play.

Again composers have sometimes called for more instruments of the same kind. In Beethoven's Third Symphony (Eroica) we find three horns instead of the conventional two, and in his Ninth Symphony he calls for *four*. That number eventually became the rule. These details, selected from a mass of potential information, give some idea, not only of the expansion of the orchestra, but of the way in which this growth matched the development of the large forms as used by the great masters.

Mozart, Beethoven, Schubert, Schumann, Brahms, in turn poured their creative genius into this lofty type of art work. Much great music has been written in other forms, but none surpasses in sheer inspiration this music of many "voices" and many colors that fills the great tonal edifices of the symphonic literature with a matchless wealth of expressive power.[*]

POINTS TO BE REMEMBERED

1. The typical symphony is a composition containing three or more separate movements, related in key but contrasting in character.

2. Of these movements at least one (usually the first) is written in sonata-form. The other movements may either be

[*] In the Layman's Music Courses, listeners have derived great pleasure and benefit from striving to follow orchestral scores long before they can literally read them in the manner of trained musicians. *Philharmonia* miniature scores, published by the Wiener Philharmonischer Verlag, contain excellent analyses of the symphonic literature. The effort of the eye to find at least the "shape" of phrases the listener is conscious of hearing further develops that consciousness and deepens the impression of the essence of orchestral music. It is like a game or puzzle at first, but very soon becomes much more.

written in sonata-form, rondo form, minuet form, extended song form or mixtures of song, rondo and sonata-form. Fugal writing is also found in some important examples.

3. The typical symphony, as we use the word to-day, is written for orchestra, that is, an aggregation of instruments.

4. Although the make-up of the orchestra is largely governed by tradition, the composer is theoretically free to choose the instruments employed. This choice of instruments is called the "scoring" of the symphony. The way in which the instruments are combined is called "orchestration."

5. Human voices may be added to the orchestra as in Beethoven's Ninth Symphony, Mahler's Second and Eighth Symphonies and others.

6. The difference in *tone quality* of each instrument in the orchestra is due to "overtone mixtures" obtained by means of the size, shape and construction of the instrument. (See Sound and the Function of Hearing.)

SUGGESTIONS FOR CORRELATED READING

Orchestration, Cecil Forsyth
Beethoven and His Nine Symphonies, Grove
From Grieg to Brahms, Daniel Gregory Mason
Grove's Dictionary of Music and Musicians, Articles on Orchestra and Orchestration
Grove's Dictionary of Music and Musicians, Article on Symphony

RECORDS

Consult large list of Classical Symphonies by Haydn, Mozart, Beethoven, Schubert, Schumann and Brahms recorded by leading orchestras and conductors of the United States and Europe. It is well to begin with Haydn, Mozart and early Beethoven (Symphonies Nos. 1 and 2).

Victor 20522 & 20523   Instruments of the Orchestra with set of charts showing different instruments.

X

SHOULD MUSIC HAVE A PROGRAM?

*"Where painting says 'this is the
meaning,' music alone says 'this is.'"*
RICHARD WAGNER

CHRISTOPHER MORLEY has expressed the idea that
"pigeon-holes are excellent—for pigeons." One might,
with equal logic, assert that in music "programs are
good—for program music." But the question whether
or not to associate extraneous meanings with our type
of art music, is not so easily disposed of. In order to
clarify it we must take into consideration not only facts
of musical history but deep-rooted impulses of the
human being.

We must remember that for thousands of years
music *was* invariably associated with other things, with
ritual and the dance, with poems and the drama, with
religion, war and ceremonial events. Throughout the
known history of the world, music has been *used* in so
many different ways that it is no wonder most people
think only in terms of "expressing" this or that "through
music," even though they belong to the civilization
that has produced abstract art music.

John Sargent once said "abstract instrumental
music is the highest art-form on earth because it does
not represent or symbolize something else."

It is not easy to follow the intricacies of vocal polyphonic scores, and the untrained listener will miss many of their beauties that give enjoyment to the musician, but wherever words give a clue, or associated ideas lend a meaning, the problem of the listener is lessened. His imaginative functioning is guided; his emotional reactions are motivated. Every alliance of music with other things diminishes his responsibility as an active listener. The absence of associated ideas is the thing that necessitated the highly-developed forms of instrumental music. It also necessitates highly-developed and active listening.

At the time abstract instrumental music began, composers unconsciously feared the lack of extraneous meaning which music had always derived from its association with other things. Early instrumental pieces often bear the most fanciful descriptive titles. Side by side with the sonatas, sinfonias, fugues and toccatas that represent the abstract development in instrumental music, we find a bewildering mass of attempts to make the innocent spinets and clavichords of the seventeenth and early eighteenth centuries "express" everything from the cluck of a hen to the combat between David and Goliath!

These artless forerunners of the grandiose program music of the nineteenth century not only exhibit the anxious intention of the composer at least to suggest an extraneous meaning; they also demonstrate the truth that a program can supply motive power for music in which high creative inspiration is lacking. Undoubtedly *abstract* instrumental music requires the *highest* degree of purely musical inspiration. This does not necessarily mean that program music cannot be great. But great program music is music that *can* stand alone; music that, shorn of its program, still retains its greatness.

Such music strictly speaking has a dual nature. It is abstract music as well as program music. It not only can stand alone without its given program, but it can teach us—if we are willing to learn—how easy it is to attach a totally different program to it. A piece of music in which the call of a cuckoo is imitated cannot be made to suggest an artillery battle but, in less literally descriptive music, all kinds of things can happen. The author once tried the following experiment with diverting results: A relatively unfamiliar symphony of Sibelius was being played by the Chicago Orchestra; during a dinner-party preceding the concert, the author managed to give five different people, who had never heard the symphony, five different programs, supposedly belonging to it. After the concert the five victims of this harmless hoax, perpetrated in the interests of layman education, rapturously reported the pleasure they had derived from knowing "the true meaning" of the music. All five programs fitted the symphony!

A still more amusing experience resulted from inducing a listener to accept, without knowing what was being played, the whispered account of a grandiose mythological tale as the "story" of Strauss's *Sinfonia Domestica*. This victim, arriving late in a box from which all programs had been shamelessly removed, revelled in exalted and impassioned imaginative impressions, until he read in the newspaper what had been played, and received a copy of a particularly detailed programmatic elucidation of the score, crying baby and all. He is not on speaking terms with the author.[1]

Richard Strauss, high-priest of program music in the late nineteenth century, often became impatient when asked about the "meaning" of his music and insisted it was "just music." This sounded inconsistent in view of the highly suggestive titles he gave his tone poems, and yet he was really claiming for them that dual nature of music that is good enough to stand alone. While program music has existed at all times since instrumental music came into the picture, it became extremely important under the influence of romanticism.[2]

[1] The Layman's Music Courses in New York and Philadelphia have afforded a rich opportunity to study this question. In many different classes, comprising laymen of all types and ages, records of unfamiliar compositions have been played without giving the listeners the program the work was supposed to express through the music. Not once have the numerous members of these classes, when asked to give their impressions, arrived at anything even approximating the "program" of the piece.
    Till Eulenspiegel of Richard Strauss was found to express everything from "soldiers returning from war" to "lovers quarreling over a woman." The nearest approach to the essence of the piece was that it was "funny music."

[2] In Eckerman's "Gespräche mit Goethe," Goethe says: "The familiar conception of the classical and the romantic arose in my mind and Schiller's. My maxims were in favor of the objective method of treatment. But Schiller preferred his own subjective method and defended it in his essay on 'Naïve and Sentimental Poetry.' He showed that I was romantically inclined in spite of my desire to be otherwise, and that my Iphigenie, because of the pre-

When, under the influence of the French Revolution, mankind became intensely interested in the newly glorified individual of the species, subjectivism logically dominated the arts. The personal destiny of man, his feelings and his thought-life assumed increased significance. Introspection was passionately indulged in by the young, who at a certain age seldom failed to find a *Weltschmerz* lurking within themselves. The orgy of expressionism in that romantic nineteenth century is too well known to need comment. Music, a marvellous medium for the expression of sentiment, soaked up romanticism as a sponge takes water.

Already in the eighteenth century we find in Haydn's symphonies such sub-titles as the "Clock" and the "Surprise." Mozart's great C major symphony has acquired the faint suggestion of the sub-title "Jupiter." Beethoven wrote definite program music in his Sixth (Pastorale) Symphony and even essayed literal descriptiveness in its thunder-storm, which, it must be admitted, is considerably more effective than such efforts usually are. In his Ninth Symphony, Beethoven goes still further and uses vocal forces and a poetic text in the last movement.

Spohr, a contemporary of Beethoven although much younger, left documentary evidence of the tendencies of the 1830's in his "Characteristic Tone-picture in the form of a Symphony after a poem by Carl

ponderance of sentiment, was by no means so antique in feeling as I thought. Later on the brothers Schlegel took up the matter; and people talk now glibly of classicism and romanticism, to which fifty years ago, no one gave a thought."

Pfeiffer." It was eventually known by the shorter title
Weihe der Töne (Consecration of Sound) but a printed
notice was appended to the score in which the composer directed that Pfeiffer's poem should be printed or
recited aloud at every performance of the symphony.
The work only enjoyed a short-lived fame. A landscape
that could not be understood or enjoyed without verbal
explanations reading "this is supposed to be a tree" or
"that represents a cloud"—would not be apt to take a
place among immortal art works. Spohr, eminent
violinist and leading musician of his day, tried to replace musical inspiration with programmatic interest.
This can be done to a certain extent in short characteristic pieces, but not in the big forms. They fall to
earth.

Berlioz was almost as insistent as Spohr in demanding that the associated ideas of his *Symphonie Fantastique* (1832) be made known to the listener. He
wrote:

"The composer has aimed at developing various
situations in the life of an artist, so far as seemed musically possible. The plan of an instrumental drama,
being without words, requires to be explained before-
hand. The programme (which is indispensable to the
perfect comprehension of the dramatic plan of the
work) ought therefore to be considered in the light of
the spoken text of an opera, serving to lead up to the
pieces of music and indicate the character and expression."

The music in Berlioz's *Symphonie Fantastique* has much more creative vitality than Spohr's *Weihe der Töne,* and yet it is questionable how much interest the listener would take in it without a knowledge of the story. Supposed to relate "episodes in the life of an artist" it has a principal theme, called "l'idée fixe," that constantly re-appears throughout the work, representing the object of the affections of the artist-hero.

Historically, the Fantastic Symphony of Berlioz is a very important work. The role of the "idée fixe," in its general plan, crystallized the possibility of having an extraneous meaning determine the use of thematic material, rather than the exigencies of an accepted musical form. Instead of being a "first subject" or "second subject," a theme became a "love theme" or a "hate theme." Just as the rhythm of text once governed the measurement of music, so the progress of a program could now condition musical form. It can easily be seen how this possibility at once freed the composer from rigid adherence to any of the existing ground-plans of musical composition. That appealed to the moderns of an age in which men were bent upon pursuing that "elusive phantom," liberty, and even imagined they had seized it.

Two important developments grew out of these early attempts at instrumental program music on a grand scale; the symphonic poem and the leit-motif [3] in Wagner operas.

[3] The leit-motif is a musical theme that definitely represents a personage, event, circumstance, or emotion. See Opera Furnishes Another Milestone: Wagner, page 199.

To Liszt belongs the credit of giving a name and recognizable character to the Symphonic Poem. Perhaps his objective is best expressed in Edward Dannreuther's definition of Romantic music:

"Romantic music is in some sense an offshoot of literature; a reflex of poetry expressed in musical terms; a kind of impressionism which tends to reject formality and aims at a direct rendering of its object; a desire to produce musical effects suggested by natural phenomena; an art eager, sensitive, impulsive, which seeks its ideal of beauty through emotional expression. With Wagner it is *ancilla dramatis*—a powerful rhetoric which, like scenery and action, is made subservient to the purposes of the theatre."

Liszt's most important successor, Richard Strauss, brought the symphonic poem to its highest point.

It is interesting at this juncture to note how every new development in the art of music makes use of preceding ones and how definitely art absorbs novel ideas without losing the valuable fundamental things that preceded them.

Without the strong sense of form that had evolved in the eighteenth century and was well understood by all educated musicians at the time under discussion, the efforts to write program music on a large scale would have been incoherent and abortive. In the best symphonic poems of Liszt, Richard Strauss and others, one finds such well defined sections and subdivisions of sections, as well as masterly handling of the elements of

contrast and repetition, that if given a letter formula
(A—B—A—C—etc.) the presence of one of the large
accepted forms, even though used with the utmost freedom, is at once revealed. Debussy's *Afternoon of a
Faun* in its big lines is a perfect example of A—B—A
divisions. The symphonic poem composers felt freer
than they really were, because, formlessness in music
being a sheer impossibility, they could not stray far
from the comprehensive discoveries in form that had
already been made.

One bad result of the instrumental program-music
development in the nineteenth century was to confuse
the issue of the essence and the essential function of
music.

In association with other things, music can lend
increased eloquence to words; it can enhance the emotional values of drama, furnish "motor-power" and
mood to the dancer, and add white heat to the expression of human passion; it can create mood, arouse
religious devotion and induce a martial spirit. In this
power of service to a purpose, it is like the element of
electricity harnessed to do the bidding of man.

In its abstract form, music can release the spirit
from all other conceptions of a definite nature and express what is inexpressible through any other medium.
It can suggest things that only the soul can understand,
things that lie deep in our subconsciousness or over the
border of super-consciousness. In form and substance it
is governed by the same law of *order* that saves the
universe from chaos and underlies all beauty in nature.

Thus, in comparison with music used for a purpose, in association with something else, abstract music might be likened to the Northern Lights that stretch across the sky, quivering, glowing with strange colors, moving for some reason of their own, the mysterious manifestations of unexplained natural forces giving us a glimpse of beauty that cannot be linked with anything on earth. The beauty is there for those who have eyes to see, and what it can mean or suggest depends on the soul of the beholder.

If we have a clear conception of these things we can approach different types of music without confusion. We can "render unto Caesar what is Caesar's" by accepting without question any definite or suggested program given us by composers. We can reject without hesitation a reliance upon the arbitrary verbal interpretations—good, bad and indifferent—that have clustered so thickly around abstract musical masterpieces that one cannot see the mountains for the clouds. If we do this we must not forget that it involves fitting ourselves to be active listeners. The highest function of the independent listener is to match the power of the genius who can create an art work through the medium of unaided musical tone by the capacity to listen to it.

POINTS TO BE REMEMBERED

1. Music, like nature, has widely differing manifestations. It has been used in connection with religion, poetic text, drama and the dance. It has served to suggest, portray or depict things that are foreign to it.

2. Perhaps the *greatest* achievement of musical genius is *abstract music*, an art form in pure sound capable of stir-

ring the emotions, the imagination and the soul of man.

3. Abstract music demands active listening.

4. It is advisable not to confuse issues by depending on someone else's imagination and considering the addition of a
program to *abstract* music as essential to enjoyment. It is
the divine right of the listener (and his highest function)
to respond independently to such music, relying on his
own imagination and emotions.

SUGGESTIONS FOR CORRELATED READING

The Romantic Composers, Daniel Gregory Mason

Grove's Dictionary of Music and Musicians, Article on the
Symphonic Poem

Musical Studies, Ernest Newman (Programme Music)

Richard Strauss, Ernest Newman

Oxford History of Music, Vol. VI, The Romantic Period
(Edward Dannreuther)

Musical Discourse, Richard Aldrich (Chapter on Programme
Music)

Strauss's Tone Poems, Thomas Armstrong, from "The Musical
Pilgrim," edited by Sir Arthur Somerwell

Claude Debussy: His Life and Works, Léon Vallas. Translated
by Maire and Grace O'Brien

RECORDS

Brunswick Record Cor- poration	*Till Eulenspiegel's Merry Pranks* by Richard Strauss recorded by the State Opera Orches- tra, Berlin, and conducted by the Composer
Victor Album M-44	*Ein Heldenleben* (A Hero's Life) by Richard Strauss New York Philharmonic-Symphony Orchestra conducted by Willem Mengelberg
Victor 6696 A and B	*Afternoon of a Faun* by Claude Debussy Philadelphia Symphony Orchestra conducted by Leopold Stokowski

XI

OPERA FURNISHES ANOTHER MILESTONE: WAGNER

"Music teaches us most exquisitely,
the art of development."

D'ISRAELI

An anonymous article which appeared in the Dresden *Anzeiger* of June 14th, 1848, contained the following paragraph:

"We shall realize that human society should rest on the activity of human beings rather than on the supposed activity of money. We shall establish from clear conviction, a principle,—and God will enlighten us so that we may find the right laws to incorporate this principle in life—and then like a bad nightmare, this devilish conception of money will leave us with all its horrible consequences of public and secret usury, swindles on paper, dividends and banker speculations. Then will come the full emancipation of the human race and the fulfillment of the teachings of Christ. . . ."[1]

Young Richard Wagner, struggling conductor and composer in Dresden, acknowledged the authorship of

[1] From Richard Wagner's *Gesammelte Werke,* edited by Julius Kapp. Vol. 12.

this article when he read it in its entirety on the following day at a meeting of the revolutionary "Vaterlandsverein."

The circumstances of Wagner's life and the changes they wrought in him led him very far from the ideals of his revolutionary youth, and the words quoted above do not fit the acquisitive Wagner of Munich and Bayreuth demanding of the world the financial means to lead a life of ease as well as to fulfill his artistic dreams. But he left a monument to the conviction of his youth in the *Nibelungen Ring,* his powerful operatic version of the old Norse-Teutonic Saga in which a golden ring, symbol of wealth, is cursed during a ruthless struggle for power and thereafter destroys all who possess it. Throughout the Nibelungen Trilogy, *Walküre, Siegfried* and *Götterdämmerung,* as well as the *Rheingold* that serves as a prologue for these operas, social problems, and ageless aspects of human nature, personified by mythical characters, provide the essential dramatic action. In all the Wagner operas except *Rienzi,* which is romantically historical, and *Die Meistersinger von Nürnberg,* the single comic opera of this colossal genius, allegory and symbolism dominate the drama. Even in the *Meistersinger,* Beckmesser personifies the stupid, prejudiced type of professional critic while Hans Sachs and Walter von Stolzing, the tutored and untutored geniuses who were not slaves to tradition in creating poetry and music, vanquish Beckmesser much as Wagner himself eventually silenced his critical adversaries—by making them look ridiculous.

Is it because Wagner in his own existence fell so far short of his expressed ideals that a fatalistic conception of life—in which human beings act, not on the basis of free moral responsibility but under the spell of a power they cannot control—runs through his operas? Even Tristan and Isolde, in the most human and passionate of Wagner's scores, are helpless under the spell of a magic love-potion administered by fate in the person of Brangäne. Only *Rienzi* and the *Meistersinger* are free from the conception of a magic power that plays such a fateful role in the *Flying Dutchman*, *Lohengrin*, *Tannhäuser*, *Tristan*, *Parsifal* and the *Nibelungen Ring*.

Or was it a profound insight into the nature of opera itself that forbade the attempt to place normal human life in that particular frame?

However that may be, Wagner has achieved, in a higher degree than any other opera composer, the long-sought fusion of drama and music. The efforts of the Greeks to achieve this fusion are veiled in mystery. The operas of the Italian composers at the dawn of the seventeenth century, important as they are historically, mean little to us as works of art. The reforms of Gluck after the debauchery of operatic form in the late seventeenth and early eighteenth centuries still live in works of formal but somewhat archaic beauty. The later Italian operas teem with luscious melodies accompanied by a discreet orchestra, and the texture of these scores enables singers to sing with the utmost freedom and beauty of tone. But while we may well worship at the shrine of bel canto, there are very few pre-Wagner operas we can take seriously as *drama*.

It was reserved for Richard Wagner—using with uncanny mastery all the existing possibilities of musical composition and stage-craft, writing his own libretti with an ear to the sound of words, and placing on his stage allegorical and symbolical characters who seldom betray the nearness of the sublime to the ridiculous in opera—to fulfill the centuries-old dream of countless artists.

The *addition* of music to other things presents no great difficulty. It can enhance most things to which it is added. But to *combine* music with other things on terms of anything like equality requires genius of the highest order because its essence is so different from anything on earth.

So far, Wagner's success in doing this in opera is unique, and it may well be considered a milestone in the evolution of music.

From a purely musical point of view, Wagner obviously could not have reached his goal without the symphonic developments that preceded him, the instrumental possibilities that had evolved and, above all, the idea of the ordered use of different themes within large forms. The fact that Wagner's themes represent personages, events and other dramatic values, does not diminish his indebtedness to the established mastery of handling thematic material that enabled Beethoven to fill his great symphonic canvases in the way he did. The leit-motif (a programmatic theme) is really an ingenious extension of the possibilities of thematic development to fill operatic needs in the Wagner scores and programmatic requirements in nineteenth-century symphonic poems.

If the layman has any realization of the long struggle to evolve *music-drama* and the true significance of Wagner's scores in this respect, he will never commit the folly of neglecting to acquaint himself with the poetic text and gain some idea of the themes that create a musical action running parallel—and yet fusing completely—with that on the stage.

Theoretically, all musical art works should reach the listener without any difficulty. Actually, in the case of Wagner, even those who have an adequate grasp of the German language, or of any language into which the Wagnerian text is translated, seldom hear enough of it really to understand. Wagner was merciless in his demands on singers. Only the greatest singers manage to give us his text with complete clarity. Again, the Wagner orchestra, symphonic in scope, is too rich for the average voice and for the acoustical conditions of the average opera house. Some people think that this problem can be solved by subduing the orchestra. Wagner knew better when he planned the shell that covers the orchestra at Bayreuth. He knew that when a conductor subdues players beyond a certain point, at moments of power and climax, life goes out of the music. The Bayreuth shell enables the orchestra to play with emotional freedom and brilliance of tone without drowning the singers. There should be such a shell in every theatre where Wagner operas are given. Until that day arrives, the layman will lose much if he does not acquaint himself with the text of the Wagner music-dramas before hearing them.

Active listening cannot be achieved without effort. Those who claim that the enjoyment of art should be effortless, forget how close that lack of effort is to passivity. Some art *can* be enjoyed without effort. It is like a peaceful meadow in which we may wander without exertion. Meadows have a charm that cannot be denied. Far be it from the author to disparage them. But other types of art are like the mountain world. They are the high places of human achievement. They involve much more than mere sense impressions and they are not easily accessible.

We have to develop within ourselves the power of perception before we can reach these lofty haunts of the greatest geniuses. At best, those who shun the effort of self-development will gaze at the heights from afar —perhaps through glasses provided by others—and guess at what is there.

A book like this should concern itself, obviously, with the less accessible heights of musical art, not in a futile attempt to bring them to the layman, but in an endeavor to show a way, as far as possible, by which the layman can reach them himself.

The third element in Wagner's music dramas, stage-craft, using that term to include all the arts that combine to give our visual impressions in the theatre, is one in which he was far ahead of his time.

At the Music Exposition in Frankfort (Germany) in 1927, there was an extraordinary department devoted to operatic stage-settings and costumes. Original Fuentes sets for *Titus* by Mozart formed the gateway for a long gallery of small models demonstrating the development of scenic and costume art. Again evolution! Candles or oil lamps for foot-lights, primitive construction, painting without perspective, a naïve realism taxing the least alert sense of humor, and all the pomp of flimsy pasteboard grandeur demonstrated the gradual advance towards the twentieth-century stage. Brunnhildes in corsets appeared side by side with prima donna Sieglindes in long trains that surely never were meant to sweep the floors of primitive dwellings.

If we play or listen to many of Beethoven's larger piano compositions we realize very definitely that he was writing for instruments infinitely more powerful than those he knew. The Beethoven Association in New York received the gift of a piano that belonged to Beethoven. There was even the skeleton of a mouse, possible contemporary of Beethoven, inside the piano. Harold Bauer, witty president of the Beethoven Association, placed this skeleton in a little coffin on which was inscribed "died in action" and with appropriate rites at a yearly meeting of members, the mouse was given a last resting-place among Beethoven relics. The piano itself is so fragile that by no stretch of the imagination could the modern pianist conceive performing the Hammerklavier Sonata or the Emperor Concerto on such an instrument. Beethoven was keenly interested in piano construction, just as Bach was interested in equal temperament, and Wagner stimulated the designing of tubas—now called Wagner tubas—that achieved effects he wanted in the brass section of the orchestra. The greatest geniuses know that the practical means of expression cannot be ignored. The popular idea of genius—an untidy, impractical individual dreaming away his life in an aesthetic sphere far from sordid realities—does not fit the prodigious workers like Beethoven and Wagner who paid the greatest attention to practical details connected with their art, any more than the general conception of an artist in relation to morals would fit the highly domestic Bach with his large family of perfectly legitimate children.[2]

It is perfectly evident from Wagner's stage directions that his flaming imagination carried him far beyond the technical possibilities of his age.

Those who profess boredom at Wagner operas (and such people almost invariably have no knowledge of the drama beyond the bare outline of the plot) are usually critical of the obvious shortcomings of the stage-craft. The Rhine-maidens in all-too-visible swings,

[2] In these United States before the war it was positively expected of artists that they should break all the commandments ordinary mortals were supposed to keep. Domesticity implied lack of temperament. Eccentricity was such a valuable asset that highly-paid press-agents supplied what the artist lacked. Since the war, such departures from the straight and narrow path have become so common that their significance in relation to the artist are somewhat clouded. As a French Countess has said with regard to make-up, "the day when one could distinguish the lady from the demi-mondaine has gone by." Perhaps the best chance for the artist to stand out from his fellow-men to-day is to be mid-Victorian!

the steam that hisses as it issues from apertures that sometimes balk in spots, the Siegfried dragon, decorated with drugstore lights, cautiously emerging from a cave which discreetly hides the last fatal combat with Siegfried, the patient horse that wags his tail as Brunnhilde in *Götterdämmerung* prepares to leap with him into the flames of Siegfried's funeral pyre, all these palpable absurdities furnish ammunition to cynical Wagner critics. But already in Bayreuth, two years ago, that imaginative master of scenic art, Emil Preetorius, achieved effects that point to an interesting possibility, namely that Wagner will come into his own in the twentieth century.

It was Preetorius who conceived the idea of painting the castle in *Lohengrin* with luminous paint giving it the glamor of a legendary atmosphere. It was Preetorius who really carried out (for the first time so far as the author's experience is concerned) Wagner's direction that the stage at the end of the *Walküre* should be "encircled by a curtain of fire." Those who are sensitive to the suggestive power of music usually receive such a tremendous musical impression at that moment that they forget the hissing steam and the "flames" of tattered fabric blown about by a breeze strongly suggestive of a hair-drying apparatus. In Bayreuth two years ago, Preetorius summoned Loge, the God of Fire, in a medium that did all but devour the theatre. His curtain of fire was produced by the combination of lights and moving pictures.

In a flash the extraordinary possibilities of Wagner

in the sound-films made itself felt. All that he dreamt, all that he imagined on the scenic side of his art could be accomplished through the sound-film. Again this medium would permit artists, who have every qualification except vocal *volume,* to take the parts that have so often been ruined—dramatically speaking—by singers whose bodily bulk and lack of talent for acting reduced their efforts to a point of absurdity in spite of the most careful coaching in the Bayreuth tradition.

When Leopold Stokowski demonstrated the wire sound-transmission of the Electric Research Products, Inc., with the Philadelphia Orchestra in Philadelphia in 1934, he performed, with Agnes Davis as Brunnhilde, the Immolation Scene from *Götterdämmerung.* The orchestra and soloist were in another part of the building, but the sound—perfectly transmitted—seemed to come from the stage of the Academy of Music. Stokowski, at the controls, could adjust balance of parts and amplify what he wished. At the point when the soprano who sings Brunnhilde is usually near the breaking-point of fatigue and battles, straining all the resources of art, to accomplish the miracle of being heard above an unleashed powerful orchestra, Agnes Davis's fresh young voice soared without strain or effort to a passionate and stirring domination of the music. The author had the sensation of hearing this music for the first time.

If we imagine all the marvels of the incredible sound-film world placed at the disposal of a really artistic director, if we imagine Wagnerian roles acted by those who could act (and look) the parts, and sung by those who, under such conditions, could sing them without strain, if we add a superb orchestra fresh and sufficiently prepared, instead of one which has rehearsed *Elektra* in the morning and performed *Aïda* in the afternoon, and above all if we imagine a public capable of understanding both the music and the drama, then Wagner would truly come into his own.

This can only come about if conservative Wagnerian authorities lose their fear of modern mediums. It can only happen when film authorities lose their fear of anything that departs from what one might call a *tabloid tradition,* and this in turn can only happen when the *public* evinces the desire to enjoy art without reference to twentieth-century tempo.

With all the much discussed leisure on the horizon, it may be that the tendency to compress all artistic experience into five-minute doses will disappear. Mutilated, tabloidized Wagner would certainly not accomplish anything. But it is not without the bounds of possibility that our children may make pilgrimages to festivals in Radio City where they will witness a complete and miraculous realization of the dreams of Richard Wagner.

In connection with active listening, which benefits the layman, it may be said that his active participation in artistic evolution could greatly benefit music. Public demand is an enormous factor in evolution. That power is seldom consciously exercised. How many are the individuals who take what is given to them without question and even allow their opinions to be governed by the newspapers. The best critics have no desire to govern opinions. It is their business to give their own and that is all that concerns them. But the indifferent or thoughtless readers of reviews are so influenced by them that one can often witness a complete change of heart in concert or opera patrons who found a composition or a performance most enjoyable until they read in the paper that it was not good.

Active listening will bring independent thinking in music lovers, and if they will go a step further and take the trouble to voice a demand, they will be assuming the significance of those patrons of art in other ages to whom we owe the existence and the preservation of our musical art treasures.

POINTS TO BE REMEMBERED

1. The many different efforts to combine music with drama.
2. Wagner's supreme achievement in doing this.
3. The necessity, in approaching his operas intelligently, of knowing the text and of being familiar with the themes (leit-motifs) he uses in building his music. A most rewarding study for the active listener.

SUGGESTIONS FOR CORRELATED READING

My Life (*Autobiography*), Richard Wagner
Letters of Richard Wagner in Two Volumes   Selected and edited by Wilhelm Altmann
Translated from the German by M. M. Bozman
Published by J. M. Dent & Sons, London

Wagner as Man and Artist, Ernest Newman
Richard Wagner's Prose Works, Translated by W. Ashton Ellis
Richard Wagner, H. S. Chamberlain
Richard Wagner to Mathilde Wesendonck, Translated by W. Ashton Ellis
Wagner's Music Dramas Analyzed with the Leading Motives, Gustav Kobbe

RECORDS

Columbia	Album 154	*Tannhäuser*—Wagner Bayreuth Festival Recording
Columbia	Album 101	*Tristan & Isolde*—Wagner Bayreuth Festival Recording
Victor	Album M–88 7843–7847	*Götterdämmerung*—Wagner Philadelphia Orchestra and Agnes Davis
Victor	6245	*Wotan's Farewell & Magic Fire Music* from *Walküre* *The Ride of the Valkyries* from *Walküre* of Wagner played by Philadelphia Symphony Orchestra
Victor	6651—9160—6789—8195 7319—9060	*Meistersinger*—Wagner (various parts by various soloists and orchestras)
Polydor	95181	
H. M. V.	D 1219	
Odeon	5117	

XII

HOW THE LISTENER'S SPHERE OF ACTIVITY DEVELOPED

> *"To listen to music is restful to the human being, because faculties are called into action and appealed to other than those he ordinarily uses, and also because it absorbs all his attention and frees him from worldly cares."*
>
> THEODORE THOMAS
> *Life Work,* Vol. 2

THE enterprising listener, who has become aware of the potential importance of his musical activity, looks about him with a new curiosity. How, when and where shall he find the way to the music he wants to hear? If he happens to belong to a musical family or live in a community rich in amateur musical activity, he can have that precious experience—"music in the home." Chamber-music evenings, group singing, all such activities, no matter how simple, will afford a fine foundation for musical life provided they are re-creatively adequate. Poor performances of music are only enjoyed by those who make them. But then comes a question that is very significant in our type of musical civilization:

Is music in the home enough?

That question may best be answered by an analogy. Let us agree that it is eminently desirable for a child to learn certain things about nature, first hand, by himself working in a garden, planting his own flowers and vegetables, watching them grow and tending them. We give the child his plot of ground, his seeds and tools, and encourage him to make the most of his possibilities. But could we feel that because he has this experience, he should not need to know the glory of the sea, the mountains, the forests, all the great manifestations of nature that lie outside of his garden? Even the best "music in the home" can never fill a rich and completely satisfying musical life for performer or listener, for the very good reason that so much great music cannot possibly be performed under home conditions. The intelligent twentieth-century layman should have his "garden" but in addition seek the experiences the wide world can give.

The public performances of music we take for granted to-day came into being to fill a real need. They are intimately bound up with the development of the larger forms and with the creation of a musical literature too important to be confined to private performance. As a rule, art treasures, in the form of painting, sculpture, etc., collected by individuals, are eventually housed in galleries or museums where they become accessible to humanity. Such a sharing of culture and beauty is one of the finest flowers of democracy. In music, it only gradually became apparent that the masterpieces of our musical civilization belong to the world, and ways and means had to be found to make them heard.

Public concert-halls and opera houses are the galleries and museums of music. In them our musical literature must be kept alive through adequate performance. Some day, the government of the United States will wake up to this fact, long recognized in Europe, and replace the generous but far too haphazard private patronage of such institutions by national subsidy so that important musical institutions can be made both permanent and secure.

But just as opera began without the conscious purpose of later developments, so the institution of public concerts crept into our musical civilization without apparent premeditation and even *before* the creation of most of the literature that fills our programs to-day. What might almost be considered as the cornerstone of a far-flung musical development, a great international industry, is described in an advertisement which was published in the *London Gazette* for December 30th, 1672. It reads:

"These are to give notice, that at Mr. John Bannister's house, now called the Musick-school, over against the George taverne, in White Fryers, this present Monday, will be musick performed by excellent masters, beginning precisely at four of the clock in the afternoon, and every afternoon for the future, precisely at the same hour."

If anyone preceded the enterprising Mr. Bannister

in organizing concerts to which the public was admitted upon payment of a fee, the author has not found any record of it. Bannister, a violinist of considerable accomplishment, succeeded Baltzar of Lübeck as leader of King Charles's new band of twenty-four violins, according to Burney, and continued to advertise "musick performed by excellent masters" for several years.[1]

It was largely due to that resourceful Parisian, Anne Dannican Philidor, who conceived the brilliant idea of giving "Concerts Spirituels" at the Académie Royale de Musique (the Opera House) when it would otherwise have had to be closed on religious feast days, that the institution of public concerts took root in Continental Europe. The only earlier developments of any consequence were the so-called Academies in Italy, and they have a rather confused history. The name is used to designate the institution which flourished all over Italy in the sixteenth and seventeenth centuries for the promotion of science, letters and art. Some of the

[1] Burney quotes North's "Memoirs of Music," then in manuscript as follows:
"Bannister having procured a large room in White Fryars, near the Temple back-gate, and erected an elevated box or gallery for the musicians, whose modesty required curtains, the rest of the room was filled with seats and small tables, ale-house fashion. One shilling, which was the price of admission, entitled the audience to call for what they pleased. There was very good musick, for Bannister found means to procure the best hands in London, and some voices to assist him. And there wanted no variety, for Bannister, besides playing on the violin, did wonders on the flageolet to a thro' base (thorough bass) and several masters likewise played solos."
It would be interesting to know how much profit Mr. Bannister and his "best hands" derived from the shilling admissions.

academies were State institutions and some private. Music was included in many of the academies and some were exclusively devoted to it, but their activities, which were largely educational, are not very clearly defined. The name was also applied to private concerts in eighteenth-century Italy and Burney describes one in his "Musical Tour" as follows:

"The first I went to was composed entirely of dilettanti. Il Padrone, or the master of the house, played the first violin, and had a very powerful band; there were twelve or fourteen performers, among whom were several good violins; there were likewise two German flutes, a violin-cello, and small double bass; they executed reasonably well several of our (J. C.) Bach's symphonies different from those printed in England; all the music here is in ms. . . . Upon the whole, this concert was much upon a level with our own private concerts among gentlemen in England."

The use of the word Académie spread to Germany and Austria where it was at first used instead of concert.

In Vienna, a quest for first public concerts leads us to performances organized in the latter part of the eighteenth century by the philanthropical Tonkünstler-Societät for the purpose of procuring pensions for widows and orphans of musicians. The society gave only two or three performances a year, but they were often important. Haydn's oratorios, *The Creation* and

The Four Seasons, had their initial hearing at these concerts and the Tonkünstler-Societät furnished the opportunity for the first public appearance in Vienna of the young pianist-composer, Ludwig van Beethoven. The program on that occasion (March 29th, 1795) announced "a new concerto played on the piano by the Master Ludwig van Beethoven and of his own invention."

It is interesting to note that public concert life in the United States began about the same time as that in Europe and has progressed parallel with it.[2]

By and large, until the revolutionary spirit at the end of the eighteenth century created the tendency to extend to the many what had formerly been the privilege of the few, musical art outside the Church and the theatre was almost exclusively confined to the palaces of rulers and nobles. As the modern millionaire has his yacht or his racing horses, the European magnate of the seventeenth and eighteenth centuries had his band of musicians. The greater his rank and fortune, the larger was his musical retinue. The development of symphonic literature owes much to the fact that the

[2] In "Grove's Dictionary of Music" the New York Philharmonic Orchestra is listed as the third oldest existing orchestra in the world, coming after London and Vienna. This might be questioned if one takes into account early concerts of the Leipzig Gewandhaus and Paris Conservatoire, but Grove qualifies the statement by the phrase "orchestral body in continuous service . . . devoted to the performance of instrumental music." The New York Philharmonic counts among its honorary members Spohr, Jenny Lind, Anton Rubinstein, Dvorak, Franz Liszt and Richard Wagner.

art-loving Princes Paul Anton and Nikolaus Esterhazy were wealthy enough to maintain a large band of musicians, and that they (successively) engaged a certain Josef Haydn to conduct and compose for them. The two things went together, for instrumental musical literature was in the making, the publication of music was still in its infancy and musicians seldom performed or conducted any music but what they had composed themselves. Improvisation was an important feature of solo performance and as late as 1824, Marx, the biographer of Beethoven, writes about a Moscheles [3] concert:

"As a concert-giver Moscheles gave the army of virtuosos who stand far below him, a lesson, by playing a composition of Kalkbrenner, and he played it with as much love as though it was his own composition."

The relation of the musician to his patrons and employers was ambiguous. The art-loving aristocracy of Italy, Germany and Austria wanted music and attached importance to the creative musicians who could give it to them. Louis XIV even conferred a title of nobility on Lully. And yet if we read Haydn's contract with Prince Esterhazy we find that the rise in the status of the professional musician from the despised jongleur of troubadour days had not gone far beyond the position of a servant in the princely household. The con-tract reads in part as follows:

[3] A famous piano virtuoso.

May 1st, 1761:

"He (Josef Haydn) will be regarded as a house officer. Whereas his Princely Highness (Prince Ester-hazy) graciously confides in him that he will, as it be-seems an honorable officer in a princely household, be sober; that he behave towards the musicians under him not brutally, but modestly, quietly and honestly. Above all when music is made before his high masters, that he and all those under him will appear in uniform and that not only he, Josef Haydn, will appear clean, but those under him will also appear clean, in white stockings, white shirts, with powder and queue all alike. That Josef Haydn will appear each day, morn-ing and evening in the antechamber and inquire whether there be a princely order for music. That he will wait, and after receiving the order will acquaint the other musicians and not only himself appear punc-tually at the hour ordered, but will see that the other musicians appear punctually or be dismissed."

The contract further provides for a modest salary and payment in kind, two uniforms a year, beef, salt, grain, candles and, occasionally, an extra grant of pork meat! Let us hope the grant of pork meat was particu-larly generous after Haydn composed some of the symphonies that still delight us at concerts where orchestral conductors receive fabulous fees for re-creat-ing the works of men who, after lives of unremitting toil, died poor or in very moderate circumstances. One might draw a lesson in comparative human values from the fact that his Princely Highness, the "high master" of this quaint document, is chiefly remembered for his association with the musician who waited upon him morning and evening in his antechamber.[4]

It is very interesting in studying the history of public concerts to try to trace cause and effect in the course of their development from early beginnings to what we now know; how the demands of composers and the sound conditions of larger auditoriums affected the improvement in many instruments and how the increasing opportunities for public performance stimulated the creation of hitherto undreamed of types of music. The accounts of early concert-giving also contain many diverting descriptions of by-gone habits and customs. To-day the Philadelphia Orchestra is seeking to meet the depression conditions by allowing its patrons to pay for tickets on the installment plan. But in eighteenth-century Germany and Austria, concert announcements bear witness to the fact that a certain part of the public was left free not only in the matter of

[4] The late Rodman Wanamaker of Philadelphia who owned a priceless collection of string instruments decided two years before his death to create a small orchestra of the eighteenth century type so that his instruments, instead of lying mute in cases, should fulfill their normal function and bring to life some of the music written for such chamber organizations. He sent three musicians, Dr. Thaddeus Rich, former concert-master of the Philadelphia Orchestra and, at that time, Curator of the Wanamaker instrument collection, Dr. Alexander Russell of Princeton, and the author, to Europe to search through the libraries for unpublished or rarely performed works suitable for chamber orchestra. This piece of research afforded an interesting glimpse into the mass of music composed for such a purpose in the eighteenth century. If Rodman Wanamaker had lived, the United States would have possessed a musical organization unique in the twentieth century.

when they paid but of *what* they paid. The following phrase often followed the regular price of tickets:

"The first four rows of seats are reserved for the high nobility whose entrance fee is left to their own generosity."

Evidently the concert-givers of those days had faith in the legend of "noblesse oblige." [5]

Sometimes at the earliest concerts in Vienna, tickets were only sold to men—it being understood that each man brought a woman—and as there were no reserved seats, the audience came in hours before the performance in order to get good places. In the twentieth century we are more accustomed to the drawn and harried faces of ticket holders battling with traffic in the large cities as they try—at the last moment—to reach the hall before the concert begins. And yet, when David Mannes conducts one of his free symphony concerts at the Metropolitan Museum in New York, many of his thousands of listeners bring their supper with them and also arrive hours ahead of time in order to obtain advantageous positions. A passer-by in Locust Street in Philadelphia, at the corner of Broad Street where the ven-

[5] In Paris of the 1890's, rumor had it that in "papering the house" for unknown artists the manager applied part of the financial investment involved to buying the presence of ladies in evening dress and gentlemen wearing the ribbon of the Legion of Honor. Measured by a sartorial yardstick, those worthy concert-goers, earning as much as twenty francs apiece, lent an air to the proceedings.

erable Academy of Music stands, seldom fails to find
a long line of music-lovers two or three hours before a Philadelphia Orchestra concert, waiting for ad-
mittance to the cheap unreserved seats of the top gallery. Love of music has not diminished.

In England as late as 1819, it was the custom to
provide refreshment for the audience between the first
and second part of a concert, because in that year
Spohr complains bitterly that he had to spend ten
pounds sterling on feeding his audience at each of his
London concerts. Spohr not only fed his audiences in
London; he introduced the conductor's baton there and
demanded a special desk at concerts, much against the
will of the Philharmonic directors who apparently
viewed this radical innovation with grave distrust. We
who are so much under the spell of great orchestra conductors like Toscanini and Stokowski have difficulty in
realizing that little more than a hundred years ago
Habeneck, director of the celebrated Conservatoire
concerts in Paris, still conducted the orchestra with his
bow from his place as first violinist. According to some
authorities Carl Maria von Weber was the first to use
a modern conductor's baton, introducing the custom in
Dresden in 1817. In early opera performances the conductor usually presided at a harpsichord upon which
he himself played the chords accompanying recitatives.
Before the introduction of the baton, the performance
of symphonies was either conducted with a bow by the
first violinist who alternately played and beat time, or

by a composer who—as in opera—sat before a clavier instrument. Haydn did both.[6]

In oratorio performances two and sometimes three conductors took part. One led the orchestra, another beat time for the singers while sometimes a third personage endeavored, with a roll of paper serving as baton, to keep the other two conductors together. Richard Wagner's interesting essay on orchestral conducting (*Über das Dirigieren*) clearly demonstrates the fact that conducting until the middle of the nineteenth century was a matter of beating time and holding the performance together, rather than the interpretative function of an artist playing upon a great living instrument such as we now consider it to be. Wagner's own vision of its possibilities seems to have been aroused by hearing Habeneck conduct a performance of Beethoven's Ninth Symphony in Paris at a Conservatoire concert. Wagner found that Habeneck, who had rehearsed the work for months, had penetrated to the very heart of the score and had caused his musicians to play it with vital eloquence in every detail. The list of famous conductors scarcely goes back a hundred years except for composers who directed in opera houses and conducted their own orchestral works. From these few facts and examples the layman can see that evolution has been at work in the listener's sphere of activity as

[6] Burney describing musical conditions in 1770, the year of Beethoven's birth, wrote: "There is no such thing as a music shop in the country. Musical compositions are so short-lived, such is the rage for novelty that for the few copies wanted, it is not worth while to be at the expense of engraving."

well as in the rest of our musical civilization and that a many-sided development was needed to bring about the conditions which now afford such rich opportunity for enjoyment: our great orchestras, opera houses, choral societies and chamber-music organizations.

The time, place and conditions under which public concerts took place in the past are not the only things in which enormous changes have taken place in the last two hundred years. A study of concert programs reveals in a most enlightening and sometimes amusing way the vagaries of public taste.[7] The program of the first Concert Spirituel in Paris means little to us to-day as most of the music it contained has been lost sight of. Dated March 8th, 1725, it included a suite for violin, a capriccio, a "Confitebor," and a Cantate Domino by Lalande and Corelli's *Nuit de Noël* (Concerto 8, op. 6). As the day on which the concert took place was the Sunday of Passion week, it is evident that no connection between the music of the concert and the religious feast-day was sought. It is interesting to think that Bach was in his prime at the time this concert was given (he died in 1750) and yet his name does not appear on its program. It is doubtful whether Monsieur Anne Danni-

---

[7] Theodore Thomas describes programs of Jullien, the eccentric conductor, prominent in London and Paris, who visited America in the early 1850's: "his programmes were all popular in character, and some of the special features of them were the 'Katy-did Polka,' the 'Prima Donna Waltz' and the 'Fireman's Quadrille.' As a feature of the latter an alarm of fire was regularly sounded, and a brigade of firemen appeared in the hall! This created great consternation in the audience the first time it was given. He also played overtures and movements of symphonies."

can Philidor knew anything about Bach or his music.
One hundred and three years later the first recorded concert of the famous Société des Concerts du
Conservatoire took place in Paris. Beethoven had been
dead just a year but we note one of his symphonies on
the program. International communication had greatly
increased. Paris was aware of Beethoven. The full program reads:

1. Eroica Symphony   BEETHOVEN
2. Duet from Sémiramide   ROSSINI
      Sung by Nélia and Caroline Maillard
3. Horn Solo composed and executed
      by   MEIFRED
4. Concerto for Violin   RODE
      Performed by Eugène Sauzay
5. Air   ROSSINI
      Sung by Nélia Maillard
6. Chorus from "Blanche de Provence"
                             CHERUBINI
7. Overture "Les Abencérages" CHERUBINI
8. Kyrie and Gloria from the
      "Coronation Mass"   CHERUBINI

We have, therefore, an orchestra conducted from
the first violin stand by Habeneck, two singers, a violin
soloist, a horn virtuoso and a chorus taking part in proceedings that must have lasted close on three hours of
a Sunday afternoon. Again, it would be interesting to
know how much—if anything—the participants in such

a program earned. Perhaps they shared the conviction Beethoven expressed in the famous "Heiligenstadt Testament" when he exhorted his brothers to teach their children *virtue* for "that alone can bring happiness, not money."

On May 7th, 1853, one finds in the Lüneburger Anzeige the following announcement of a concert:

"The undersigned propose to give a concert on Monday evening, the 9th inst. at 7:30, in Herr Balcke's Hall, and have the honour to invite the attendance of the music-loving public. Amongst other things, the concert-givers will perform Beethoven's Sonata for Pianoforte and Violin in C minor, op 30, and Vieuxtemps' grand Violin Concerto in E major.

"Tickets to be had, etc.
(signed) Edward Remenyi
Johannes Brahms"

This concert, taking place on Brahms's twentieth birthday, was part of his tour with Remenyi, and Florence May, in her delightful biography of Brahms, mentions the profits of a concert given by the two musicians a few days before in Winsen as amounting to something over nine (English) pounds. The entrance fee was eight-pence, and of course the profits had to be divided. These concerts cannot be regarded as typical of the period for Brahms was young and unknown and the small towns of Germany were not the most brilliant field for concert-givers, but the announcement and program just given point—even though in a humble way—to an institution that had grown up in the first half of the nineteenth century—the travelling virtuoso. In the eighteenth century musicians travelled, but they usually established themselves in some place (preferably one where there was a court) for a considerable length of time. There they would endeavor to be heard in some established series of concerts and run around "making connections" while playing in leading salons so as to create a following for their own concerts. It was a precarious life, depending largely on the bounty of the privileged classes.

The author now invites the reader to imagine himself on board a swift Atlantic liner in the year 1912. The ship will soon land in Europe. At a festive table a group of famous musicians are celebrating the last night on board. Champagne flows, amusing stories are exchanged, a care-free gayety animates the group, for each member of it is returning from a successful concert season in the United States. On the passenger list each name of this group is followed by "maid," "valet," or "secretary." The captain has singled the artists out for special privileges during the voyage. The other passengers seek acquaintance with the celebrities who are going to fulfill concert or opera engagements in London and Paris before betaking themselves to cures in Vichy or Marienbad, or to luxurious summer homes acquired with American dollars. The concert business has become a great international industry. The earnings of a successful virtuoso in a single season sometimes run into six figures. The salaries of the most successful orchestral conductors (who do *not* conduct from the place of first violinist!) rival those of bank presidents. The musical unions of the United States have brought the earnings of the musician in the orchestra above what famous composers were once glad to receive. Is all this an unmotivated mushroom growth resting on some hysterical hero-worship? Not at all. It rests squarely on the development of music itself. It rests on the skill required to re-create the music written in the last two hundred years.

Humanity has always been ready to pay highly for two things—for something very rare, and for a high degree of skill.

Some musicians of lesser talent have perhaps won a disproportionate reward because of glittering virtuosity, but in the main the musical artists who have captured the imagination of the international opera or concert public have not only been fine musicians but have possessed qualities of personality, a capacity for work and a level of intelligence that would be apt to win success in any field. The general requirements for a successful musical career have been constantly increasing. Instrumental musicians who once played their own music almost exclusively, when they began to master other men's music always used the score. Now they are called upon to accomplish almost incredible feats of memory. The usual repertory of a modern instrumental virtuoso requires a memory and a degree of technical skill undreamed of a hundred and fifty years ago. The Wagnerian and modern opera roles make terrific demands on singers. Conductors of orchestras, many of whom also conduct without a score, have become civic personages. Whereas Haydn's duties were to keep himself and his musicians clean, report in the antechamber and carry out princely orders for music, the modern conductor has, besides his huge musical task, endless executive work, and all the demands upon time and strength that devolve upon an important man in public life. Musical education has had to keep pace with all this. Yehudi Menuhin has had the education of a young prince; private tutors, sojourns in various countries to make him the polyglot that royalty, diplomats and musical virtuosos are supposed to be, and every advantage that develops a polished man of the world have been his.

One thing to be regretted in the rise of the musician in general is, that it has not sufficiently included the most important type—the *composer*. Creative musicians still battle with poverty and insecurity, probably because our estimate of their work is so uncertain and recognition often so tardy.

The layman may ask "what has all this to do with my becoming an active listener"? Some understanding of these developments, brought about by the very nature of our musical civilization, is essential if the layman is to take an active part in that life, and above all, if he wishes to preserve certain things he *needs*. Since the World War, the profession of music has suffered like everything else. Artists of established reputation have kept afloat even though their earnings are far less than they once were. But the fate of the oncoming generation of musicians is a matter of grave concern, particularly to educators. The difficulty of entering the concert field is great, but the problem of making a living, even after a successful debut, is still greater. The same is true of opera, particularly in the United States where so little operatic opportunity exists. Meanwhile the old idea that Americans, nationally speaking, are unmusical is so completely exploded that the great problem to-day is, what to do with the tidal wave of talent rising from a vast country that contains the blood heritage of every race in Europe. Unexcelled educational advantages now exist in the United States. Some unthinking writers advocate educating fewer musicians. It would be an easy way out, but let the layman imagine looking into the eyes of an ardent gifted young being who longs to be a musician and is willing to starve as well as work without limit, and say: "No, you may not be educated. There are too many musicians. You are not wanted. Go away and do something else." That young being might well respond to-day with an unanswerable question: "Do *what?*" *Where* is the field to which highly gifted musical children should be diverted to-day?

Other people argue that musical performers should be content with music as an avocation. This is sound advice for those without pronounced talent. But can the musician who is a real artist by nature be content to strive for less than perfection in re-creating the music he loves? And if he gives the years of work necessary to this striving, can we tell him, "All well and good, but you must not expect to make a living by your work!"

Is it not still more impossible to refuse the possibility of development to a pronounced *creative* talent even though we have not yet discovered the means of detecting just how great such a gift will prove to be? The problem is difficult, but there is one very clear issue: *we must not, under stress of a passing depression, commit musical race suicide.*[8] If we, in the United States, shun the responsibility to try to increase the *demand,* rather than choke off the *supply* of musicians, we shall not only miss the opportunity of a great national musical development, *including our creative contribution to musical literature,* but we may some day awake to find ourselves without the musicians we *need adequately to re-create our existing musical literature for us.* The radio and the phonograph can spread the performance of a single artist over a wide field without his presence; but he has to exist in order to broadcast and make the records.

The active listener, in these days of perplexing upheaval, will find absorbing interest in the efforts being made to keep his sphere of activity richly supplied with what he needs in order to enjoy musical literature of the past and present—living performers, fine phonograph records and high-type radio broadcasts. If the listener be civic-minded, he can himself take an active part in these efforts and thereby contribute to a musical

[8] See Appendix, Page 287.

development in the United States that is potentially one of the most important the world has ever known.

POINTS TO BE REMEMBERED

1. Opera houses and concert halls are the museums and galleries of music in which our great musical art treasure must be kept alive through adequate performance.
2. Music in the home is enormously valuable but it is not enough as a sphere of activity for the listener.
3. The phonograph is the logical "practice instrument" of the listener (see Foreword) and should be used in connection with scores in exploring musical literature.
4. The layman can play an important part in demanding the things he needs in his sphere of activity as listener, namely, adequate living performers, fine phonograph records, and high-type radio broadcasts. He will be even more important if he can become one of the invaluable minority that in every age has the interest to seek, the intuition to find, and the vision to support the creative art of his day.

SUGGESTIONS FOR CORRELATED READING

Beethoven the Creator, Romain Rolland
Beethoven, Impressions of Contemporaries, published by G. Schirmer, Inc.
Mozart, Marcia Davenport
J. S. Bach, Albert Schweitzer
Bach, A Biography, Terry
Letters of Clara Schumann and Johannes Brahms, Litzman
Letters of Robert Schumann, Storck
The Well-tempered Musician, Francis Toye
The Life of Liszt, Guy de Pourtales
Wagner as Man and Artist, Ernest Newman
My Musical Life, Rimsky-Korsakoff
My Musical Life, Walter Damrosch
Music Education in America, Archibald T. Davison
Correspondence between Richard Strauss and Hugo von Hofmannsthal, published by Alfred A. Knopf Inc.

XIII

MUSIC WE HEAR IN THE CONCERT HALL

"It is not we who revive the masterpieces. It is the masterpieces which revive us."

JULES JANIN

Once the layman has entered into his sphere of musical activity he encounters such an embarrassment of riches that he may be puzzled to know the significance of different types of music in the general scheme of things. One so often finds orchestra enthusiasts who never go near opera, chamber-music adepts who hardly ever listen to the recitals of individuals, amateur solo instrumentalists who utterly ignore singers' concerts, and music-lovers capable of enjoying all these categories who take no interest whatsoever in performances of choral music. It is one thing to wander aimlessly, guided only by chance through the richly-varied realm of music, developing personal taste in a haphazard way, and quite another for the listener, whose potential field of enjoyment is so wide, to approach this field with some knowledge of its manifold possibilities. Obviously, no layman can know in advance how he is going to react to any type of music of which he has had no past experience; therefore it will aid him in finding his way about in the world of music if he gains a general idea of the essence and significance of certain types of music that have not yet been touched upon in this book.

Chamber Music

Some years ago, the author was visiting a Boston family, well-known for its general culture and special love of music. In the course of an animated conversation about musical conditions, centering largely in the affairs of the Boston Symphony Orchestra, the hostess said: "A great deal of propaganda is being made here for a new chamber music organization. I have been asked to subscribe, but I will not do it. *I do not like chamber music.* I cannot stand string quartets. They bore me to death. Do *you* like to listen to a string quartet?" Thus challenged, the author inevitably became the champion of chamber music in the lengthy argument that ensued. Why should one like chamber music? Why listen to a few instruments when one can hear a whole orchestra? Why do musicians act as though chamber music were so lofty and virtuous that they almost imply the rest of music is sinful and unworthy? These were some of the questions asked.

One reason for liking any type of music is very simple. *If great music has been written for a certain medium, we cannot have that music in its original form without the medium.* This seems almost too obvious to put on paper and yet a long experience has taught the author how often the fact is lost sight of. It had been lost sight of by those delightful music-lovers in Boston.

Instead of asking why the listener likes or dislikes any particular kind of music we might well ask why the *great composers* have liked chamber music so much that they have created a wonderful literature for the various instrumental and vocal combinations included in this category. If we look back to the days when music had to be performed either in the Church, the theatre, or the home, we can realize the importance of chamber music as the main outlet for secular art music outside of opera. We must also remember that centuries of concerted vocal music preceded all instrumental forms. This deeply-rooted habit of concerted music is essentially a product of polyphony which, in turn, is the foundation of our particular musical civilization. If it is true that "men make systems and systems make men," it is easy to understand why centuries of concerted vocal music, first great manifestation of the polyphonic system, in turn produced men who thought and felt music in terms of collectivity. The sixteenth-century caption, "apt for voices or viols" heralds the realization, towards the close of the great vocal polyphonic era, that several instruments could perform the lines of a vocal polyphonic score. Very soon composers realized that the possibilities of instruments *exceeded* those of voices in building interesting musical edifices of tone.

The "era of patronage," as Colles rightly calls the period when musicians depended entirely on princes and nobles for a livelihood and for musical activity, greatly stimulated the type of music under discussion.

Great virtuosos have always been rare, but the composer who was creating music for a princely patron could rely on maintaining a small band of musicians sufficiently skilled to perform concerted music, and therefore he composed for such a group. By the time the concert hall brought with it a different kind of outlet, composers had consciously realized the value of certain purely *artistic* features of concerted music on a small scale as a type of composition. Purity of line, intimacy of expression and economy of means proved to be distinctive advantages of the genus. The balance of parts when each line is taken care of by an individual whose attention is concentrated on the perfection of his part, is apt to be much finer than when a pianist or organist tries to adjust all the relative values of a score on a single instrument. At the same time, the limited number of performers enables chamber musicians to achieve an ensemble without a conductor. For all these reasons composers have continued to be drawn to what we still call chamber music although, in its finest manifestations, it is now heard in the concert hall.

The superior attitude of chamber-music enthusiasts referred to in the course of the above-mentioned argument in Boston—if and when such an attitude really exists—is probably an unconscious revolt against exhibitionism and the tendency of many solo performers to consider and use music as a vehicle for self-expression or—in extreme cases—self-exploitation. Neither self-expression nor self-exploitation has a place in chamber music. Self-*effacement* is more nearly the requisite for a good chamber-music player, even though the quality and skill of each individual performer plays a great part in the general artistic result. Again, the highest kind of musicianship is necessary in chamber music. If a painter undertook to copy a portrait he would not make the nose of the subject twice as long as the original. Solo players, sometimes through ignorance but more often through carelessness, treat musical values [1] in a manner that does just as much damage to music. They are certainly much less accurate than orchestral or chamber-music players, and they often do strange things in the name of self-expression to the actual values of the music they interpret. The chamber-music player cannot permit himself any such liberties with the score. The one hope for a good ensemble is to have the values just right. Therefore the chamber-music player, obliged by the very nature of his art to keep all the musical commandments, may sometimes assume a somewhat self-righteous attitude towards others.

The layman, in addition to making the acquaintance of many great masterpieces written for string quartet, for piano and various numbers of string instruments, and for combinations that include wind instruments as well as the human voice, can greatly accelerate the possibility of following orchestral records with a score by first undertaking such activity in the field of

---

[1] By values, the author means pitch and duration of single tones, positions of chords, phrasing, time value of rests, accentuation and dynamics, in short, all the aspects of music that can be definitely conveyed by means of musical notation and textual directions.

chamber music. He should certainly not neglect this high type of musical art.

The Concerto

Many are the problems of the officers and directors of a modern symphony orchestra. The cost of such organizations is prohibitive and continues to mount. Endowments that seemed adequate a few years ago no longer suffice for increased deficits. One particular problem is whether or not to have soloists at orchestral concerts. An attractive list of soloists undoubtedly increases the seasonal subscription as well as the ticket sale for single concerts, but the type of artist that can be depended upon to act as a box-office attraction is so expensive that his ultimate financial value is questionable. If an orchestra is blessed with a primadonna conductor, the public is not only less interested in soloists but frequently resents their presence. The author remembers occasions when this question was the subject of bitter controversy in a certain city where the concerts of the local orchestra were sold out. Because of box-office conditions the financial value of the soloist had dropped to zero so far as the management was concerned, and a large part of the population had apparently lost sight of the obvious fact that it is impossible to banish soloists from orchestral concerts without the loss of a rich literature of masterpieces—the concerto literature. Again, they were not thinking *in terms of music itself*.

The concerto and chamber music have a common ancestry.

When Ludovico Viadana (in 1602–03) published motets for voices and organ called "Concerti ecclesiastici" (such works were also called Concerti da Chiesa) he was as far from the idea of exhibiting the skill of a solo virtuoso as he was from including an orchestra in his musical scheme.

As late as 1686, a Concerto da Camera by Giuseppe Torelli (who is sometimes called the father of the concerto) was written for two violins and bass. Even Bach and Handel in writing their concertos had concerted music in mind rather than what we now call a concerto, a composition for one or more soloists together with an orchestra. But a gradual development towards the present type showed itself in the "concerti grossi" of the late seventeenth and early eighteenth centuries, when a "concertino" or small group of solo instruments was often given an important part within the whole. Bach wrote concertos for one, two and three pianos [2] accompanied by string orchestra, as well as for other instruments, but he treats his solo instruments rather orchestrally. They do not display solo virtuosity in the manner that subsequently became a dominant feature of the concerto.

Haydn used the form, but Mozart was the first of the great composers to write important concertos along the lines of those we hear most frequently in orchestral

[2] In the complete collection of Bach's works there is a concerto for four claviers inscribed "after Vivaldi."

concerts to-day. The typical classical concerto (Mozart left about fifty for various instruments) has three movements. The animated first movement is in sonata-form, but with the peculiarity that there is a double exposition section. The themes are first given out by the orchestra and then by the solo instrument in conjunction with the orchestra. Sometimes the orchestral (or to use the technical term *tutti*) exposition is not quite complete, the second subject being omitted, and it does not close in the key in which an exposition section of sonata-form *should* close (dominant or relative major) but in the tonic, thus preparing the way for the entry of the solo instrument. A feature of the first movement of a typical classical concerto is the interpolated *cadenza,* a short, free fantasia which may be of the soloist's own invention, although it may also be composed by someone else or by the composer of the concerto.[3] Handel was one of the first to introduce this custom. In the second movement of his D minor organ concerto, no less than six places are marked "organo ad libitum." The rests in the orchestra parts indicate a complete pause for the other instruments during which the soloist improvises his own *cadenza.*

The tradition of the cadenza does not give the soloist unlimited freedom. He must improvise his interpolated solo *on the themes of the concerto-movement* in which the cadenza occurs. If he is a real artist he will

---

[3] Cadenzas are sometimes placed in other movements of a concerto but those near the close of the first movement are usually longer and more elaborate.

try to make his treatment of the themes interesting without going too far afield in the matter of tonality and without departing too radically from the style and period of the piece. The cadenza has an historical interest because it is all that remains of the once prevalent custom of musical improvisation in concerts.[4]

The second movement of the average classical concerto is usually slow and expressive, although the composer sometimes allots many florid and ornamental passages to the solo instrument while the orchestra sings the melodies.

The third movement, frequently written in rondo form, provides a brilliant and animated close in which the virtuosity of the soloist is brought to the fore.

As instruments improved and the virtuosity of players increased, technical skill began to play a part in instrumental music not unlike the orgy of vocal agility in early opera. Reaching a peak in the case of such virtuosos as Paganini and Liszt, technical display became a great factor in the composition of music as well as in the careers of performers. This had its good and bad sides. Much of the music for the violin was written by violinists (especially in the days when men played chiefly music "of their own invention") and the fact that the composer-player sought to display technical skill, revealed possibilities of the instrument which

---

[4] As concertos became more symphonic and players lost the habit of improvising or never developed the ability to do so, composers considered it more prudent to make their own cadenzas integral parts of the concerto, as in the Schumann A minor piano concerto and many others.

composers who were not specialists subsequently had at hand to use for purely musical ends. The same thing is true of the piano and other instruments. The net result of the orgy of technical display in the late eighteenth and throughout the nineteenth centuries, is an enormously high general level of professional proficiency on all instruments. Technical skill of a high order is now necessary for the performance of the important music that has been composed.

The *worst* side of the above-mentioned orgy was the creation of a great deal of empty music that contained little beyond technical fire-works, and this in turn furnished players with ample opportunity for sterile exhibitionism. It also had a very bad influence on the public, which, for some reason, is always prone to lavish money and applause on the mere exhibition of technical skill. The concerto was a form peculiarly adapted to the display of virtuosity. The soloist, standing out against the background of the orchestra, afforded a logical opportunity for exhibitionism and lesser composers availed themselves to the full of this possibility. Innumerable superficial compositions, in which the orchestra modestly accompanied the pyrotechnical display of the soloist, served as vehicles for nineteenth-century virtuosos. But the greatest composers saw other possibilities and created magnificent concertos in which the solo part serves chiefly as an interesting use of a different sonority medium in connection with the orchestra. Even when an orchestra instrument like the violin or cello is used, there is a distinct difference between the tonal effect of the single instrument and the respective section of the orchestra. The piano, probably because of its totally different tone quality and its polyphonic possibilities, has been particularly popular with concerto composers and a highly important literature for the combination of piano with orchestra has come into being. Beethoven wrote only one violin concerto but he composed five for piano and orchestra. Brahms wrote one for solo violin and two for piano. In the Brahms concertos we have the most complete fulfillment of the gradual development which, since Mozart, has brought the concerto nearer and nearer to a type of symphonic proportions in which the solo instrument is used as an important but integral part of the whole instead of a brilliant vehicle for virtuosity accompanied by orchestra. Let us think twice before we banish the masterpieces written in concerto form.

The Art-Song

Vocal music, that oldest branch of the art, shows perhaps more varied manifestations than any other type. Explained by text, it reaches the consciousness of the listener without difficulty although with many varying degrees of appeal. Without some idea of its significance, plain-song, for instance, soon wearies the average twentieth-century listener. Troubadour songs, sung without accompaniment (for nobody really knows if or how they were accompanied), cannot arouse in the modern listener the feeling they evoked at the time they were created. Even the florid type of operatic aria that enchanted our forefathers no longer exercises the fascination it once did, although an occasional coloratura singer with a phenomenal voice and abundant charm still uses it successfully as a display vehicle. The song, belonging equally to poetry and to music, has to satisfy our taste in both respects in order to evoke the emotional response which, however, is always easier to arouse with vocal art than with instrumental music.

According to most authorities, France was the cradle of the art-song and one of the earliest examples is a "Complainte on the Death of Charlemagne," in a manuscript in *fonds-latin* dated 1154, in the Bibliothèque Nationale in Paris. From that time on, the history of this particular type of music fluctuates between songs in which text is secondary to music and the reverse. Popular songs, epic songs, religious songs and national songs appeared in all occidental countries, revealing the strong urge for expression in this form.

Just when romanticism had brought an outburst of lyric poetry in Germany in the early nineteenth century, and the technique of writing for the piano had been so wonderfully developed by the classical masters, a genius who was destined to raise song to a new plane of artistic significance came into the musical world—Franz Schubert. Endowed with an inexhaustible melodic inventiveness, but lacking the sense of form that produces great abstract instrumental tone-structures, Schubert found his ideal medium in the art-song where the poetic text, to a certain extent at least, determines form. The art-song (Lied) of the type composed with such inspiration by Schubert and afterwards by Schumann, Brahms, Franz, Wolf, Richard Strauss and others, is a composition in which text, melodic line and accompaniment have an almost equal importance. The Germans use the word "durch-komponirt" to indicate that the composition of the song preserves this correlation throughout, without the refrains and the repetition of the same melody for different verses which are common to other types. The piano accompaniment is often descriptive or dramatic, affording powerful support to the voice and adding greatly to the interest of the composition as a whole. The melody itself is often declamatory and so full of harmonic implication that divorced from its accompaniment it would be completely ineffective. It is distinctly a part of a whole art work, not an independent tune. In one great song, *Death and the Maiden,* Schubert achieves an effect of extraordinary solemnity by having the utterance of Death, in a dialogue with the Maiden, chanted for several measures on a single reiterated tone.

The singing of these nineteenth-century Lieder requires great art on the part of the vocalist and the accompanist. The layman who wishes to enjoy to the full the possibilities of the art-song as an imaginative and musical experience would do well to prepare himself by examining scores and records listed below so as to be fully aware, in listening to the concert of some fine Lieder singer, of the subtlety and beauty of this type of music.

Choral Music

No further attempt to discuss solo instruments and their literature will be made here inasmuch as the layman who is familiar with the larger forms, that hold such an important place in the repertory of instrumental soloists, the Fugue, the Suite, the Sonata and the Concerto will have little difficulty in understanding the Variations, Toccatas, Ballades, Nocturnes, Etudes, Rhapsodies, Intermezzi, Capriccios and smaller pieces with still more descriptive titles that he will find on the programs of recitalists.

But the significance of choral music in our civilization demands discussion.

It is an ideal musical *activity* for laymen who can read a score and sing true to pitch. According to recent reliable information, over four hundred choral festivals take place in the British Isles in the course of a year. The author witnessed an extraordinary demonstration of the way in which this British aptitude for choral singing can be transferred to distant colonies, at a music festival in Regina, Province of Saskatchewan, Canada. For several days musical events of every description succeeded each other. Choral groups, amateur orchestras, brass bands, chamber music organizations and soloists (totalling thousands of entries), took part in the festival. The author, engaged in an advisory mission for the Carnegie Corporation, acted as judge in conjunction with eminent musicians imported from England for the special purpose of fulfilling this function at various Canadian festivals, and thus had a unique opportunity to study the entire development. Without a doubt, the highest musical achievement on this occasion was the *choral singing*. There was something profoundly impressive and stirring in the vitality of this art form that had taken such firm root in the vast plains and mountain lands of northwest Canada.

The innumerable *Sängerbünde* and *Singvereine* of Germany have many sturdy offshoots in the United States. Russia sends us choirs displaying a peculiar gift for choral singing that in precision and in flexibility has an almost instrumental quality. Vienna has her *Sängerknaben* to demonstrate how alive is the art of choral singing among the very young in the Austrian capital. If any patriotic American is afflicted with an inferiority complex regarding the musical possibilities of the youth of his own country, let him listen to one of the Intercollegiate Glee Club Contests. Throughout the United States, groups of citizens ranging from high school age to that at which it becomes undesirable to count the years, include choral singing among their major interests.

This vital and widespread musical activity rests on a twofold foundation: love of group singing peculiar to our polyphonic civilization, and a rich and diversified literature, the creation of which extends as far back as the beginning of the notation that made it possible. All important European composers from the dawn of polyphony to the seventeenth century contributed to this literature, and most great creative musicians of later periods have added to it. What Gregorian music was to the early Christian Church, choral singing has been to western religion, both Catholic and Protestant, since the discovery of polyphony. No loftier musical compositions exist than Bach's B minor Mass and his Passions according to St. Matthew and St. John. In writing for chorus Bach displays an unmatched degree of inspiration. In no other form is the *spiritual* power of music more evident.

Choral music found its way not only into the Church and into opera, but into symphonic literature. Beethoven, for example, introduced it into the last movement of his Ninth Symphony. Mendelssohn employs a chorus in his *Lobgesang* (Hymn of Praise) which is listed as a symphony-cantata. Gustav Mahler has used a chorus most effectively in his Second and Eighth Symphonies. Choral literature in oratorio form is rich in masterpieces. Ultra-modern composers have made notable choral contributions, such as Schönberg's *Gurrelieder,* Honegger's *Roi David,* Prokofieff's *Sept, ils sont sept* and Paul Nordoff's *Secular Mass.* No development of active listening could be complete without some experience in this important branch of musical art.

In considering musical literature in its many aspects, one general fact stands out—the extraordinary *living* quality of the art. A portrait shows us the way someone has looked. If the painter is great, it may even reveal what the person *was,* for portraiture can capture human traits. But the figure on canvas is inanimate. Ancient buildings can help us reconstruct—imaginatively—the life of other people in other ages, but the life itself is not there. Music alone can give us in *living* vibrant tones, an art work to all intents and purposes fresh from the brain of its creator.

Music has been called a universal language. It might with far greater truth be called the most living link between the ages.

POINTS TO BE REMEMBERED

1. The value of exploring musical literature with some plan and purpose.
2. The realization that music composed for any medium cannot be heard without that medium; therefore we should think primarily in terms of music itself.
3. The advisability of becoming acquainted with important works of various kinds so as to have some idea of different types of music. The broader the listener's culture, the wider his field of enjoyment.

SUGGESTIONS FOR CORRELATED READING

The Story of Chamber Music, Nicholas Kilburn
Chamber Music, a Treatise for Students, T. F. Dunhill
The Development of Chamber Music, R. H. Walthew
Brahms Chamber Music, Henry Drinker
Grove's Dictionary of Music and Musicians, Article on Chamber Music
Grove's Dictionary of Music and Musicians, Article on the Concerto
Grove's Dictionary of Music and Musicians, Article on the Song

Schubert, H. F. Frost
Schubert the Man, Oscar Bie
Grove's Dictionary of Music and Musicians, Article on Oratorio
Oxford History of Music, Vol. IV, First Five Chapters

RECORDS

Victor Album M–34	9241–9245 A	Quartet in D Minor (*Death and the Maiden*)—Schubert Played by Budapest String Quartet
Victor Album M–10	6571–6575	Quintet in F Minor—Brahms Played by Harold Bauer and the Flonzaley Quartet
H. M. V.	1940–1944	Concerto #3 in C minor —Beethoven Played by Artur Schnabel and the London Philharmonic
Victor Album 155		Concerto #5 (*Emperor*) —Beethoven Played by Artur Schnabel and the London Philharmonic
Victor Album 156		Concerto #4 in G major —Beethoven Played by Artur Schnabel and the London Philharmonic
Victor Album M–80	7237–7241	Concerto in Bb major—Brahms Played by Arthur Rubinstein and the London Symphony Orchestra

Victor Album M–209	7783–7787	Concerto in D minor—Brahms Played by Wilhelm Bachaus and the B. B. C. Symphony Orchestra
Victor Album M–36	8098–8102 A	Concerto in D major—Brahms Played by Fritz Kreisler and the Berlin State Opera Orchestra
Victor Album M–99	8208–8211	A Minor Double Concerto—Brahms Played by Jacques Thibaud & Pablo Casals and Barcelona Orch.
Odeon	5144	*Tod und das Mädchen*—Schubert Sung by Karin Branzell
Polydor	67051 A	*Erlkoenig*—Schubert Sung by Heinrich Schlusnus
Columbia	50182 D	*Feldeinsamkeit*—Brahms Sung by Alexander Kipnis
H. M. V.	E 546	*Die Mainacht*—Brahms Sung by Maria Olszewska
Odeon	5136	*Von Ewiger Liebe*—Brahms Sung by Lotte Lehmann *Aug Fluegeln des Gesanges*—Mendelssohn Sung by Lotte Lehmann
Parlophone	RO 20096	*Traum durch die Dämmerung*—Strauss *Ständchen*—Strauss Sung by Lotte Lehmann
Victor	11285–11286–11287–11289 11291–11292–11293–11295 11296	*St. Matthew Passion*—Bach, sung by St. Bartholomew Choir

Victor 7275 A	*Aus Liebe Will Mein Heiland Sterben* from *St. Matthew Passion*—Bach, sung by Elisabeth Schumann
H. M. V. EJ 195	*Kommt Ihr Tochter* from *St. Matthew Passion*—Bach, sung by Philharmonic Choir of Berlin
Parlophone 9414 1	*Nun beut die Flur das frische Gruen* from *The Creation*—Haydn, sung by Lotte Leonard
H. M. V. EG 1065	*Vollendet Ist Dies Gross Werk* and *Stimmt an Die Saiten* from *The Creation*—Haydn, sung by the Singakademie Chor
Columbia Albums 101, 102 (Foreign Recording)	*Messiah*—Handel
Victor 6555	*O Rest in the Lord* from *Elijah* — Mendelssohn, sung by M. Matzenauer
Victor 9104	*Hear Ye Israel* from *Elijah* — Mendelssohn, sung by Lucy Marsh
Victor 35829	*He, Watching over Israel* from *Elijah*—Mendelssohn, sung by Mormon Tabernacle Choir
Victor 35873	*Behold God the Lord* from *Elijah*—Mendelssohn, by Mormon Tabernacle Choir and Organ

XIV

MODERN TENDENCIES

*"In art, each step that is gained
opens a fresh vista; but often, till the
new position is mastered, what lies beyond is completely hidden and undreamed of. In fact, each step is not
so much a conquest of new land as the
creation of a new mental or emotional
position in the human organism."*

PARRY

A SOUND and intelligent approach to modern developments in this disquieting twentieth century is perhaps
more difficult in music than in most things. When
Schönberg's ultra-modern *Variations for Orchestra* were
performed by the Philadelphia Orchestra in New
York, the author sat between two conservative music-
lovers. As the piece progressed a glance at the author's
left-hand neighbor revealed a facial expression of such
astonished anguish that curiosity prompted a turn to
the right, and there the author beheld not only on the
face of the nearest neighbor but on those of rows and
rows of people as far as the eye could reach, outward
and visible signs of acute distress, utter bewilderment
or unmistakable indignation. This geometry [1] in music

[1] In connection with the geometric character of some ultra-
modern music, as well as modern painting, it is interesting to re-
call what Plato said of the "beauty of shapes."

"By beauty of shapes I do not mean, as most people would

was obviously giving no pleasure to the most sophisticated audience in the most modern of cities.

This experience reminded the author of another occasion, the première of Stravinsky's *Sacre du Printemps* in 1913 in Paris, where similar feelings found audible expression in true Gallic fashion, and the bravos of an adventurous minority were almost drowned by hisses and uncomplimentary epithets from the rest of the audience. The remark most frequently heard while leaving the hall was: "Mais, ce n'est pas de la musique, ça, voyons. . . ." This particular phrase is the most significant adverse criticism to be found in all that is said and written about modern compositions: "*That* is not *music.*" It proves so clearly that the speaker or writer does not admit of the possibility of any music outside of the kind he has accepted. It is like the religion which claims that all those of a different faith are damned.

It is for this reason that The Listener's Music Book begins with a picture of totally different musical civilizations. This seems especially important in view of the fact that we are living in one of those transition ages

suppose, the beauty of living figures or of pictures, but, to make my point clear, I mean straight lines and circles, and shapes, plane or solid, made from them by lathe, ruler and square. These are not, like other things, beautiful relatively, but always, and absolutely."   PLATO: Philibus 51 C

Schönberg and some other ultra-modern composers seem to be inspired by a similar ideal in music for they work with groups of tones that form distinct patterns of sound. This is not new in itself. Bach did the same thing in a different way but the relations of the single tones to each other and to the whole in ultramodern music are unfamiliar and therefore seem to lend novelty to the device.

in which profound changes take place. They are not comfortable, these transition ages, and the author has sympathy with those who take refuge in the peaceful enjoyment of the established order of the past and refuse to be disturbed by the artistic turmoil of the present. But for those who wish to participate fully in the musical life of their own day, there is no better way of approaching it than through the study of musical evolution.

If, after reading a harmony textbook of the nineteenth century and observing the strict prohibition of "consecutive fifths" in composing music, we realize that in the days of early organum (tenth century A. D.) the only intervals *permitted* and *used were* "consecutive fifths" (or consecutive fourths) we could almost agree with Sir Richard Burton when he says in Book Five of the "Kasidah":

> "There is no good
> There is no bad
> These be the whims of mortal will.
> What works me weal, that call I good,
> What harms and hurts, I hold as ill.
> They change with place
> They shift with race
> And in the veriest span of time
> Each vice has worn a Virtue's crown
> All good was banned as sin or crime."

The layman has an advantage over the conservative, trained musician in approaching ultra-modern musical developments with equanimity. He does not have to rid himself of strong pre-conceived ideas. The type of trained musician to whom the perfect authentic cadence [2] means an immutable law of nature, is, of course, entirely logical in turning away from music that is not based on this law. That settles his personal problem. One can choose to live inland and ignore the ocean. But that does not do away with the ocean.

Schönberg, in his "Harmonielehre" says: "This book I have learned from my pupils." The author can certainly echo that sentiment for it is only from innumerable layman pupils that certain truths contained in this book have been learned.

In the average ear-training course, for example, the most untutored ear is supposed to "expect" the seventh tone of the scale "to lead into" the tone above—the tonic. The reader is already acquainted with the fact that music existed for thousands of years, and exists today, in many different musical systems in which this "expected" progression does *not* take place. And it is very easy to prove that the really untutored ear does *not* "expect" it. Another feature of even the best ear-training classes is the conventional belief that the untutored ear, by some unexplained miracle, will recognize without trouble the tones composing the common chord, the major triad, called the "chord of nature" because it is made up of the lowest (and strongest) partials of the

[2] The harmonic progression from dominant to tonic with the seventh (leading) tone of the scale in the upper voice proceeding to the tonic tone above.

harmonic series of a single tone. The author, even though somewhat mystified by the idea that a layman who did not hear the difference between C and F#, should be able to perceive the harmonics of a single-tone, trustingly assumed ear-training experts to be right until innumerable experiments with laymen proved conclusively that unless they had had some initiation into *our harmonic system,* or extensive contact with music employing that system, they did *not* hear the 1—3—5—8 degrees of the diatonic major scale (the tones of the "chord of nature") any more easily than they did the other scale degrees. Let us therefore establish as a basis for a sane and simple consideration of modern music the indisputable fact that our accepted musical civilization is not the only one or the only kind in the world. It is a man-made, or let us say *genius*-made system in which the rules are all devised *a posteriori,* crystallizing the discoveries and the organization of sound used by creative musicians. This system has been in a constant state of flux owing to new departures of creative geniuses in every period into which the history of the art can be divided. There is no good reason for believing that any living art will cease to be in a state of flux at any time. There may be longer and shorter periods of conformity; there will be periods following radical innovations that need more time for adjustment; but no generation of creative geniuses can be forced to remain within established traditions, particularly if these traditions, like a gold mine, are worked out to the point of exhaustion.

It is the belief of the author, and of many musicians, that such a point of exhaustion had been reached in the first decade of the twentieth century. Innumerable well-made musical compositions passed through our concert halls and opera houses on their way to the limbo of forgotten art. One veteran orchestra player, after a rehearsal of a new work entitled *Festivals* said: "I like the original better." A bystander asked what he meant by "the original" and he answered "Why, Debussy's *Fêtes,* of course." This remark might have been applied to hundreds of pieces in which the ghosts of Wagner, Brahms, Richard Strauss, or Debussy flitted by, while existing rules were piously observed.[3]

[3] Debussy puts a scathing criticism of such music into the mouth of Monsieur Croche (Mr. Eighth-note) with whom he held imaginary discussions during his activity as music critic in Paris. Saint-Saëns appears as the immediate victim in this attack on academic composition.

"Monsieur Croche, an old friend of mine, when speaking of M. Saint-Saëns, would gravely remove his hat and say in a faint, wheezy voice: 'Saint-Saëns knows more about music than any other man in the whole world.' Then, lighting a horrible little cigar, as black as a crow, he would continue: 'His profound knowledge of music, has, moreover, prevented him from ever subjecting it to his own personal desires. . . . Nevertheless, we owe him our appreciation of Liszt's tumultuous genius; and he professed his worship of old Bach at a time when such an act of faith was also an act of courage. Let us then make no mistake. Saint-Saëns must be defined as the musician of tradition. He has accepted its aridity and enforced submission. He never allowed himself to go further than those whom he had chosen for his masters. This is marvellously shown in the "Variations" for two pianos which he wrote on a theme of Beethoven's. That master's style is so faithfully copied that one can only think of Beethoven. . . . I know of no more perfect example of disinterested respect! This devotion to form suggested symphonies which are models of logical development; and one asks oneself how he could ever have strayed so far as to find pleasure in *opera,* and pass from Louis Gallet to Vic-

When Stravinsky's *Sacre du Printemps* was performed in 1913 in Paris, the tocsin was sounded. In those pages no Wagner, Brahms, Debussy or anybody else could be detected. Something had happened.

The World War followed, with a crashing of barriers in every direction, and an orgy of experimentation in music began. Many youthful composers of slight talent and great arrogance took the attitude that the world had begun the day they were born. They scorned the masters of the past, took no trouble to acquire a technique of composition and improvised incoherent music that did little but antagonize the world in general. Groups formed in various countries, took themselves very seriously and were voluble in explaining their "style of 1916" and their "style of 19– something else" to a waiting world. Bewildered critics either tried dutifully to find some sense in the confusion or laid about them angrily with pens dipped in vitriol. Without the influence of the World War and all the subsequent upheavals in human life and thought, this whole process of musical change might have taken a much more normal course, extending over a longer period. All we can do now, however, is to try to understand things as they are.

Let us therefore examine, as far as possible, what has really happened in musical evolution to bring about

torien Sardou, thus propagating the odious heresy that one must *compose theatrical works,* as if this could ever be reconciled with the *composition of music. . ; .' "*

the existence of a twentieth-century music as distinctive as that of any definable period in the past. As a practical basis for such an examination let us discuss in turn the way modernists are employing the fundamentals of musical art: melody, harmony, rhythm, and form.

The *melodic* content of twentieth-century music sometimes fails to reach the listener for any one of three reasons or for all of them:

It is often fragmentary and deliberately avoids the appeal to sentiment which romanticism lead us to expect of melody—

It often has no *harmonic implication* or, at least, none that is familiar to ears attuned to eighteen- and nineteenth-century music—

It is often so surrounded by dissonant counterpoint or unaccustomed harmonies that it is not readily discerned.

If we attempt to discover reasons for these things we shall find that the fragmentary character of many melodies in modern songs and in opera is a result of the effort to obtain a complete unity between text and music, rather than to achieve a long and flowing melodic line. The composers of nineteenth-century art-songs had already achieved a close unity between text and music in this sense and Wagner's declamatory style and free use of accompanied recitative is the direct ancestor of more recent developments, whereas the kind of text employed in connection with twentieth-century music often helps to intensify the change from a more romantic type of melody.

In instrumental music the fragmentary type of melodic ideas, often used by Richard Strauss and Debussy, is the forerunner of more recent developments. In Strauss's fin-de-siècle music, however, these fragments are held together by skilfully wrought passages in which the modulations and contrapuntal writing, rich in imitation and varied use of thematic material, create a feeling of continuity: in Debussy's impressionistic music the fragments are joined by passages in which sheer sonority effects charm the senses and create atmosphere.[4] But the fragmentary melodic ideas of twentieth-century music often appear and end with an abruptness that seems almost brutal, and they are apt to be linked—as in certain parts of the *Sacre du Printemps* —by nothing more than persistent rhythmic patterns or geometric tonal designs. Such music is not unlike a certain type of modern thought, stripped bare of illusion and mysticism and yet alive with undeniable power as it strives for clarity in a baffling universe. The melodic lines of ultra-modern music stand out like a

[4] Craven, in his "Men of Art," writes that impressionistic painters practice "the use of atmosphere as a circumambient medium to hold fragments together as fog seems to give coherence to unrelated things." The examination of many of Debussy's compositions, and of other works of the impressionistic school, reveals the same tendency. Passages, so contrived that their sonority effects produce a kind of tonal "mistiness," form the connecting link between themes or fragments of melody that appear from nowhere and vanish again with the elusive quality of an unreal realm of the imagination.

jagged, irregular silhouette against a strong rhythmic background.

The deliberate avoidance of appeal to sentiment is something in which music most obviously reflects the spirit of the times. The World War jostled us rudely out of the beautification of human life and feeling. It could not destroy deep, elemental things like human passion, but the lover no longer bends the knee and woos his lady in courtly language. Perhaps the lover, with divorce statistics daily before his eyes in the newspaper, does not even use the word "eternal" as frequently as his grandfather did. The World War forced several weary generations to contemplate ugly realities. Beauty and sentiment seemed far away. Art and literature were saturated with satire—an escape for wounded sensibilities. Bitterness tinged the music of such scores as *Wozzeck* of Alban Berg and the *Glückliche Hand* of Schönberg. Bitterness was the keynote of both realism and symbolism in many of the subjects chosen for operas and ballets. Such music does not lend itself to relaxation in pleasant social hours.

Wagner contemptuously referred to Haydn's music as "Unterhaltüngsmüsik" (music for diversion) and claimed that music belonged with the deeper things of life. Certainly the music written between 1912 and 1935 by what one may call the twentieth-century (ultramodern) composers, reflects the age in which it was created.

Let us take the *Sacre du Printemps* as an outstanding example. It brings to our consciousness the grim.

relentless side of nature. The ballet for which Stravinsky's music was written depicts the stern struggle of the frozen earth in pagan Russia to achieve renewed fertility. Man seems like a puppet in the grip of these primeval forces; the dancers portray the agonized effort of the human race to cope with them. The music expresses foreboding, fear, and ruthlessness. The culmination of these Rites of Spring is the sacrifice of a living being, that supreme act of propitiation of unknown forces that has found its way into so many religions.

This sophisticated music expresses primeval things much more powerfully than primitive music ever could, because of the musical resources in the hands of a masterly genius like Stravinsky. By no stretch of the imagination could a work like this take a place in "music in the home," except through the medium of the phonograph or radio. It is an experience for the listener like a visit to the Grand Canyon, not to be indulged in too frequently but powerfully stirring to the imagination as it reminds one of things that lie beyond the comfortable, smoothed-out routine of ordinary life.

The second point in our general consideration of the characteristics of twentieth-century melody—lack of harmonic implication—is enormously important. Musicians were perhaps not clearly aware how completely melody and harmony were bound together in the music of the eighteenth and nineteenth centuries. When the tones forming a melody are so disposed that they suggest *no* harmonic progressions, or if the harmonies that actually accompany them are in themselves strange and unfamiliar, the melody scarcely seems like melody.

Not only the unfamiliar harmonic idiom but dissonant counterpoint is significant in connection with melody because typical twentieth-century music is so often written in contrapuntal style, the various voices pursuing their independent course without any apparent regard for the conceptions of consonance and dissonance prevalent at the close of the nineteenth century. The music of Richard Strauss already abounds in dissonant counterpoint, foreshadowing twentieth-century developments, but every once in a while he indulges in passages, mellifluous and almost trite, in which progressions of the tonic, dominant and subdominant chords soothe aching nerves as though a storm-tossed air-ship were gliding smoothly to earth. The listener is back on familiar ground. The ultra-modernist affords no such relief. He is very apt to conclude an entire work with an apparently unresolvable discord instead of one of the orthodox cadences.

In considering the element of *harmony* itself as a major issue in the general picture of twentieth-century music, let us bear in mind two points, *the laws of sound vibration and the fact that all chords, if they are to have relation to each other, must be built on degrees of a recognized scale that determines the relationship.*[5]

[5] The following chart, taken from Marion Bauer's "Twentieth Century Music" cleverly divides the first twenty-one partials of a single tone (C) into sections that demonstrate how both scales and

The layman who is familiar with the laws of sound vibration that produce the harmonic series of a single musical tone (see page 44) can readily understand the following quotation from Henry Cowell's "New Musical Resources":

"Considered as a matter of musical practice, if we combine overtone relationships into chords, it is found that the ear has accepted most readily such combinations as are made by the lower tones of the series. Combinations so accepted are known as simple or consonant chords. As tones higher in the series are incorporated into chords, the effect increases in complexity, and the ear accepts less and less readily, until a point is reached where the ear fails to rest satisfied with the resultant chord, and what is known as dissonance begins. If in a given dissonant chord the shifting of the tone causing dissonance to a step next lower, or by certain other

the progressive development of harmony in Western Music follow the harmonic series of the single tone.

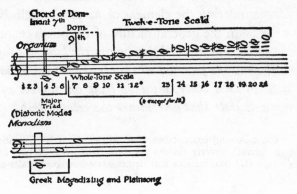

methods, restores the chord to what seems consonant harmony, the dissonance is said to be *resolved*. Dissonant tones, then, are those for which the ear, in a certain state of musical development, demands resolution. What has been called discord results either when still higher overtone relationships are formed into chords, or when the tones of a dissonant chord are so spaced that the possibility of resolution is not suggested to the ear.

"It is a notable fact that certain combinations accepted as satisfactory by one listener are found to be unsatisfactory to another, and this acceptance or rejection of a given chord depends very largely upon the familiarity of the ear with the chord in question—that is to say, upon the musical experience of the listener. The points in the series, therefore, where consonant chords leave off and dissonance begins, and where dissonance leaves off and discord begins, are not rigidly fixed, as was assumed by most theorists, but depend upon the ear of the particular listener, who is in turn influenced by the musical age in which he lives. It is this fact, proved by the history of musical progress, in conjunction with the fact that, acoustically speaking, there is no point at which any other than an arbitrary difference between them can be shown, which establishes the relativity of consonance, dissonance, and discord."

In considering building chords on the degrees of a scale that determines their relation to each other, we arrive at two distinctive features of twentieth-century musical composition:

Atonality

and

Polytonality

Atonality, as its name implies, refuses to recognize the scale as a scale in the sense of tonality. C is C and G is G, but the relation of tonic to dominant no longer exists. Every tone of the twelve semi-tone division of the octave is an independent entity. The pleasant "family life" of tonality with its ordered relation between tones and chords is thrown overboard. Consequently chords can be built in perfect freedom. All traditional restrictions disappear.

In polytonality the relation between scale tones and their respective chords is retained, thus preserving tonality as a concept, but the composer refuses to be confined to a *single* tonality. He freely uses two or more simultaneously. A simple illustration can be obtained by playing the melody of the *Blue Danube Waltz* in C major and the accompaniment in B major. Yasser's contention that in atonality as well as in polytonality, composers are really—although unconsciously—building their music on a new scale (which he defines in his "A Theory of Evolving Tonality") has a precedent in history; for during the transition from mediaeval modes to the exclusive use of our major and minor scales, composers increasingly—and also unconsciously—em-

ployed the regular progressions of these scales that subsequently became the acknowledged basis of so much
great music in the eighteenth and nineteenth centuries.

In connection with the element of *rhythm* in ultra-
modern music we should again consider several salient
points: its dominant role in ultra-modern music, the
freedom with which it is used, and the adroit manipula-
tion of polyrhythms (several different rhythms occurring simultaneously). The layman who knows that
music prior to the twelfth century A. D. was measured
only by the rhythm of verbal text, and who has gained
some conception of the subsequent developments that
gave us our ordered mathematical measurement of
music, will be able to understand modern developments
better than many a trained musician of the old school.

Rhythm of some kind, if only the free speech-
rhythm of prose text, has always existed in music. It
exists even in the single musical tone which can only
become a tone through a certain definite number of
regular periodic vibrations. The *duration* of the single
tone, the grouping of several successive tones and the
accentuation which defines the group, are the very life-
pulse of music, and yet at no point in the evolution of
the art has rhythm played such a dominant role as in
twentieth-century music. Briefly, while rhythm has always been an important *part* of music, twentieth-century scores often contain passages in which rhythm is
the *only* interesting element, and all else is subordinated
to it. In this respect twentieth-century music is akin to
primitive music.

As an example, in the Dance of the Adolescents, the second division of Part I of the *Sacre du Printemps,* the same chords are repeated in a monotonous rhythmic pattern in the strings for eighteen bars, interrupted only by four bars of a different figure. During these measures the rest of the orchestra contributes only occasional chords and motifs that sound like ejaculations. The music is entirely dominated by the persistent rhythm, varied only by displaced accents.[6]

When rhythm in general is thus given a dominant role, it has to be made interesting through *variety.* Continuous duple and triple time, even with occasional syncopation and a multitude of subdivisions, is not enough. If we study the score of the *Sacre du Printemps* we find in the division entitled *Cercles Mystérieux des Adolescentes* seven successive bars in which the time is indicated as follows:

Is this just a mannerism, or a devilish contrivance to worry orchestral conductors? The "strong beat of the bar," that stress on the first beat in each measure, which makes the line dividing the bars from each other on paper audible to the listener, is something the player observes subconsciously. If Stravinsky tried to gain the effect he wanted in these seven bars by dividing them into seven regular measures of duple or triple time and

[6] By displaced accents, the author means stress moved from the first beat in the bar which is the "naturally strong beat" to other points in the measure.

then placing accents (>) on the beats he wanted stressed, the result would not be satisfactory because the player would give *definite, obvious* accents instead of the more subtle *pulse* of the "strong beat" stress. The way Stravinsky has divided these bars gives just the subtle variety he wants in the natural pulse of the music. This example of what twentieth-century composers are doing with rhythm could be multiplied ad infinitum. To sum up, ultra-modern composers are seeking to combine the advantages of unmeasured music and measured music. The ingenuity that has evolved through the long development of measured music is being applied with consummate skill to the irregular and unexpected pulse of apparently *un*-measured music while at other times the strongest kind of measurement is used with startling effectiveness.

In connection with *form,* the ultra-modern composer is not nearly so ready to abandon acknowledged types as was Debussy, who claimed that "every musician should create the forms necessary to the expression of his genius. He should not employ standard forms, however admirable may have been the masters who established them in other days, with different motives and without anticipating that they would become rigidly stereotyped." On the contrary, when the twentieth-century composer is not writing operas, ballets, songs or straight program music he usually pours new wine into the old bottles of traditional forms. The nearest approach to something new in form was essayed by Anton von Webern, a pupil of Schönberg.

Apparently inspired by a desire to escape from "the twin principles" of musical form—contrast and repetition—as well as from the necessity of erecting a tonal structure without these inevitable elements, he composed little wisps of music, the longest of which—if I remember correctly after a single hearing—boasted fifteen or twenty measures. Obviously there was nothing to do but let his musical ideas die a natural death at the end of their few measures. So far as the author knows, no one has followed in his footsteps.

An "opera" by Milhaud entitled *Les Malheurs d'Orphée* which was produced in concert form in New York on January 31st, 1927, was divided into three acts, each of which lasted fifteen minutes.[7]

[7] The following description of Milhaud's opera appeared in the author's review of the work in the *New York Evening Post* of January 31st, 1927:

"It employs the overworked legend of Orpheus and Eurydice transposed to Camargues, France. Orpheus is 're-imagined' in the person of a village apothecary-veterinarian.

"The listener struggles with the question why the adventures of the said apothecary-veterinary could not be used as a theme for an opera without any reference to Orpheus, who seems to be, even in his most mythical aspects, about as remote from Saturday's proceedings as possible.

"The apparatus of opera is reduced to dimensions eminently suitable to the harassed conditions of modern life. The listener is only required to concentrate for fifteen minutes—Act I—on Orpheus in the person of the apothecary-veterinarian of Camargues, the picture of the village street, his fellow villagers, the blacksmith, basket-weaver and wheelwright, his sudden love for a Bohemian, 'Eurydice,' passing through the village on a pilgrimage, her return of his passion, and those aspects of her character which shock the community to the extent of bringing about the banishment of the amorous pair.

"Another fifteen minutes—Act II—disposes of their sojourn in the refuge of a forest, the affection and devotion of animals (represented by four devoted singers who, I should say, stand in need

This tendency towards brevity was perhaps the extreme point of a reaction against the enormous proportions of orchestral works by Mahler, Bruckner and others at the close of the nineteenth century, a similar development to which, in opera, is represented by Wagner's Nibelungen Trilogy. Giganticism in concert music had reached a climax in Mahler's Eighth Symphony, which employed a huge orchestra, mixed choruses and soloists, totalling a thousand performers, and lasted over two hours.

In this general discussion of modern tendencies we shall make no further attempt to discuss individual composers, their works or their style. The examples and illustrations given above and the tendencies here discussed will not be found in all the music written since 1900, but only in that part of it which unmistakably differs from music of the past and is distinctive enough in its essence to be called twentieth-century music. History teaches us that in every transition period within

of a robust sense of humor), Eurydice's illness and death, her funeral cortege composed of the said devoted and dolorously lamenting animals and her previous recommendation of her lover to their care.

"A third very *mauvais quart d'heure*—Act III—accomplishes Mr. Milhaud's and Mr. Lunel's idea of the grief-stricken Orpheus's return to his village, the accusations made by the peripatetic sisters of Eurydice that he has murdered her, the prompt offer of one of the accusing sisters to replace her, his rejection of this unseemly proposal and the prompt decision of these singular relatives to murder him as a punishment for his fidelity to the memory of the already defunct member of the family, accomplished in the orchestral score by means of an instrument which sounds like a spanking machine. In death, Orpheus, of course, meets Eurydice.

"The music combined extreme poverty of invention with equally extreme sophistication."

which vital musical changes occur, there are corresponding instrumental developments. The tendency towards the use of intervals smaller than the semitone will require changes in all keyboard instruments. Already quarter-tone instruments have been constructed in America (by Hans Barth) and in Europe. The electric instruments which are being developed by Theremin and Hammond in America as well as by Martenot and others in Europe, seem destined to fill the needs of modern composers, not only in the matter of smaller intervals but also in the control of tone quality which is becoming more and more possible through scientific regulation of overtone "mixtures." Impossible as it is to

"Look into the seeds of time
And say which grains will grow and which will not"

it would seem that the modern tendencies of the early twentieth century, worked out by a genius greater than any that has yet appeared, may, with the aid of a perfected family of electric instruments, produce a music of strange and other-worldly beauty. Perhaps this music will be less of a momentary pleasure to the senses and more of an experience that stretches the imagination and widens the scope of life.

The layman may well be confused by the radical differences of opinion on modern music he will encounter, not only in the writing of professional critics, but among musicians who have every right to his respect and confidence. Throughout the ages mistakes, apparently inevitable and usually sincere, have been made in evaluating modern art. We have only to remember Ruskin's criticism of Whistler's "Nocturne" [8] to realize that music is not the only field in which such absurdities can occur.

From the time Artusi of Bologna wrote his famous comments on "The Imperfections of Modern Music" in a righteous effort to save the art from the menace of those two dangerous radicals, Monteverdi and Gesualdo, to the present day, there has always been someone to immortalize the standpoint of the indignant reactionary and remind us of the Aesop Fable of the Mountebank and the Countryman: "It is easier to convince a man against his senses than against his will."

Let the layman who finds the music of *Tannhäuser,* perhaps, a trifle old-fashioned, remember what Chorley wrote of it in 1840:

"Throughout the opera, beyond a whimsical distribution of instruments, such as a group of flutes above

[8] Ruskin wrote: "For Mr. Whistler's own sake, no less than for the protection of the purchaser, Sir Coutts Lindsay ought not to have admitted works into the gallery in which the ill-educated conceit of the artist so nearly approached the aspect of willful imposture. I have seen, and heard, much of cockney impudence before now; but never expected to hear a coxcomb ask two hundred guineas for flinging a pot of paint in the public's face."
The "Nocturne—Blue and Gold—Old Battersea Bridge" which Ruskin thought not worth two hundred guineas was purchased in 1905, two years after Whistler's death, for two thousand guineas for the British National Gallery in London. Whistler sued Ruskin in 1878, but was only awarded one farthing damages.

the tenor voice or some lean stringed sound to harass, not support, the bass, I recollect nothing either effective or agreeable, but grim noise or shrill noise and abundance of what a wit with so happy a disrespect designated 'broken crockery' effects—things easy enough to be produced by those whose audacity is equal to their eccentricity."

And lest we forget how unacceptable Brahms once was to some people, let us read the exasperated outburst of a superior being named Hirsch who wrote musical criticisms for the *Wiener Zeitung:*

"We are always seized with a kind of oppression when the new John in the wilderness, Herr Johannes Brahms, announces himself. This prophet, proclaimed by Schumann in his darkening hours, who for the rest has his energetic admirers in Vienna—we mention this in our position from pure love of truth—makes us quite disconsolate with his impalpable, dizzy tone vexations that have neither body nor soul and can only be products of the most desperate effort. Such manifest, glaring artificiality is quite peculiar to this gentleman. How many drops of perspiration may adhere to these note-heads?"

Perhaps this explains the joke that went around Boston at the time Symphony Hall was built when some wag advised the Orchestra authorities to place over the exits: "This way out in case of Brahms." [9]

Adolf Weismann has said: "Conservatism and striving forward are the conflicting powers within art. But this conflict is fruitful. The progress of music could not do without the one or the other." Such a belief enables us to contemplate with greater equanimity,

---

[9] The music of Richard Strauss inspired the following poetical effusion in the London Spectator:

ODE TO DISCORD
(Inspired by a Strauss Symphony)

Hence loathed Melody, whose name recalls
The mellow fluting of the nightingale
  In some sequestered vale,
  The murmur of the stream
  Heard in a dream,
Or drowsy plash of distant waterfalls!
But thou, divine Cacophony, assume
The rightful overlordship in her room,
And with Percussion's stimulating aid
Expel the heavenly but no longer youthful maid!
Bestir ye, minions of the goddess new,
  And pay her homage due.
First let the gong's reverberating clang
  With clash of shivering metal
Inaugurate the reign of Sturm and Drang!
  Let drums (bass, side, and kettle)
Add to the general welter, and conspire
To set our senses furiously on fire.
Noise, yet more noise, I say. Ye trumpets, blare
In unrelated keys and rend the affrighted air,
Nor let the shrieking piccolo refrain
To pierce the midmost marrow of the brain.
Bleat, cornets, bleat, and let the loud bassoon
Bay like a bloodhound at an azure moon!
  Last, with stentorian roar,
To consummate our musical Majuba,
  Let the profound bass tuba
Emit one long and Brobdingnagian snore.

even though with undiminished amazement, the ever-recurring phenomenon of change and resistance to change in the evolution of music, and the manifestation of the latter in a long comedy of critical errors.

The layman—like the musician—must find his way in the maze of modern music as best he can, but his mental attitude will greatly affect the development of his taste. In approaching all modern art there is just one thing worse than prejudice and that is *indifference;* in music there is something worse than mistaken judgment, and that is *refusing to listen.*

If we look about us in some of the beautiful houses of our wealthy fellow-citizens we find only too often that there is literally nothing to be seen—except perhaps some living plants or cut flowers—that is a product of this century. Paintings, sculpture, furniture, fabrics, rugs, all visible objects in many such houses are antique. They testify that the owner has contributed greatly to the wealth of dealers, for antiques are costly, but it would be interesting to know if the possessor of such treasures ever reflects upon the fact that they would not be in existence if somebody had not ordered and bought them—probably for very little—in the days when they were modern.

After a lecture the author once gave on Modern Music in an eastern city, there was a lively debate in which many challenges to the views that had been expressed were made by members of the audience. One gentleman arose and asserted that he felt conductors of symphony orchestras had no right to impose modern

music on subscribers. "I do not pretend to know anything about music," said this vigorous opponent of the
new, "but I am a lawyer and I *do* know something
about *logic*. It is not logical that a conductor who is
paid to give concerts—presumably for the enjoyment of
the community—should be entrusted with the choice
of programs which gives him the freedom to inflict pain
instead of pleasure. *Audiences* should choose the programs and if they did there would be no modern
music!" The author, obliged as a woman and a musician to disclaim any understanding of logic, ventured
to suggest that audiences could scarcely exercise a
choice involving a modern composition unless they had
heard it at least once!

Each layman, as he explores musical literature and
its history, might ask himself whether he would rather
take his place among the few who, in each generation,
have the interest to seek, the intuition to find, and the
vision to support creative artists of their own day, or
join the many who, in each age, live and die without
knowing or appreciating the things posterity enjoys.

Of one thing we can be sure. We are not living in
a stagnant, unproductive age. The twentieth century is
sometimes confusing and often irritating but it is unmistakably creative. We may still be in an experimental
stage, but enough is happening to stimulate us to look
about us and to listen, with a strong probability of the
thrill of discovery.

Perhaps the fountain of youth, eternally sought by
man, really lies in the power to participate so com-

pletely in evolution that we derive from some general creative current of thought and feeling the possibility of living fully *in* and *with* our own age.

POINTS TO BE REMEMBERED

1. Our musical civilization consists of a genius-made system which has been in a state of flux since its inception.
2. There has been *modern music* in every age.
3. The history of our musical art makes it seem impossible to assume that any concept of consonance and dissonance is final and unalterable.
4. A rich musical life should include the greatest things of the past and a vital interest in modern creative music.

SUGGESTIONS FOR CORRELATED READING

Twentieth Century Music, Marion Bauer
The Relation of Ultramodern to Archaic Music, Katherine Ruth Heyman
New Musical Resources, Henry Cowell
A New Esthetic of Music, Ferruccio Busoni
Arnold Schönberg, Egon Wellesz, translated by W. H. Kerridge
American Composers on American Music, edited by Henry Cowell
Music of our Day, Lazare Saminsky
Modern Music, edited by Minna Lederman (A Quarterly Review published by the League of Composers, New York, 1924–1935)

MUSICAL ILLUSTRATIONS

Stravinsky   *Le Sacre du Printemps,*
                Victor recording by Leopold Stokowski and the Philadelphia Orchestra

Paul Hindemith   String Quartet, opus 22
                    Played by the Amar String Quartet
                    Foreign recording, procurable through The
                    Gramophone Shop, New York, N. Y.
    For a wide choice of records see *A Summary of Twentieth Century Music* by Marion Bauer, published by G. P. Putnam's Sons.

APPENDIX

Information for Teachers *

SINCE the work of the Layman's Music Courses has become known, many music teachers have applied to the author for information as to how they could organize courses along similar lines. This book together with "The Gist of Music" by George A. Wedge (published by G. Schirmer, Inc.) should enable any trained musician to use the particular approach and continuity they contain, but the author offers the following suggestions based on practical experience:

These books are addressed to the trained mind of the adult, therefore an attempt to adapt them for younger students should only be made by a teacher well-versed in child and adolescent pedagogy.

The best results can be obtained by adding to the material contained in the books *visual* impressions through black-board work and charts or slides.

For the benefit of any teachers or study clubs that might wish to use "The Listener's Music Book" and "The Gist of Music" for class work, the Layman's Music Courses is prepared to furnish sets of the lantern slides used by the author.

Larger and smaller sets with corresponding differences in price can be procured from:

* See page 287.

The Layman's Music Courses, Inc.
The Town Hall
123 West 43rd Street
New York City

For information address Olga Samaroff Stokowski.

A regular Initiation Course of the Layman's Music
Courses comprises twenty lectures given with the distinctive
visual aid of specially designed lantern slides and appropriate phonograph records for musical illustration. These
should be followed by twenty ear-training classes for listeners who have had no previous musical education. No outline
for ear-training lessons can be furnished but competent
teachers may find practical direction in *The Gist of Music*
by George Wedge.

The Function of Hearing

The layman who wishes to have a clear picture of his
potential activity as a listener, is usually interested in the
following description of the act of hearing.

"Behind the bony partition, and between it and the
brain, we have the extraordinary organ called the *labyrinth,*
filled with water, over the lining membrane of which are
distributed the terminal fibres of the auditory nerve. When
the tympanic membrane receives a shock, it is transmitted
through the series of bones above referred to, being concentrated on the membrane against which the base of the
stirrup bone is fixed. The membrane transfers the shock to
the water of the labyrinth, which, in its turn, transfers it to
the nerves.

"The transmission, however, is not direct. At a certain
place within the labyrinth exceedingly fine elastic bristles,

terminating in sharp points, grow up between the terminal nerve-fibres. These bristles, discovered by Max Schultze, are eminently calculated to sympathize with such vibrations of the water as correspond to their proper periods. Thrown thus into vibrations, the bristles stir the nerve-fibres which lie between their roots. At another place in the labyrinth we have little crystalline particles called *otolithes*—the *Hörsteine* of the Germans—imbedded among the nervous filaments, which, when they vibrate, exert an intermittent pressure upon the adjacent nerve-fibres. The otolithes probably serve a different purpose from that of the bristles of Schultze. They are fitted by their weight to accept and prolong the vibrations of evanescent sounds, which might otherwise escape attention, while the bristles of Schultze, because of their extreme lightness, would instantly yield up an evanescent motion. They are, on the other hand, eminently fitted for the transmission of continuous vibrations.

"Finally, there is in the labyrinth, an organ, discovered by the Marchese Corti, which is to all appearance a musical instrument, with its chords so stretched as to accept vibrations of different periods and transmit them to the nerve filaments which traverse the organ. Within the ears of men, and without their knowledge or contrivance, this lute of three thousand strings (according to Kölliker, this is the number of fibres in Corti's organ) has existed for ages, accepting the music of the outer world, and rendering it fit for reception by the brain. Each musical tremor which falls upon this organ selects from the stretched fibres the one appropriate to its own pitch, and throws it into unisonant vibration. And thus, no matter how complicated the motion of the external air may be, these microscopic strings can analyse it and reveal the constituents of which it is composed. Surely, inability to feel the stupendous wonder of what is here revealed, would imply incompleteness of mind; and surely, those who practically ignore or fear them, must be ignorant of the ennobling influence which such discoveries may be made to exercise upon both the emotions and the understanding of man."

—Tyndall

Equal Temperament

To the scientifically minded, equal temperament presents no great problem. Those less versed in physics can obtain some idea of this important development through the following explanation based on the circle of fifths.

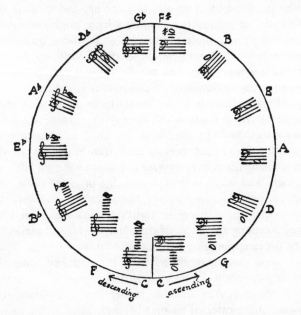

Between each tone and the fifth tone above or below it, there is a fixed ratio of vibration frequency. Taking a tone produced by a stretched string as an example, this ratio is determined by the relative vibration frequency of the whole string and that of one third of its length. If beginning at the right-hand "C" at the bottom of the circle (the lowest C on the piano), we ascend by quint strides to F sharp, and at the same time *descend* in quint strides from the left hand C at the bottom of the circle (the highest C on the piano), *we could not arrive at the same tone* IF *the piano were so tuned that each fifth had the ratio of vibration frequency of the natural law.* F sharp would not be the same as G flat. That means we should have to have double the amount of keys and corresponding strings on our keyboard instruments in order to sound these fractional differences, because any progression similar to the example given, i. e., a progression beginning on any given tone, would bring the same problem. Each of the fifths in the ascending and descending progressions would be a little too large to permit arriving at the same point. By reducing each fifth, i. e., tempering it, through subtracting so slight a fraction of its vibrations that the average ear could scarcely detect the change, we arrive at the same tone. We also achieve through this adjustment the possibility of dividing each octave *into twelve equal semi-tones.* The adoption of this method of tuning keyboard instruments has had an enormous influence on the general evolution of music. Bach, that far-seeing "musician of the future," helped in bringing about the adoption of equal temperament and celebrated it in his great collection of Preludes and Fugues, *The Well-tempered Clavichord.*

1	2	3	4	5	6
Elements	Name of Neume	Elementary Form	St. Gall IX Cent.	North Italy X Cent.	Germany XI Cent.
Grave accent	Punctum	●	●	●	●
Acute accent	Virga	╱	╱	╱	╱╱
Acute and grave accent combined	Clivis or Clinis	∧	⌐	⌐	∧
Grave and acute accent combined	Podatus or Pes	⌄	⌄	⌄	⌄
Two grave and one acute accent	Scandicus	╱	╱	╱	╱
Acute accent and two grave accents	Climacus	╲	╱	╱	╱
Grave, acute, and grave accents	Torculus	⌒	⌒	⌒	⌒
Acute, grave, and acute accents	Porrectus	ᴎ	ᴎ	ᴎ	ᴎ
Grave, acute, and one or more grave accents	Podatus subpunctis or sub-bipunctis	⌄	⌄	⌄	⌄
Acute, two grave, and one acute accents	Climacus resupinus	╱	╱	╱	╱
Two grave, one acute, and one grave accents	Scandicus flexus	⌐	⌐	⌐	⌐
Two grave, one acute, and two grave accents	Scandicus subpunctis or sub-bipunctis	╱	╱	╱	╱
Grave, acute, grave, acute accents	Torculus resupinus	W	⌶	⌶	⌶
Acute, grave, acute, grave accents	Porrectus flexus	M	⌶		⌶
Acute, grave, acute, and two grave accents	Porrectus subpunctis	ᴎ	ᴎ		ᴎ

[1] "Grove's Dictionary of Music and Musicians," The Macmillan Company.

Development of our Notation [1]

7	8	9	10	11	12	13	14	15
Lombardy XI Cent.	Aquitaine XI Cent. on one line.	Germany XII Cent.	Gothic XIII Cent.	Sarum Gradual XIII Cent. on four lines.	Gothic XIV Cent.	South Italy XV Cent.	Ratisbon 1889	Solesmes 1902

Comparative Table of Ancient Greek and Mediaeval (Ecclesiastical) Modes.

Additional Notes

The layman should note that scientists disagree on the numbering of the partials of a single tone. Some scientists regard the fundamental as the prime tone or harmonic generator and the octave above as the first partial or overtone. In many of the most recent scientific works, however, the numbering of the partials is given as on pages 43 and 44 of The Listener's Music Book.

In addition to the sets of slides mentioned on page 279 the following equipment is now available for those desiring to inaugurate Layman's Music Courses:

1. The Layman's Music Album issued by the R. C. A.-Victor Company and including musical illustrations of milestones in the evolution of the art of music as presented in The Listener's Music Book.

2. The Layman's Keyboard Guide devised by Olga Stroumillo and published by J. Fischer & Bro. This Guide will enable the layman to find his way about at the piano keyboard and includes concrete reminders of musical fundamentals such as scale building, notation, the harmonic series and other important information.

INDEX

Aeschylus, 35
Allemand, 144, 146
Aristotle, 68 f., 160
Art music, 18, 19, 138, 157, 185;
  occidental, 20 ff., 80, 115, 120 f.,
  134, 139; and opera, 120, 232;
  and instruments, 161 ff., 181;
  and chamber music, 232 (*See
  also* Art-song)
Art-song, 240 ff., 257
Artusi of Bologna, 130, 271
Atonality, 264
Augmentation, 107 ff.

Bach, Johann Sebastian, 203, 221,
  251, 255; motets, 95; fugues,
  106 ff., 163; suites, 143; concertos, 236; choral, 245; *A
  minor English Suite,* 146; *B
  minor Mass,* 245; *St. Matthew
  and St. John Passions,* 245; *Well-
  Tempered Clavichord,* 108, 113,
  283; *Art of Fugue,* 106 f., 109 ff.
Bach, Karl Philipp Emanuel, 150,
  180
Ballet, 130, 141
Bannister, 211 f.
Bauer, Harold, 202
Bauer, Marion, 261 f.
Beethoven, 165, 202 f., 222 f.; and
  phonograph, 14; symphony, 41,
  46, 139, 182 f., 199; sonata, 150,
  154; first public appearance,
  214; concerto, 240; choral music,
  245; *Eroica* (Third) *Symphony,*
  183, 222; *Ninth Symphony,* 183,
  189, 220, 245; *Pastorale* (Sixth)
  Symphony, 189; *Hammerklavier
  Sonata,* 202; *Emperor Concerto,*
  202

Berg, Alban, 259
Berlioz, *Symphonie Fantastique,*
  190 f.
Boston Symphony Orchestra, 31,
  231
Boulton, Laura C., 67 f.
Brahms, 255 f., 272, 273; chamber
  music, 31 f.; and symphony, 183;
  tour with Remenyi, 223 f.; con-
  certo, 240; lieder, 242
Brain, in reception of music, 39 ff.,
  46 ff., 281
Bruckner, 269
Burney, 212 f., 220
Burton, Sir Richard, 252

Cadence, 253, 261
Cadenza, 237 f.
Canon, 99 f., 102
Canzonetti, 124
Carnegie Corporation, 244
Chamber music, 95, 231 ff., 236;
  Brahms', 31 f.; and rondos, 154
Chants, 71 ff., 89 (*See also* Grego-
  rian)
Cherubini, 222
Chicago Orchestra, 187
Chopin, 154
Choral music, 243 ff.
Chord, 124 ff., 152, 261 ff.; pro-
  gressions, 176; of nature, 253 ff.;
  in modern music, 264, 266
Church music, 60, 71 ff., 88 ff.,
  126 ff., 214, 232, 245
Clavier, 163
Coda, 151 f., 154
Colles, 137, 232
Concerto, 235 ff.
Concerts, history of, 180, 211 ff.;

conductor, 219 ff.; programs, 221 ff.; in U. S. S. R., 287
Confucius, 60
Consonance, 68 f., 121 ff., 137, 261, 263
Corelli, 149, 221
Counterpoint, 81 ff., 98, 105 f., 121, 261
Courante, 144, 146
Cowell, Henry, 79, 262 f.
Craven, Men of Art, 258
Cristofori, 163, 165

Dance music, negro, 76; in opera, 138; in suites, 141 ff.
Dannreuther, Edward, 192
d'Arezzo, Guido, 92
Davis, Agnes, 205
Debussy, 22, 193, 255 f., 258, 267
Diminution, 107 ff.
d'Indy, Vincent, 77
Dissonance, 68, 121 ff., 137, 176 f., 261, 262 f.
Drinker, Henry, Jr., 31 f.

Emerson, 40
Equal temperament, 109, 282 f.
Esterhazy Princes, 215 ff.

Faure, Elie, 161 f.
Folk music, 18 f., 53, 69, 77, 137, 139, 142
Form, history of, 137 ff.; and suites, 141 ff.; and sonata, 147 ff.; and program music, 191; and modern music, 267 ff.
Forsyth, Cecil, 91, 162 f., 164
Franz, 242
Freschi, Domenico, 130 f.
Fugue, 186; history of, 98 ff.; theme of, 100 ff.; voices in, 102 ff.; Bach on the, 106 ff.; and prelude, 146; and sonata, 152

Galliard, 141 f.
Gesualdo, 130, 271
Gigue, 145 f.
Gilman, Lawrence, 32 f.
Gluck, 198
Greek music, 19; moral value of, 60 ff.; polyphony in, 68 f., 78;

notation in, 92; and drama, 122, 126, 198 (See also Modes)
Gregorian chant, 71 ff., 77, 87, 245; notation of, 91
Grove's Dictionary, 74, 91, 95, 132 f., 214, 284 f.

Habeneck, 219, 220, 222
Hale, Philip, 31
Half-tones, 50, 53
Handel, 132, 236, 237
Harmonic series, 42 ff., 48, 178, 254, 261 ff.
Harmony, 82, 121 f., 124 f., 134, 137, 260 ff.
Haydn, Josef, 220, 259; sonata, 150; symphony, 181, 189; oratorios, 213 f.; and patron, 215 ff., 226; concerto, 236
Hearing, function of, 38 ff., 280 ff.
Helmholtz, 41, 45, 177
Honegger, 245

Instrumental music, abstract, 21, 26, 147, 160, 186 f., 193 f.; history of, 138 ff.; modern, 258
Instruments, 138; history of, 160 ff., 178 ff.; of modern orchestra, 165 ff.; and orchestration, 177; and technical skill, 238 f.; modern, 270
Inversion, 107 ff., 112

Juillard Graduate School, 11, 15

Krehbiel, Henry, 18 f.
Kuhnau, 149 f.

Lalande, 221
Layman's Music Courses, 11 f., 15 f., 183 f., 188, 251, 279 f.
Lieder, 242
Liszt, 192, 238, 255
Lully, 130, 141, 215
Luther, Martin, 75

Madrigals, 95, 126 ff.
Magadizing, 68 f., 78
Mahler, Gustav, 245, 269
Mannes, David, 218
Marx, 215
May, Florence, 223
Measurement of music, 87, 137;

triple-time, 88 ff.; duple-time, 90; modern, 266 f.
Meifred, 222
Melody, 66 ff., 260 f.
Melody-types, 56
Mendelssohn, 245
Menuhin, Yehudi, 226
Milhaud, 268 f.
Minstrels, 127
Minuet, 145 f., 153
Modes, Greek and Mediaeval, 54, 57 ff., 92, 264; table, 286
Monteverdi, 129 f., 140, 179, 271
Moral value, of music, 60 ff.
Morley, Thomas, 141
Moscheles, 215
Motets, 95, 236
Mozart, sonata, 150; symphony, 181 ff., 189; concerto, 236 f., 240; *Titus*, 202
Musica Enchiriadis, 78, 83 ff.
Musical education, 82, 154, 187; in 19th century, 20 ff.; in 20th century, 30 ff., 226; and criminality, 62 ff.; in U. S., 227 ff.
Musical tone, 87, 108, 160, 265; essence of, 38, 41 ff.; vibrations, 42 ff., 51, 59, 262; Chinese, 55; of scale, 58, 262; instrumental, 177 f.

Negro music, 76 f.
Neidhardt, 109
Neumes, 91; table, 284 f.
New York Philharmonic Orchestra, 214
Niemann, 32
Nordoff, Paul, 245
Notation, 14, 69 ff., 74; development of, 91 ff., 245; table, 284 f.
Nottebohm, 107

Occidental art music, *see* Art music
Opera, 21, 113, 138; history of, 119 ff.; and harmony, 121 ff.; and words, 126 ff.; and oratorio, 133; overture, 140 f., 179 f.; and choral music, 245; modern, 259, 268. (*See also* Wagner)
Oratorio, 21, 133; conductors, 220; and choral music, 245
Orchestra, 21, 129, 134; instru-

ments of, 165 ff.; history of, 178 ff.; and soloists, 235, 239
Orchestration, 177
Organ, development of, 162 f.
Organum, 78 ff., 83 ff., 252
Oriental systems, 19, 54 ff.
Overtones, 41, 48, 262 f.
Overtures, opera, 138, 140 f.; instruments used, 179 f.
Oxford History of Music, 88

Paganini, 238
Palestrina, 125
Papal Bull (1322), 89
Parry, 19, 137 f., 140, 142 f., 147 f.
Partial tones, 42 ff., 58, 177, 253 f.
Part-songs, 70, 138
Pater, Walter, 42
Patronage, 211, 214 ff., 226; American, 227 ff.; era of, 232 f.
Pavan, 141 f.
Peri, Jacopo, 120, 124, 129, 178 f.
Philadelphia Orchestra, 205, 217, 219, 250
Philidor, Anne Dannican, 212, 221 f.
Phonograph, 48, 260; educational value, 13 f., 34 f., 152, 234, 242; in U. S., 29 f., 33, 228
Piano, 120, 161; history of, 163 f.; and Beethoven, 202 f.; and technical skill, 239; in concerto, 240; in lieder, 242
Pitch, 42, 46, 56, 74, 108; and notation, 91 f.; of modern instruments, 164, 174 f.
Plain-song, 71, 88, 89, 240
Plato, 250 f.
Polyphony, 26 f.; definition of, 66; history of, 67 ff.; organized, 83; 81, 121, 124 f., 137, 176, 232, 245
Polytonality, 264
Pratt, Waldo Selden, 72, 127
Preetorius, Emil, 204
Prelude, 142, 146
Primitive music, 17 f., 42, 139, 185; scale-basis of, 51 ff.; and words, 126; and dance, 142; and modern, 260, 265
Professionalism, 27 f., 224 ff.
Program music, 30 ff., 147, 154,

185 ff.; and romanticism, 188 ff.; symphonic poem and Wagnerian leit-motif, 191 ff.
Prokofieff, 245
Pythagoras, 57, 126

Quagliati, Paolo, 130
Quinault, 141

Radio, 48, 260; educational value, 13 f., 34 f.; in U. S., 29 f., 33, 228
Raginis, 55 ff.
Rags, 55 ff.
Rameau, 125 f.
Recitative, 132 f., 257
Remenyi, Edward, 223
Rhythm, 17, 60, 76; in organum, 87, 91; in modern music, 265 ff.
Rhythmic modes, 88
Riemann, 67, 69, 107
Rinuccini, 120, 129
Rode, 222
Rondo form, 153 f., 238
Rossini, 222
Ruskin, 271

Saint-Saëns, 255
Samuels, Harold, 146
Sarabande, 143, 145 f.
Sargent, John, 185
Scales, 47, 50 ff.; in primitive music, 51 ff.; five-tone, 53; diatonic-major, 53; chromatic, 53; Chinese, 54 ff.; of India, 55 ff.; major and minor, 108 f., 264; follow harmonic series, 262; in atonality and polytonality, 264 f. (See also Modes)
Scarlatti, Alessandro, 132
Scherzo, 146, 153
Scholia Enchiriadis, 85 f.
Schönberg, Arnold, 245, 250 f., 253, 259
Schubert, 183, 241 f.
Schumann, 183, 238, 242, 272
Schweitzer, Albert, 75 f.
Science and music, 160 ff., 177 ff.
Self-expression, 23, 25 ff., 33, 233 f.
Sibelius, 187
Solmization, 92

Sonata, 113, 146 ff., 186; form, 149 ff., 180, in concerto, 237
Sound, 27, 38 ff.; definition of, 41; interpreted in light of experience, 38, 47; physical laws of, 54, 57, 261 ff.
Sound films, 48, 204 ff.
Specht, 32
Spohr, 189 ff., 219
Stamitz, Johann and Carl, 180 f.
Stanford, Sir Charles Villiers, 62
Stanford-Forsyth, History of Music, 70, 90, 162 f.
Stokowski, Leopold, 205, 219
Stradivarius, 165
Strangways, Fox, 57
Strauss, Richard, 22, 187 f., 255, 258, 261, 273; symphonic poem, 192; lieder, 242
Stravinsky, Sacre du Printemps, 251, 256, 258 ff., 266 f.
Suite, 141 ff.
Symphonic poem, 191 ff., 200
Symphony, 113, 146; and rondos, 154; and instruments, 160, 165; and orchestration, 176 f.; development of, and orchestra, 180 ff.; conductor, 219 f.; and choral music, 245

Toccata, see Overtures
Tonality, 152, 155, 264
Tone, see Musical tone
Torelli, Giuseppe, 236
Toscanini, 219
Tovey, 107
Troubadours, 126 ff., 240
Tyndall, 280 ff.

Valle, Pietro della, 130
Variation form, 153
Vecchi, Orazio, 128 f.
Viadana, Ludovici, 236
Vieuxtemps, 223
Vibrations, see Musical tone

Wagner, Richard, 133, 165, 255 f., 259; leit-motif, 191 f., 199; philosophy, 196 ff.; fuses drama and music, 198 ff., 257; and Bayreuth orchestra shell, 200 f.; and stage-craft, 201 ff.; and sound film, 204 ff.; on conduct-

ing, 220; *Nibelungen Ring*, 197, 198, 269; *Walküre*, 197, 204; *Siegfried*, 197; *Götterdämmerung*, 197, 204, 205; *Rheingold*, 197; *Parsifal*, 198; *Rienzi*, 197, 198; *Die Meistersinger*, 197, 198; *Flying Dutchman*, 198; *Lohengrin*, 198, 204; *Tannhäuser*, 198, 271, overture, 25; *Tristan*, 198
Wanamaker, Rodman, collection, 217
Ward, Justine, 72 ff.
Weber, Carl Maria von, 219

Webern, Anton von, 267 f.
Wedge, George A., *The Gist of Music*, 12, 47, 94, 279
Weismann, Adolf, 273
Werckmeister, 109
Whole-tones, 50, 53
Williams, Vaughan, 109
Wolf, 242

Yasser, Joseph, 50 ff., 264

Zarlino, 109